OLD MONSTERS NEVER DIE

A STORY COLLECTION

OLD MONSTERS NEVER DIE

A STORY COLLECTION

TIM WAGGONER

BRAM STOKER AWARD-WINNING AUTHOR

NEW YORK   LOS ANGELES

Jacket design by Rejenne Pavon
Jacket Copyright 2024 by Winding Road Stories
Interior book design by A Raven Design
ISBN#: 978-1-960724-20-5 (pbk)
ISBN#: 978-1-960724-21-2 (ebook)

Published by Winding Road Stories
www.windingroadstories.com

This one's for Cynthia Pelayo, an amazing writer and an even more amazing human being. She does so much to lift up other writers, and the horror genre is a far, far better place because of her.

CONTENTS

A Touch Of Madness	1
The Crying Man	19
No One Sings In The City Of The Dead	38
The Girl Who Bled In The Tree	51
In The Monster's Mouth	64
The Garden Of Love Is Green	79
God Spelled Backward	90
Forever	101
Old Monsters Never Die	115
The Ashes Of Our Fathers	128
The White Road	145
Going Home	163
Negative Space	180
The Gray Room	196
Voices Like Barbed Wire	211
In The End There Is A Drain	228
Cast-Offs	244
Til Death	260
How To Be A Horror Writer	277
Acknowledgments	287
Publication History	289
About the Author	291

A TOUCH OF MADNESS

Kristina Lawson sat at a corner table in a small cafe, coffee sitting in front of her, gloved hands tucked beneath her legs. Folk-pop music played over the cafe's sound system in a vain attempt to give the place a relaxing atmosphere, but it was filled with so many people—ordering at the counter, sitting and talking to one another, working behind the counter and operating various whirring, whooshing, or grinding machines—and the air thrummed with tension.

She glanced around at the other customers. A couple sitting at a table, each involved in whatever was displayed on their phone screens instead of looking at each other. A father sitting with his twin daughters—who were five at the most and dressed in superhero outfits complete with capes, one green, one red—sipping juice boxes while their dad drank his coffee. A pair of middle-aged women in blue medical smocks talking over coffee and pastries after a long hospital shift. And a dozen more, including the staff behind the counter. All of them appeared completely normal. Completely *sane*. But she knew better than most that appearances didn't mean shit.

Anything could be happening behind their eyes, their thoughts a chaotic maelstrom of wild imperceptions and barely restrained homicidal impulses. Any one of them could be on the verge of succumbing to the lunacy raging inside, and then all hell would break loose. Pam would've told her she was being paranoid, and maybe so. But she'd seen it happen before, and if it had happened once, it could happen again.

She wasn't sure why Pam had asked to have their session in a public place like this instead of her office. No doubt she thought there was a good reason for it, maybe some new type of therapy that she wanted to try, but Kristina wasn't comfortable around people, especially this many. She looked down on the tabletop to avoid meeting anyone's gaze. She flexed her hands, felt them move under her legs, was reassured to know they were still protected. She made no move to touch the coffee in front of her. She didn't want it, didn't really like coffee much. She'd only bought it so she wouldn't look any stranger sitting here than she already did.

Pam rushed into the shop then, blond hair a frizzy mess, make-up slightly askew, as if she'd applied it too fast. She looked around, saw Kristina, smiled, and hurried over to her table.

"Sorry I'm late," she said. "Do you mind if I order something before we get started?"

Kristina *did* mind. She wanted to get whatever this was over as soon as possible. But she shook her head. Pam smiled again then headed to the counter. There was a line, and Kristina watched her stand there for several moments until it was her time to order. She trusted Pam—as much as she trusted anyone, that is. She'd seen a number of therapists over the years, most of whom had treated her as if *she* was the crazy one. Pam had been the first to treat her as if she was a person instead of merely a psychologically fascinating puzzle to be solved, a shattered porcelain doll whose pieces needed to be put back together. She'd been seeing Pam for almost two years, and she couldn't deny they'd made progress together. Two years ago, she never could have come into a place like this by herself, order a drink, sit, and wait for someone. But here she was, and if she wasn't comfortable, so what? She was *here*.

Pam returned to the table carrying a large cup that most likely contained a latte with an extra shot of espresso. During one of their earliest sessions, she'd mentioned it was her favorite drink. She sat down opposite Kristina and took a long sip before setting the cup down on the table. Normally, Pam began their sessions with some chit-chat. *How have you been since we last talked? Anything new going on with you?* But not this time.

"I'm sure you're wondering why I asked you to meet me here today."

Kristina smiled. "The thought had crossed my mind."

"I'd like to try something different today, and I thought this would be a good place for it."

Called it, Kristina thought. "Were you late on purpose in order to give me a chance to handle being by myself?"

Pam took another sip of her latte.

"The thought had crossed my mind," she said, and despite herself, Kristina laughed. "So what was it like?" Pam asked.

"Tolerable. Although if you'd been much later, I'd probably have left."

"Good thing I wasn't any later then, huh?"

Pam's expression grew more serious, became what Kristina thought of as her *doctor face*, and she knew their session was about to start in earnest.

"How are you feeling about the TV show this week?"

Kristina grimaced. "Okay, I guess. The bastards have stopped trying to contact me, so that's a relief."

The producers of a lurid true-crime TV show called *Unnatural Acts* were doing a segment on Kristina's mom. For a month they'd bugged her nonstop, desperate to get an on-camera interview with her, but she'd ignored them and they'd finally decided to go ahead without her participation. She'd had enough media attention over the last decade to last her a lifetime. News reporters who fought to be the one to interview her first. True-crime authors who wanted to write books about what had happened. One was eventually published—*Blood on Campus*—and it had become a modest success. She hated the attention, hated how it always brought the memories of that awful day back full force. For the last ten years she'd hoped people would forget and find a new atrocity to be fascinated by. But it hadn't happened yet, and she was starting to wonder if it ever would.

"That's what I wanted to talk to you about," Pam said, then added. "Kind of."

"Oh, god. Don't tell me the producers hired you to be a consultant."

Pam's eyes widened in surprise, and then she laughed.

"No, and even if they asked me, I'd turn them down. It would violate doctor-patient confidentiality. Plus, it would be a total dick move."

Kristina relaxed. The thought of Pam betraying her like that was too awful to think about.

"So what *do* you want to talk about?" She felt her defenses going up. She didn't like to remember that day, let alone talk about it. But Pam had done a lot to help her, so she'd go along with whatever she wanted to do. To a point.

Pam took another sip of her latte, a long one, as if fortifying herself for what came next.

"We've talked about that day before," she began. "Several times. And during those conversations, I never questioned the truth of what you told me, never disputed the reality of any of it."

Kristina nodded cautiously. She didn't like where this seemed to be going. Her other therapists *had* questioned, had tried to convince her that it hadn't happened, or at least that it hadn't happened the way she remembered. One of the things she liked about Pam is that she'd never done that. But maybe she'd just been waiting for what she thought was the right time to bring up the subject.

"I went to the university yesterday."

An ice-cold hand gripped Kristina's heart, and she began trembling. Pam went on, speaking faster as if hoping to get everything out before she freaked.

"I'd never been there. I went to college in Chicago before my husband and I moved to Ohio. It's a beautiful campus. Lovely old buildings, lots of grass and trees… Very different from the downtown campus I attended. The Science Center's not there anymore. They tore it down years ago and planted trees there. They put up a remembrance plaque, too. I think you might find it healing to see it."

Kristina trembled harder now, and her mouth and throat felt dry as desert sand. She didn't want to reply, but if she tried, her words would've likely come out in a hoarse croak.

Pam continued.

"I looked for the fountain, but I couldn't find it at first. I thought maybe it had been torn down, too. But I found it eventually, and it was peaceful and relaxing, just as you described it." She paused, and then added, "I took some pictures with my phone."

Sudden nausea erupted in Kristina's gut, and her vision blurred. She wanted to jump up from her chair and run toward the exit, but she feared that if she tried, she'd pass out before she made it halfway.

"I'd like to show them to you, if that's okay."

She wanted to shake her head violently, but she was unable to move. Taking her silence for assent, Pam removed her phone from her purse, brought a picture up on the screen, and then held it out for Kristina to see. She scrolled through a series of images, and although Kristina wanted to look away, wanted it more than she wanted her next breath, she watched the pictures go by, one after the other.

———

KRISTINA SAW the statue on a hot afternoon in late July when she was thirteen years old. She was supposed to be attending the second morning of a weeklong summer science workshop for middle school kids run by the university, but after her mom dropped her off in front of the Science Center and drove away in her Lexus, she'd decided to wander the campus instead. She *hated* science and never got good grades in it—which was the reason her overachieving parents had insisted on signing her up for the workshop. But as much as she hated science, she hated being told what to do even more. Rules, regulations, do this, don't do that, be a good girl, don't be a bad girl... Why couldn't everyone just leave her alone to do *what* she wanted *when* she wanted? Her parents, teachers...all her life people had told her what to do, and she was sick of it. The only rules she was interested in following were her own.

Her parents might've enrolled her in the workshop—and paid for it—but they couldn't make her attend if she didn't want to. Yesterday had been so *boring!* All they'd done was make "inventions" out of cardboard, tape, glue, plastic straws, popsicle sticks and other odds and ends. More arts and crafts than science. Kid stuff. Today she planned to skip out and kick around campus for a couple hours until it was time for Mom to pick her up, and then she'd meet her back in front of the Science Center and feed her some bullshit about what the instructors had the kids do today. Her parents were smart—Mom was a lawyer, Dad a pediatrician—but they were so busy they only ever paid partial attention to what she did. Lying to them was almost embarrassingly easy.

This wasn't her first time at Ash Creek University. Her parents were both alums and had been dragging her to campus concerts, art shows, and theater productions since before she could walk. But in all those visits—dozens of them—she'd never gotten the chance to explore the place. High time she rectified that, she decided. But after a half hour of walking around in the sun and heat, she was not only bored but miserable. She supposed the campus was pretty enough. Red brick buildings, well-landscaped grounds, large trees… But there wasn't anything to *do*, and because it was summer, there weren't many people around, which made the place feel empty and lonely. She did like the fact that no one paid any attention to her. The few people she passed—students, professors—didn't so much as glance at her, as if a thirteen-year-old walking around campus by herself was completely normal. It made her feel very grownup.

But she'd been walking nonstop since her mother left, and she was tired and sweaty. And while the campus was pleasant for the most part, there was a lot of construction going on—parking lots being resurfaced, buildings being remodeled—and that meant noise. Machines running, tools striking metal and concrete, people shouting to each other as they worked. She wanted someplace quiet where she could sit in peace for a bit, preferably in the shade. She was on the verge of saying to hell with it and going back to the Science Center and attending the stupid workshop when she saw the red dumpster. It contained odds and ends from campus construction—chunks of broken concrete, lengths of discarded wood. It was in no way remarkable. She'd seen a dozen like it during her self-guided tour of the campus so far.

But what *was* remarkable was what lay behind it. She almost missed it, so completely did the dumpster block the view. But there was a tiny sliver of space between the side of the dumpster and an old oak tree, and through it she caught a glimpse of what looked like a fountain. Intrigued, she slipped past the dumpster and found herself standing at the entrance to a—well, she wasn't sure what it was exactly. A place for people to sit, relax, and think, she supposed. A stone fountain sat atop the third level of a dais, a curving half circle of stone wall behind it with an arched open doorway in the middle. Wooden benches rested on either side of the doorway, where people could sit and watch the fountain and listen to the gentle trickle of water. The water bubbled up from the center of a large round stone surface to flow over the edges and into a pool beneath. The water emerged from the edge of the dais in a small waterfall surrounded by large stones placed to look like a natural formation. Trees surrounding the fountain, separating it from the rest of the world, making it seem as if it were a place out of a fairy tale, a secluded, magical setting that only a lucky few ever found.

There was shade here, along with a pleasant breeze, and the sound of the gently rustling tree leaves—combined with the running water—soothed Kristina. She knew where she'd be spending the rest of the time until her mother came to get her.

Then she looked to the left of the fountain and saw the statue. Her parents had both had been raised Catholic, but they weren't religious. Ash Creek University was a private Catholic institution with a reputation for academic excellence, and that was the only reason her parents had come here for their undergraduate degrees. Kristina sometimes wondered if they still considered themselves Catholic, culturally if not spiritually. They took her to Christmas Eve and Easter mass every year—to "broaden her horizons," they said—and on the way home they'd give her a speech about how religion was nothing more than a way to instill moral values in its followers by using metaphor and symbolism, and it wasn't to be taken literally.

Thanks to her "broadened horizons," she recognized the statue as the Virgin Mary, the mother of Jesus. Mary stood atop a granite pedestal, bare feet sticking out from beneath the hem of her robe. She held her hands out before her, fingers steepled as if praying, her hood-covered head bowed. There was no expression on her face. Her eyes were closed and her mouth was little more than a line with only a suggestion of lips. But the detail that stood out the most to Kristina was what looked like a thick reptilian tail protruding from the back of her robe and curling around her left foot. She frowned upon seeing the tail—for that's what it had to be, couldn't be anything else. She was no expert on Catholic theology, but she felt confident that Mary wasn't supposed to have a lizard's tail.

There was something written on the granite base the statue stood on, and she walked over to read it. It was a single word.

PANDEMONIA.

And beneath that, in smaller letters, a quote: *If there is a universal mind, who says it has to be sane—Charles Fort.*

Was this some kind of weird piece of art or maybe a joke of some kind?

And then the tail twitched. Just the tip, and it happened so fast she wasn't sure she'd really seen it. She looked up at the statue's face and ice-cold fear hit her when she saw its eyes were now open. They weren't the same gray-white as the rest of the statue, though. Instead they were a glossy obsidian, and while she could read nothing within their empty blackness, she could feel the weight of the statue's gaze upon her.

You do well to shun the false god of science, child.

The statue's thin mouth didn't move. Its voice—cold as midnight and dry as ancient bone—echoed in her mind.

Science pretends there is order to existence, that for every question, there is an answer. This is a lie. Existence is random and meaningless, and that is glorious.

The statue bent toward Kristina and stretched it hands toward her. At first she was so terrified she couldn't move, could only stand and watch the stone fingers draw closer. But then her survival instincts kicked in, and she threw off her paralysis and turned to run. But before she could take more than a single step, the stone tail lashed out and encircled her waist, stopping her. She pulled and tugged, but she couldn't break free of the tail's stone coils.

The statue closed its hard fingers around Kristina's right wrist and held her hand steady as its lips parted and a pearl of thick dark liquid emerged. It fell onto the back of her hand and sat there for a moment, burning cold on her skin, before flattening against her flesh and slowly disappearing into her body. She felt no different, but a shudder raced through her just the same.

The soothing rhythm of the fountain ceased, and the sudden silence drew Kristina's attention. She glanced over to see the water had stopped flowing, and an instant later blood welled up from the center of the round stone, crimson and thick. It oozed across the surface, overflowing the stone's edges, falling in ropey threads into the pool below, before finally emerging as a red waterfall. She looked into the statue's obsidian eyes, its face only a few inches from her own now.

Go forth and share the gift I have bestowed upon you, my daughter. Free them. Free them all.

KRISTINA HAD no memory of the statue releasing her, no memory of beginning to run. One moment she was standing there, trapped in the statue's embrace, staring into its obsidian eyes, and the next she was running full out, heart pounding, lungs heaving, sweat pouring off her. She had no destination in mind, wasn't capable of anything approaching rational thought at that moment. Her body operated on autopilot, returning her to the place she'd started from: the Science Center. She was relieved to see her mom's Lexus parked in front of the building, and she ran straight to it, only partially aware of the tears streaming down her face. She ran to the driver's side window and began pounding on it to get her mother's attention. It was several moments before she realized the car was empty.

"*There* you are!"

Kristina stopped pounding on the window and looked up to see her mother exiting the Science Building, her face a mask of anger. She continued chiding Kristina as she walked toward her.

"I was in a meeting with a client when the workshop director called to ask me why you weren't present today. I hauled ass down here, grinding my teeth to nubs the whole way. Why can't you, for once in your life, do what you're supposed..." She trailed off as she reached Kristina, her expression softening. "Are you okay, honey? Why are you crying? Did something happen?"

Before Kristina could respond, her mom took hold of her hands and gave them a reassuring squeeze. The instant their flesh came in contact, her mother stiffened, and her eyes widened in shock. She began shaking her head, as if trying to deny something only she could see. She paled, an expression of absolute horror coming onto her face, but instead of turning away from the unseen whatever-it-was, she continued looking and slowly her features slackened and her expression became placid. She remained like that for several heartbeats, still holding onto Kristina's hands, and then she spoke in a calm, almost toneless voice.

"Thank you. I understand now." She looked at Kristina, and in the same flat voice said, "I'm going to go tell the director I found you and you're safe. I'll be back in a minute."

She released Kristina's hands, turned, and walked back into the building.

Kristina's tears subsided to a trickle, but she was no longer aware of them. She stared at the glass door that was the entrance to the Science Building, unable to escape the feeling that something was terribly wrong. For a moment she forgot about the statue, or rather she forced herself not to think of it. When Mom got mad—*really* mad—she stayed that way for a while, sometimes hours. Kristina had never seen her calm down so quickly and completely. It was like a switch had been thrown inside her, shutting off all her emotions. It was beyond weird.

And that's when the screaming began. It was muffled, but the sound was unmistakable. It came from somewhere inside the building, and when she looked toward the second floor— where the science workshop was taking place—she saw a smallish, child-sized hand slap the window from the inside. The hand was covered with blood and left a red smear on the glass as it slid away.

Her own paralysis was broken by the sight, and she ran into the building and went up the stairs, taking them two and three at a time. The screams grew louder and fewer the closer she got to the second floor, and they were punctuated by moans of pain. She slowed as she approached the classroom where the workshop was held. She didn't want to go in, didn't what to see whatever waited for her, but she *had* to. Her mother was in there.

The door was open, and by the time she reached it, the

sounds had stopped. No more screams, no more moans. Just silence. She stepped inside, not far, only a foot or so. The room was set up the same way as it had been yesterday—ten circular tables with chairs around them, materials for students to use in constructing their projects in the middle. It was more like art class than science, which had been one of the reasons she'd found it so boring. But what she saw now wasn't boring. Far from it.

Bodies were scattered around the classroom, mostly kids her age but there were a couple adults as well. Some lay on the floor in various positions, while others had collapsed into chairs or onto desks. They had sustained numerous cuts and blood was everywhere—on their clothes, on the desks and chairs, on the floor and walls...and all the corpses, around twenty in total, appeared to have died the same way, by having their throats cut.

Kristina's mother stood in the middle of the room, holding a pair of box cutters, her clothes, hands, and face covered in blood. She turned to face Kristina and smiled, her teeth a startling patch of white in her otherwise crimson face.

"Thank you for helping me to see how things really are, sweetie. Thank you for setting me free."

She raised both box cutters and pressed the tips of the razors to the small hollow at the base of her neck. And then with a pair of vicious outward swipes, she laid open her throat. Blood fountained from the wound to join that which already covered her. If she felt any pain, her face didn't show it. Her smile widened, and her eyes seemed to almost glow. Kristina didn't know the word *beatific,* but if she had, that's how she would've described her mother's expression.

Her mother stood like that for a time, but eventually the box cutters slipped from her hands and thunked to the floor. A moment later, she joined them, collapsing and staring up at the ceiling with wide, unblinking eyes. Her smile, however, remained in place.

And then it was Kristina's turn to scream.

KRISTINA SAW THE FOUNTAIN, the stone wall behind it, the rocks in front of it, the trees surrounding it—but there was one thing she didn't see on the phone's screen: the statue.

"I checked with the campus groundskeeper's office," Pam said, "and they told me that not only isn't there a statue next to the fountain, there never has been in the university's one hundred and twenty-two year history." She closed the phone's photo app and replaced the device in her purse. "There *was* no statue, Kristina. In your mind, yes, but not in the physical world. It didn't infect you with…" She frowned, as if unsure how to put it. "With its madness. And you didn't pass it on to your mother when she grabbed your hands. You aren't responsible for what she did, and you never were."

All of Kristina's therapists had argued that the statue wasn't real, at least not the way she'd perceived it. But none had gone so far as to visit the campus and take pictures, let alone check to see if the statue had ever existed. A part of her that was still thirteen, and maybe always would be, wanted to shout at Pam, accuse her of lying. But the rest of her, the woman she'd become in the last ten years wanted to believe her. What a comfort it would be to believe that her mother had done what she'd done for some other reason than because she'd touched her daughter's hand and come in contact with a contagion that Pandemonia had infected her with.

"I know how to prove that you had nothing to do with what happened," Pam said. "But you'll have to trust me. Do you trust me, Kristina?"

She hesitated, but then she managed a single nod.

"Good. Put your hands on the table."

Kristina stared at her, not quite sure she'd heard correctly.

"You told me that you've worn gloves every day for the last ten years, that you won't even take the right one off to bathe. All because you don't want to risk infecting anyone else."

"Yes." She'd been extremely—no, *obsessively*—careful over the years.

"But if there was no statue, there's no infection to pass on. And that means you can touch someone without anything bad happening. So you can touch me."

Pam put her left hand on the table, palm up.

Katrina looked at Pam's hand, head swimming with vertigo.

"What's more likely to be true? That some...*thing* chose you to spread some kind of psychological plague, or that your mind made up that incident so you wouldn't have to believe your mother was responsible for killing all those people?"

Katrina knew which of the choices was the most logical, but that didn't necessarily make it the correct one. Still, she took a deep breath and slid her hands out from under her legs. She wanted to get better, she truly did, and she recognized that this would be a huge step toward making that possible. She removed her left glove—the one that she didn't really need to wear—and placed it on the table. And then, after another moment's hesitation, she removed the right and placed it next to the left. The air felt cold on the exposed skin of her hands, but it felt stimulating, too. Then slowly, fighting every instinct inside her that screamed she shouldn't be doing this, she lowered her right hand onto Pam's, and for the first time since that day, she touched another human being. Pam curled her fingers upward to grasp hers, and tears of joy welled in Kristina's eyes. Pam had been right. The statue *hadn't* been real, it *hadn't*...

Pam's eyes glazed over and her features went slack. She pulled her hand away from Kristina's.

"No," Kristina whispered. "No, no, no, no, no!"

Pam didn't respond. Instead, she rose from the table and walked toward the counter. But instead of stopping in front of the register, she continued on, stepping behind the counter where the staff were working. They looked at her for a moment, as if uncertain what to say or do. Then one of them, a skinny twenty-something with a goatee and a man bun, stepped forward to block her way.

"I'm sorry, ma'am, but you're not—"

Pam reached down and from somewhere—Kristina couldn't see from the table—grabbed hold of a knife. It was long and sharp, with a black plastic handle, one of the implements the staff used when preparing sandwiches or slicing bagels. Man Bun started to raise his hands, as if he thought he could ward off Pam by gesture alone. But before he could complete the gesture, Pam swiped the blade across his throat in a single swift motion. Flesh parted, blood spurted, and Man Bun clapped his hands to his throat in a ridiculously ineffective attempt to stop the bleeding.

People started screaming at them, and while some stared at Pam, dumbfounded, the majority bolted for the door. Too many tried to go through it at the same time, but the crowd behind them pushed until the jam was broken and everyone could get through.

Pam turned away from the bleeding man, whose mouth kept opening and closing like a fish as he attempted to speak, but all he managed were wet clicking sounds, and then his eyes rolled white and he slumped to the floor. His coworkers gaped at his prone form for a second, but when Pam came out from around the counter and started back toward Kristina, they saw the opportunity to get the hell out of there, and they lost no time in doing so, fleeing into the street after their departed customers.

By the time Pam returned to the table—still gripping the knife, blade slick with blood—the café was empty except for the two of them.

Kristina wanted to look away from Pam's gaze, wanted to close her eyes and wait to feel the knife edge's kiss on her own throat. But she forced herself to meet her therapist's eyes. She half expected to see they had become a glossy obsidian, but they looked the same as they always had, save for the complete and total lack of anything resembling human emotion within them.

"You were given a gift." Pam spoke in a toneless voice that reminded Kristina of the way her mother had spoken before going inside the Science Building. "And you've wasted it."

Moving so swiftly that Kristina hardly saw her move, Pam grabbed hold of her right wrist and pressed her hand to the table.

"Time to return what you've squandered."

She pressed the sharp edge of the knife against the tender skin of Kristina's wrist.

Kristina impressed herself by not feeling afraid. It would be a relief to be rid of Pandemonia's dark gift. And if she bled to death after Pam performed her impromptu amputation, what of it? At least she would've kept her sanity at the end. She gritted her teeth to steel herself for the pain to come and curled her right hand into a fist, the tips of her fingers pressing hard into her palm.

Ten years she had avoided touching herself with her right hand, terrified of what might happen. Now she knew. More, she *understood.*

Pam kept the blade pressed against her skin for another moment, but then she pulled it away and released her grip on

Kristina's wrist. Face still expressionless, eyes still dead, she handed the knife to Kristina, and then stood there, waiting. Katrina examined the blade, turning it this way and that to see how the light played across the metal. The barista's blood still clung to the knife, and she brought the blade to her mouth and licked it clean. She cut her own tongue in the process, but she didn't care. The pain was exquisite, and the blood she swallowed —hers mixed with his—tasted sweeter than any wine.

She looked at Pam.

"Thanks for everything," she said, and then rammed the blade into the woman's chest, expertly slipping it between a pair of ribs and into her heart. The non-expression on Pam's face didn't change as she slipped free of the blade and collapsed to the floor, dead. Instead of licking the knife this time, Kristina wiped it on her cheeks, smearing them with Pam's blood.

Many times over the years, she'd tried to imagine what it had been like inside her mother's mind after she'd experienced the dark touch. The closest she could come to was to imagine Mom's skull as a hive filled with angry buzzing bees furiously trying to sting one another to death. She was surprised to discover she hadn't been far off the mark. The sound—one of absolute and total disorder—was magnificent. It was the song of discord and upheaval, of malady and torment, of decay and dissolution, and she couldn't wait to share it with the world.

She heard Pandemonia's voice one last time.

That's my girl.

Kristina tossed the knife onto Pam's lifeless body and started walking toward the door. She flexed the fingers of her right hand, as if limbering them up. She had work to do— *important* work—and she couldn't wait to get started.

THE CRYING MAN

Martin Foster walked down the stairs, carrying a portfolio case in his left hand, gripping the handrail with his right to steady himself as he descended. He was fifteen pounds overweight—okay, twenty—and during his last checkup his doctor had told him he needed to get more exercise. Martin was in his thirties, but the doctor said it was never too early to start taking care of yourself.

If you can't find time to hit the gym, try exercising in small ways as you go through your daily routine. Increase your speed when walking, park farther away from store entrances when you shop, take the stairs instead of the elevator.

That had been a week ago, and so far Martin hadn't heeded his doctor's advice. But today he'd finally decided to do so, so when he left his cubicle to head downstairs for a meeting, he passed up the elevator and entered the stairwell instead. As exercise went, this was easy enough, but of course, he was going down. The return trip was going to be a different story, but he decided not to think about that right now and focus on the positive instead. He was taking a first step—even if it was only a baby step—toward a healthier lifestyle.

As he continued downward, he realized that in all the time he'd worked for Pinnacle Advertising—seven years and change—he'd never taken the stairs, had never been in the stairwell before. The walls and ceiling were a dull, dingy white, the handrail a thick metal pipe, cold to the touch, and the steps plain gray concrete, marred by occasional cracks. The stairwell looked like it belonged in a different building, one that housed some kind of industrial business, like a tool manufacturer or a food packaging plant. The air here had a stale, flat quality, as if it had been trapped in here too long and gone bad. It felt like it gave his lungs no nourishment when he breathed it in. Instead of echoing, his footsteps seemed muffled, as if the air was too weak to conduct sound properly.

Halfway down, he heard another set of muffled footsteps, and he realized someone was approaching. They met on the second-floor landing, and while Martin recognized the man's face, he couldn't immediately put a name to it. This wasn't a surprise. Martin made it a point to keep his distance from people in all aspects of his life, not just at work. He was happy that way—safer—but it sometimes made for awkward encounters, like meeting someone who might expect you to know their name.

The man had one of those faces that made it hard to judge his age. He could've been anywhere from forty to sixty. His brown hair was thinning, his face was clean-shaven—with the beginnings of five o'clock shadow—and he wore a white shirt, navy blue tie, and slacks. The outfit was practically a work uniform at Pinnacle. Martin dressed the same, except his tie was yellow. Unlike Martin, the man wasn't carrying anything. Also unlike Martin, he didn't hold onto the rail, and he jogged effortlessly from step to step. When he reached the landing, he smiled at Martin in a generically friendly way.

Martin smiled back, then stepped to the side so he could move past the man and continue down the stairs.

"Careful," the man said. "There's a swirl of elevators at the bottom." He lowered his voice and leaned closer. "I think they get jealous when people spurn them for the stairs."

And then he was jogging upward again, stepping so lightly he barely made any sound. Martin turned to watch him go, staring at him until he reached the next landing, turned, and disappeared from Martin's sight.

What the fuck?

Martin continued down the stairs, but when he drew near the ground floor landing, he hesitated. He looked down but saw nothing strange—certainly no swirling elevators—and he breathed a heavy sigh of relief. Face slick with sweat, shirt damp against his body—not from exertion but anxiety—he opened the door to the first floor and stepped through.

"JUST SIT HERE, Martin. I'll only be a few minutes."

Martin—who'd turned thirteen a month ago—acknowledged his aunt's words with a nod. They stood in a small lounge area. Four uncomfortable-looking couches—chrome armrests and legs, cushions covered in orange vinyl—were arranged around a square coffee table. The couches were empty, but the table had a half dozen magazines fanned across its surface. They all looked boring as hell. News, entertainment, sports. No comics.

Aunt Leslie—who was *Doctor* Foster here—looked at Martin for a long moment, her eyes narrowed, as if she were trying to read his thoughts. He'd pointed out this habit to her once, and she'd laughed and said, *I'm a psychologist. It's an occupational hazard.*

She didn't look much like a psychologist to him right now.

The ones in movies and TV shows wore white lab coats a lot of the time, but Leslie wore a light blue blouse, a dark blue skirt, and black heels. She looked more like one of his teachers than a doctor. He wore a Teenage Mutant Ninja Turtles T-shirt, jeans, and sneakers, making him look like exactly what he was: a bored kid forced to accompany his aunt on an errand.

She gave him a parting smile and left to do whatever it was she needed to do. Picking up paperwork, signing it, something like that. There was no one else in the lounge, so Martin had his choice of seats. He sat on the couch that was closest and picked up a magazine that was about health and wellness and started flipping pages, barely noticing the words and pictures that passed before his eyes.

He'd never been to Leslie's work before, had only the vaguest notion what she did here. *She listens to people talk about their problems and gives them useless advice on how to fix them.* That's what his dad—her brother—said. Martin like Leslie well enough, but he wasn't happy about staying with her. His parents had left on a couples' cruise, which Martin knew was less of a vacation and more a last-ditch effort to save their marriage. They'd left him in Leslie's care, but she lived on the other side of town, which meant he couldn't see his neighborhood friends after school. She didn't own a television, either, which Martin thought was weird as hell. Who didn't have a TV? Without a TV, he couldn't play videogames, which meant he had nothing to do but read. That was okay—he liked to read—but he liked to do other things too, which meant he was bored most of the time at Leslie's. Bored as shit. And Leslie and her husband had divorced before having children, so he didn't have any cousins to play with either.

She'd picked him up after school today and asked if he minded if they stopped in at the hospital where she worked. It wasn't really a question, so he hadn't bothered answering. Now that he was here looking at an article on keeping your colon in tip-top condition, he wished his parents hadn't gone on the stupid cruise. It wasn't as if it was going to help. Their marriage was already over; they just hadn't admitted it yet.

He didn't hear anyone enter the lounge and take a seat. The first he was aware he was no longer alone was when the person spoke.

"I had babies."

Martin looked up from the magazine. A middle-aged man wearing a long-sleeved gray pullover, jeans, and blue slippers sat directly across from him. The man's blond hair was cut close to his scalp, and he had dark splotches on his nose and cheeks, like freckles, only larger. He was smiling, showing gaps in his teeth, and his brown eyes were open wide, giving him a look of perpetual surprise.

Martin had no idea how to respond to the man's statement, so he said nothing.

"I was pregnant for almost five years. It went on so long because I had so many babies in me. It took a while for all of them to bake. Like cookies. Cookies are good, aren't they? I like snickerdoodles the best."

The man's voice was calm, as if what he was saying was perfectly normal. That was creepy enough, but it was the way the man kept his too-wide eyes fixed on him that most disturbed Martin. The man didn't seem to blink, and the way the overhead fluorescents hit his eyes made them appear to gleam with an inner light.

"Uh, me too," Martin said. "About snickerdoodles, I mean."

Martin felt a strange disconnect from reality combined with a crawling sensation of fear deep in his gut. Something was *seriously* wrong with this guy—and Martin was alone with him, no grown-ups in sight that could come help. He wanted to get up and go in search of Leslie before this situation got any more bizarre, but he feared the man might react poorly to losing his audience. So Martin sat and listened, doing his best to look calm and interested in what the man would say next, while inside he shouted, *I want to go! Now!*

"After I gave birth, there were so many babies I had to use a school bus to take them home from the hospital. Not this hospital. A different one." The man's smile fell away, and the gleam in his eyes dimmed. "But while I was driving, I got angry. They were crying so *loud*. I got so angry that I turned into a tornado and hit the bus. It went spinning around and around before it finally crashed. All my babies died. I killed them. Killed my poor babies."

Tears began to slide down the man's face, and his shoulders heaved up and down as he silently sobbed. Martin watched, fingers tightening on the magazine, crumpling the pages. He had no idea what to do, and so he sat, unable to take his eyes off the crying man, feeling more and more as if he might start crying himself.

A hand came down upon his shoulder then, gently, but the touch still made him jump. He jerked around so hard he tore one of the magazine's pages. Leslie stood there, but she wasn't looking at him. Instead she was looking at the crying man.

"It's all right," she said in a quiet voice. "He's not dangerous. He's just…confused." She attempted a smile, but it wasn't very convincing. "Let's go. On the way out, I'll tell someone to come check on him."

Martin turned back to look at the man but made no move to stand. Leslie came around to the front of the couch, took the magazine from his hands, and placed it on the table. She then took hold of his arm in a firm grip and pulled him to his feet. As she led him away from the lounge, he glanced back. The man had turned around on the couch, one arm draped over the back, and he was looking at Martin. He was smiling once more—grinning this time, actually—and although it had to be a trick of the light, Martin's imagination, or both—the man's tears were now red as blood.

MARTIN NEVER LEARNED the crying man's name, so he just thought of him like that, capitalizing the first letter of each word to make it a proper name: the Crying Man.

Leslie tried her best over the next several weeks to do damage control, and Martin responded to her efforts in whatever way he thought she wanted. He listened quietly, nodding or shaking his head as appropriate.

I should've told you the residents in that section of the hospital are free to move around. That man wouldn't have hurt you. All of the patients there are nonviolent. In fact, most people with mental illness would never hurt anyone. He was probably more afraid of you than you were of him.

She gave variations of this speech numerous times, and Martin wanted to believe her—*needed* to believe here so he could put this upsetting experience behind him. But her words rang hollow, and no matter how many times she told him the Crying Man hadn't been a threat, Martin couldn't stop thinking about the man's gap-toothed grin, and the tears of blood that streamed from his eyes.

Eventually Leslie let the subject of the Crying Man drop. But Martin didn't forget him. Not at all. He didn't believe the man had actually cried blood, of course. That part had to have been his imagination. What he *did* believe was that you couldn't always tell there was something wrong with a person just by looking at them. The Crying Man had seemed completely normal until he opened his mouth and his crazy poured out. And despite what Leslie claimed, Martin knew the Crying Man was dangerous. How could he not be with a mind that messed up? Martin came to understand that anyone, anyone at all, could be crazy. The only person he could be certain was sane was himself. And so he made a decision. From that moment on, he decided to keep other people—*all* of them—at arm's length. And if any of their masks should slip and reveal the madness that lay behind, he'd know to stay far, far away.

When he was fifteen, he almost had a girlfriend. Lora Young sat next to him in art class, and she took every opportunity to brush against him whenever she could, sitting so close her leg or shoulder touched his. And when she reached to borrow a pastel or piece of charcoal from him, her fingers touched his for the briefest of moments. She looked into his eyes a little too long when she talked to him, laughed a little too loud when she thought he said something funny. But her nails were always chewed to the quick—an unhealthy sign—and he asked Mrs. Everhart to assign him to another seat.

In college, he failed an exam because as the professor passed out the test, Martin noticed one of the man's eyes blinked more often than the other. He got up from his desk and walked out of the room without saying a word.

Several years later he bailed on a job interview when the woman interviewing him kept reaching up to touch her left earring. In addition, her R's sounded more like W's when she spoke. He cut her off in the middle of a question, thanked her for the opportunity, then left, the woman looking after him in confusion.

He refused to meet the eyes of anyone on the street, declined making chit-chat with servers, supermarket clerks, and bank tellers, and he gave panhandlers a wide berth. The less contact he had with strangers the better, as far as he was concerned. Better, and more importantly, *safer.*

His constant wariness didn't help his dating life, and the longest relationship he'd ever managed lasted only one month. He'd been seeing a pharmacist named Alexis Cross whose hobby was training border collies to run agility courses. At first this seemed a bit odd to him—it wasn't exactly a *normal* hobby—but he accompanied her to a couple competitions, and he came to admire the discipline and precision that lay at the core of the activity. Then one night, while they were in the middle of having sex, Martin broke off when he realized something.

"You don't have any eyelashes." And she didn't, not a single one.

She smiled, seeming amused.

"I thought you'd have noticed by now. I have trichotillomania. It means I pull my hair out. Usually just my eyelashes. It doesn't bother you, does it?"

There was so much about Alexis that he liked. She was smart, orderly, and attractive, and so for the first time since the day he'd encountered the Crying Man, he decided to let a person's...*idiosyncrasies* pass. They continued dating for another two weeks, but no matter how hard he tried, he couldn't feign being comfortable when he looked at her and saw those hairless eyelids. Her lack of eyelashes gave her a strangely robotic appearance, kind of like a department store mannequin.

Eventually, he couldn't stand it any longer, and he decided to break up with her. She'd stayed over at his house the night before, and he couldn't bring himself to face her, so— knowing it was a complete dick move—he wrote a note and left it on her purse in the kitchen as he headed out for work, leaving Alexis still sleeping upstairs since the pharmacy where she worked didn't open until 10:30 each morning. He hoped she'd wake, read the note, and be gone by the time he got home that evening.

He didn't hear from her that day. No calls, no texts. He wasn't sure if that was a good sign or not. On the one hand, the less drama there was about the break-up, the better. But he expected some kind of reaction from her. When he got home from work, he was dismayed to see her car still parked in the driveway. He considered driving on past his house and giving her a few more hours. Once she realized he wasn't coming home any time soon, maybe she'd get tired of waiting and leave. But he didn't want to do that. Why, he wasn't sure. Maybe twenty years of being on guard against the slightest hint of crazy in other people had worn him down. Maybe he was tired of avoidance. Maybe, for once, he wanted a confrontation. Whatever the reason, he pulled into the garage, got out of his car, and went inside.

He found the note on the kitchen counter. He stared at it for a moment before finally picking it up and reading it. It was the one he'd left for her, but she'd crossed out what he'd written with a black marker and wrote a message of her own at the bottom in large capital letters.

YOU DID THIS TO ME.

He felt a prickle on the back of his neck, accompanied by a sharp jab of pain between his eyes. He didn't call out her name, didn't race through the house frantically searching for her. He moved slowly, calmly up the stairs toward the bedroom, knowing what waited for him there. Alexis needed control of all things in her life, and when she couldn't control him, couldn't stop him from breaking up with her, she'd plunged into a massive depression and lost control of the most important thing: her mind.

She was a pharmacist, and so he assumed he would find her lying on his bed, an empty bottle or two of some powerful narcotic sitting on the nightstand. She would be lying on top of the covers with her eyes closed, hands folded on her chest in a classis death pose, not so much as a single wrinkle on her clothes, demonstrating complete and total control in death, as if to rebuke him. But the scene which confronted him when he opened the bedroom door couldn't have been further from what he expected. The covers had been pulled off the bed and thrown onto the floor. The drawers from the nightstand and dresser had been yanked out and their contents dumped. The curtains had been torn down, and the clothing removed from his closet and strewn around the room. Alexis wasn't on the bed, but the mattress was smeared with blood, as were the walls, crimson streaks and whorls, along with an occasional handprint.

At first he could only stare at the chaos, not understanding. But then he realized what he was looking at. Alexis hadn't lost control so much as willfully abandoned it. Hurt and angry, she'd gone wild and ravaged his bedroom. The door to the master bathroom was open and the light was on. He didn't want to go inside, didn't want to see what waited for him there, but he knew he had to.

Alexis lay sprawled on the tiled floor, naked, her flesh riven by dozens of cuts, some short and shallow, many more long and deep. A large kitchen knife was grasped in her right hand, and she'd torn handfuls of hair from her head and pubis, and the bloody clumps lay on the floor around her. Blood was everywhere, bright red on white porcelain. Martin imagined her cutting herself over and over, running through the bedroom, spinning around in the bathroom, flinging and smearing her blood wherever she could, like a suicidal animal marking its territory. In contrast to the bloody scene, almost as if a last sign of rapidly dwindling sanity, were her clothes, which she had placed in the tub, folded and stacked neatly.

He held his breath, as if he were standing in the presence of someone who'd fallen to an extremely virulent strain of plague and feared he might become infected himself. He continued holding his breath until he was outside standing on the lawn. Only then did he draw in a loud gasping breath, take his phone from his pocket, and call 911. While he waited for someone to answer, he imagined Alexis' insanity inside him, tiny particles of madness floating around in his lungs, entering his bloodstream as they began to colonize his body.

THE POLICE QUESTIONED HIM, of course, but not very hard. There was no evidence Alexis' death had occurred by any hand other than her own. Her parents took care of the funeral expenses, but Martin wasn't invited to the service. He might not have killed her directly, but her family viewed him as the cause of her suicide. He wouldn't have gone if he had been invited, though. Alexis might be dead, but he feared some remnant of insanity might linger around her body. He couldn't risk further exposure.

The police gave him the name of a professional cleaning crew that took care of crime scenes, and he hired them to come clean his bathroom and bedroom. For an additional fee, they also removed any clothing Alexis had gotten blood on. When the cleaners were finished, Martin painted the walls and replaced the carpet. He then contacted a realtor—no way would he continue to live in this house any longer than he had to—and then he returned to work. Less than a week had passed since Alexis' death, but if anyone at Pinnacle thought he'd come back too soon, no one said anything.

He'd only been back two days when Shari Mitchell, the art director, asked him to work up some ad designs for HizStyle Menswear, and one day after that, he was scheduled to present these designs in a meeting. He was glad to be back at work, grateful to have a project to occupy his mind. But he still couldn't help thinking about Alexis' sudden explosion of madness. He'd been so careful for so many years. How could this have happened? How could he not have seen the signs? And if he had been infected by her insanity, how would he know? He hadn't recognized the signs of madness in her, so how could he hope to recognize them in himself?

EVERYONE ELSE WAS SEATED and waiting for him when he arrived: Sherri, along with Albert Watkins from Sales, and Nancy Barber from Website Development. Martin entered the small meeting room, closed the door behind him, and put his portfolio case on the table. His skin crawled with sweat and his shirt clung wetly to his body, as if he'd just gotten back from a several-mile run in summer heat. If the others noticed anything strange about him, they gave no reaction. Maybe they were cutting him some slack because of Alexis. He'd told no one at Pinnacle about her suicide, but he was certain it was common knowledge. It had been on the news, and a gruesome story like that was too juicy not to get around. But whatever the reason for their ignoring his damp hair and sweat-sodden shirt, he was grateful.

"Sorry I'm late," he said, having no idea if he truly was late. It was simply something to say. "Just give me a minute to set up."

The meeting room had a long narrow table, and at the far end was a wall-mounted screen. A laptop sat at the head of the table, already on, projecting a blank image on the screen. Martin went to the computer, plugged in his flash drive, and called up his presentation. He then returned to his portfolio and removed three large mockups of images and text. He knew from experience that even though the exact same images were in his presentation, people liked to see and hold physical artwork before making a decision.

As the others began to pass around the sketches, Martin

returned to the computer, picked up the wireless mouse sitting next to it, and began. The three listened quietly and attentively as he went through the three different versions of the HizStyle ad artwork, and as usual, he saved his favorite—in this case three images of the same model wearing different suits with the tagline *Whatever Your Taste in Clothes, HizStyle's Got You Covered*—for last. When he was finished, he thanked the others for their attention and asked for their thoughts.

Sherri, the art director, was the first to speak. She was a handsome woman in her late fifties who dressed in vivid colors and liked to dye to her hair. Today it was electric blue.

"Mama's eyes are red."

Martin frowned, uncertain if he'd heard her correctly. There was no mother in any of the designs he'd presented. No women of any sort, red-eyed or otherwise.

Cold shivered down his spine, and a fidgety nervousness took hold of him. Any other time he would've asked Sherri to repeat what she'd said, but not today. He was afraid she'd say the same thing word for word—or something worse.

He nodded slowly.

"Thanks for your input, Sherri." He turned to Albert. "What do you think?"

Albert was in his mid-forties, a lean man with a shaved head and neatly trimmed black goatee. He wore a navy-blue suit with a lavender tie. He always looked like he was ready to meet with a client on a second's notice.

"If something's lost, it will only get more lost."

Albert put no special emphasis on any of the words, injected no particular emotion into his voice. But the sheer normalcy of his tone made what he said seem even more sinister.

Nancy was in her late twenties, blond, short and overweight, and she favored loose blouses and pants which she thought concealed her weight but which only drew attention to it.

"I'll scream," she said. "I'll do it."

Martin couldn't stop himself from responding this time. "Please don't."

He thought of the man on the stairs, of the bizarre statement he'd made. *Careful. There's a swirl of elevators at the bottom.* Did Sherri, Albert, and Nancy have the same thing wrong with that that that guy had? Whatever it was, was it contagious? A desperate hope occurred to him then, and he forced a smile.

"This is some kind of joke, right? You guys are just playing with me, trying to ease me back into the swing of things by putting me on."

If they *were* joking, it was goddamned cruel of them, but he wouldn't call them on it. He'd be too relieved to learn they were faking. But they just looked at him, gazes empty, faces expressionless.

Finally, Sherri stood and walked to the head of the table. Martin shrank back from her approach, but she ignored him. She picked up the laptop and carried it to Albert. He took hold of the screen and the two of them yanked. The screen separated from the laptop's bottom half, and Albert held onto the former, Sherri the latter. They then walked around the table until they stood next to Nancy. She didn't look up at them, kept her gaze fastened on Martin.

"I have helicopters in my ears," she said, and then smiled at him.

A second later, Sherri and Albert smashed their laptop sections against Nancy's head. The woman didn't make a sound as she fell out of her chair and slumped to the floor. Sherri and Albert looked at her for a moment, and then in unspoken agreement they bent down and began hitting her again, over and over. Her body jerked and quivered with each blow, but still she made no sound. Eventually, she stopped moving, but Sherri and Albert continued striking her, flinging arcs of blood into the air.

It's happening again, Martin thought. The Crying Man. Alexis. The madness that lay behind the fragile veneer of existence had broken once more. He had to get out of here before it came for him.

It's already got you.

He heard these words in Alexis' voice.

You caught my madness when you found my body, and you brought it with you when you came back to work. It took a couple days to spread—you do try to keep to yourself—but your coworkers caught it. The only question now is how much longer you'll hold out. You have a lifetime of keeping insanity at bay, and that experience has protected you so far. But it won't last forever.

Martin ran for the door, keeping to the other side of the table to put a barrier between Terri, Albert, and himself. They were still hitting Nancy's head—or what remained of it—and the wet smacking sounds of their blows caused hot bile to rise in his throat.

He burst out into the hallway, expecting to see a crowd of men and women committing atrocities on one another. But the hall was empty. He didn't wait around for anyone else to show up. He headed straight for the exit. Once he reached his car, he'd get in, peel the fuck out of here, and only when he was miles away from this place would he call 911 and report what had happened. The police would likely think him crazy, but he didn't care about that. All he cared about was getting away from this madness. But as he reached the lobby, he saw Alexis standing in front of the double glass doors, knife in hand, naked body covered with cuts and slick with blood from head to toe.

She smiled, displaying teeth smeared crimson.

"The tigers come at night," she said. She started walking

toward him, feet smacking wetly on the tiled floor, leaving a trail of bloody footprints behind her.

Martin turned and ran back the way he'd come.

"You can't escape!" she called out after him. "Wherever you go, there you are!"

She laughed then, a thick gurgling sound, as if her throat was filled with blood.

Martin was too terrified to think clearly, but if pressed, he would've said that this moment was when the protective shield he'd worked so hard to construct around his psyche over the years shattered like thin, cheap glass.

He ran on instinct, retracing his steps, and he found himself standing in front of the door that led to the stairwell. He yanked it again and hurried through, no destination in mind, no plan for escape, nothing but the irresistible compulsion to run and keep running, no matter what. But once he was inside the stairwell, he stopped dead. The ground floor landing was gone, and in its place was a spinning maelstrom that extended downward as far as he could see. And caught within that whirling vortex—which resembled nothing so much as a massive, subterranean tornado—were rectangular metal objects, hundreds of them, tumbling end over end as they spun around.

"Elevators," Martin said. "A swirl of them."

The roaring sound inside the stairwell was deafening, like a dozen trains rumbling past at the same time.

Martin was beyond terror now, and as he looked down into the maelstrom he thought that, in its own impossible way, it was the most awe-inspiring sight he'd ever seen. *This was what he'd been so frightened of all these years? This was a thing of wonder, a great mystery forbidden to those whose minds remained closed, remained safe. The man he'd been before dating Alexis could never have seen something like this. But now the scales had been removed from his eyes, and for the first time in his life, he could truly *see*. And what he saw was magnificent.

"What's so great about sanity anyway?" he said with a crooked smile.

He saw the man he'd encountered earlier standing on the stairs, laughing and clapping. Alexis burst through the stairwell door, knife raised high, lips pulled back from her teeth in a savage grin. Terri and Albert followed close behind, faces and clothes stippled with blood. Nancy accompanied them, her head a misshapen pulp, features unrecognizable.

Martin turned, gave them all a farewell wave, and fell backward into the maelstrom. As he plunged downward, he saw Alexis and the others peer over the edge, but they remained where they were. He sighed contentedly, enjoying the freedom, the release that came from letting go of his struggle against the unreal and the mad.

*If you can't beat them...*he thought.

Elevators spun around him, doors closed, giving no hint as to what—if anything—lay inside. He thought he could hear a faint keening, as of babies crying, but he wasn't sure. Then one of the elevators came rushing toward him, its door sliding open. He slammed painfully into something solid with a loud *whump*, and he lay there, trying to catch his breath as the elevator door closed. Standing in front of the control panel was the Crying Man. He looked exactly as he had when Martin had seen him two decades ago. Twin trails of blood ran from his eyes, dripped from his chin, and pattered to the floor like soft rain.

Martin reached up, grabbed the handrail, and pulled himself to his feet. He was sore from his collision with the elevator's interior, but otherwise unhurt.

The Crying Man looked at him. "There's a new monster every day."

Martin smiled, his own crimson tears welling in his eyes.

"I'm counting on it."

He stepped past the Crying Man and saw there were only two buttons on the control panel. One was labeled *Outward,* the other *Inward.* Martin pressed the latter, and the car's interior was plunged into darkness as the elevator began to descend.

NO ONE SINGS IN THE CITY OF THE DEAD

"I honestly didn't think I'd see you again. I *hoped*, sure, but I didn't *believe*, not deep down."

Keith doesn't respond. He looks at me with eyes that don't blink, and his mouth—wet with blood—remains closed. Crimson stains mar his hospital gown, and while a cold, strong wind is blowing, the thin fabric doesn't stir. Neither does his hair. It's dusk, so there's still some sun left, but the cemetery is surrounded by tall oaks, and their reddish-brown leaves block much of the light, paint shadows on the ground, drape old, crumbling gravestones in darkness.

I step forward, but I immediately stop. I want to go to Keith, touch him, prove that he's real, but I'm afraid. What if his form is tenuous? What if I touch him and he pops like a soap bubble, here one instant, gone the next? I can't take losing him a second time. So I stand here, motionless, just like him, fifteen feet between us, maybe less, the wind tearing leaves from the trees, causing them to dance in the air around us before falling to the ground.

A woman's voice comes from close behind me.

"What's wrong? Not what you were expecting?"

Her tone is both amused and cruel. She's enjoying this.

The Clown Lady.

I don't take my eyes off Keith, as if I fear he'll vanish the instant I stop looking at him.

"Is…*this* all he is now?"

"Not good enough for you? I can always send him back if—"

"No!"

I hesitate another moment, then I start walking toward him. Behind me, cloth rustles on the ground, and something whimpers, unhappy in the cold. I ignore it and keep moving, leaves crunching beneath my feet. Keith shows no sign he's aware of my approach, but I feel something change in the atmosphere between us. At first, I don't know what it is, but as I draw closer, I feel it more strongly, and now I can name it.

Anticipation.

His stink hits me then, a rank combination of spoiled meat, blood, shit, and piss. I don't mind it, though. It's evidence he's really here.

When I reach him, I put my arms around his cold, stiff neck, stand on the tips of my toes, lean forward, and press my lips to his mouth. His lips don't yield right away, so I push my mouth against his harder. Eventually, his lips grow warmer, and—if they're not exactly soft—they become more pliable.

I pull my face away, my mouth smeared with his blood. It's foul, diseased, and I've never tasted anything sweeter.

I look into his empty eyes and smile, my teeth streaked red with what used to run in my husband's veins.

"Happy Halloween, my love."

HE LIES on his hospital bed, eyes closed, chest barely moving when he breathes. I rise from my chair and step to the side of the bed, wanting to get a closer look, to make sure he's still alive. Without opening his yes, Keith smiles weakly.

"I'm not dead yet," he says.

His voice is thin and tired, but I'm glad he can still joke. I take his left hand, careful not to squeeze too tight. His skin is dry as paper, the bones beneath fragile as balsa wood, and I fear if I tighten my grip, these bones will snap like desiccated twigs.

"How long have you been here?" he asks.

"Not long," I lie. I didn't leave his room after he fell asleep last night. I spent the night here, sleeping in the chair.

His eyes open slowly, as if this takes a great effort.

"What time is it?" he asks.

The bed controls are attached to the inside of railing, and his hand fumbles for them. I want to work the controls for him, but he's a proud man, determined to do as much for himself as he can, while he can. So I stand by and wait while his fingers search for the right button. They finally find it, he presses it, and the head of his bed raises him into a sitting position. When he's satisfied with the angle, he takes his finger off the button, and his hand falls limply onto the mattress. His breathing picks up speed, as if this small exertion has exhausted him. He's connected to various types of medical equipment—an IV drip of isotonic solution, blood oxygen monitor, heart monitor, blood pressure cuff, and more. It's all about the blood right now.

Speaking of blood, he coughs once, and a dark line of the stuff rolls down the side of his mouth. If he's aware of it, he gives no sign.

"Do you need to go to the restroom?" I ask, eyeing the blood nervously.

I think about the last time this happened, when I didn't get him to the toilet in time and he vomited a gush of dark-red blood all over the room's tiled floor. It took forever for the staff to clean up the mess.

He shakes his head. "I'm good." A pause. "For now, anyway."

I hope he's right.

Keith was diagnosed with liver disease in his twenties, and doctors told him he'd need a transplant by the time he hit middle age, if not sooner. He made it to thirty-six before his liver started giving out, and it was almost a year after that until a donor organ became available. The transplant procedure went smoothly, and all signs were that Keith was going to be fine. And for a few weeks, he was. But then he started throwing up blood. Not a lot at first, but then more began coming up, and we returned to the transplant doctor. Tests were run, results were inconclusive, and Keith ended up back in the hospital. After yet more tests, the doctors determined the cause of Keith's problem was that there'd been an "incident" during surgery—perhaps an artery was nicked, and the transplant team didn't see it and closed him up. The leaking blood was backing into his stomach, and when the amount became too much, Keith's body ejected it the only way it could.

Three months in the hospital and six surgeries later, the problem still wasn't fixed, and this morning, one of the doctors took me aside and told me Keith's body couldn't take anymore. His new liver was dying, and he'd developed an infection that the docs couldn't get rid of. She told me Keith had a week left, maybe less.

I went out to my car and cried for the better part of an hour. Then I came back to Keith's room to wait for him to wake up. Being here was hard before, but knowing what I know now, it's unbearable. But I won't leave him. He's my husband, and I want to spend every moment with him that I can before he dies. Thank god we never had children. I can't imagine trying to deal with their grief while I'm grieving too.

"Has the doc been by this morning?" Keith asks. "Did I miss her because I was sleeping?"

"I haven't seen her yet." This is a lie. If I tell him the truth, he'll ask what she said to me, and I don't want to tell him. I *can't* tell him.

He settles his head back against the pillow, eyes now half-lidded.

"I'm so sick of this place. I can't wait for them to fix me up so I can go home."

"Me too."

There's a catch in my voice, but Keith doesn't register it.

"I'm *so* sleepy. Why am I so sleepy? I just woke up."

I squeeze his hand a bit tighter, but he grimaces in pain and I quickly loosen my grip.

"It's all the meds they have you on. Why don't you go ahead and take a nap? I'll be right here."

"Okay, but only a short one."

He closes his eyes, and a moment later his breathing deepens.

I think he's asleep, but then he mumbles, "Sing something for me."

I work in phone sales, but singing is my hobby, and, if I do say so myself, I'm not too shabby at it. I'm okay singing in front of an audience, but I'm uncomfortable singing for only one person. I'm too aware of them looking at me, listening, judging... But this is Keith. I've sang solo to him before. Of course, none of those times did I know he was dying.

"Sure, sweetie."

I'm not sure what to sing, so I pick a song at random—a slow ballad about two lovers saying goodbye for the last time. Tears stream down my cheeks as I sing softly. Keith doesn't open his eyes, and I'm glad. I don't want him to see me upset like this.

I manage to make it to the end of the song, and I use my hands to wipe tears off my face. It looks like Keith is asleep, so I'll go into the restroom and get some toilet paper to blow my nose. But before I stand, I look at his chest again to check his breathing, and I see his chest isn't rising anymore.

"No," I whisper, then louder, "*no!*"

Keith doesn't stir at the sound of my voice. In fact, he'll never stir at anything ever again.

Now that the dark miracle has occurred—now that Keith's back—I don't know what to do.

I turn to the Clown Lady.

"Can I take him away from here? Or is he stuck in this place?"

"Do you *want* to take him home the way he is? It would be more than a little difficult to explain him to friends and family, don't you think?"

She has a point. Even if he was completely restored to normal, how could I explain that he's returned from the dead?

The pillowcase at the Clown Lady's feet moves as the thing inside it wriggles. We both notice, but neither of us says anything.

"We could go somewhere, a place no one knows us."

"And do what?" the Clown Lady asks. "His physical and cognitive functions will improve somewhat over time, but he'll never be the Keith you knew. You won't be able to take him out in public. People will know instantly that something's wrong with him. They won't know what it is, not on a conscious level, but instinctively they'll sense that he's *wrong*. More, that he's a *violation*. Some may even attack him. The living are compelled to destroy the Returned to maintain the balance between this world and the next." Her too-red lips stretch into a poor simulation of a smile. "That's why you tend not to see many dead people walking around."

My eyes narrow with suspicion. "It sounds like you're trying to talk me out of this."

"Not at all. But I insist my clients be fully informed before any deal is finalized. Customer satisfaction is extremely important to me. Say the word, and I'll send him back, and you can take your payment and leave."

She nudges the pillowcase with her foot, and the thing inside wails, cold and scared. I do my best to shut out the sound. I turn back to Keith, reach up, stroke his cheek, find it hard as marble.

"No. We'll find a way to make it work…somehow."

"If you're sure…"

I stare into Keith's glassy eyes as I answer.

"I am."

"Very well."

I keep my gaze on Keith, but I can hear the Clown Lady pick up the pillowcase, remove its contents, and then begin to greedily eat. For a moment, the baby's screams drown out the wet sounds of tearing meat and enthusiastic chewing, but then the child's voice is cut off, likely because the Clown Lady has torn out its throat.

I smile at Keith, place my hand on his chest, feel no heartbeat.

"Everything's going to be okay, sweetie. Now that we're together again."

The wind continues swirling leaves around us as the Clown Lady eats, slurping and swallowing, moaning in pleasure.

ANOTHER HALLOWEEN, almost thirty years ago.

I'm seven, it's Trick-or-Treat, and I'm dressed as the pink Power Ranger. My friend Lindsey is Wednesday Addams, and Lindsey's older brother Marcus is one of the Teenage Mutant Ninja Turtles. I can't remember which one. I can never keep them straight. Our parents came along to "keep an eye" on us, which I hate because I'm not a baby, but the four of them hang back and stay on the sidewalk when we go up to people's houses, talking about whatever grownups talk about when kids aren't around. So it's *kind of* like we're on our own.

The sun has gone down, and the fluorescent glow of streetlights create eerie circles of light on the sidewalks, and we make a game of running from one to the next, so the Boogeyman won't get us. I don't believe in the Boogeyman, though. Not really.

We started in our neighborhood, and now we've moved on to the next street over. We stop at several houses, yell "Trick-or-Treat!" and get candy. Some of it's good, like full-sized Hershey bars, and some of it's not-so-good, like rock-hard pieces of cheap taffy. The farther down the street we go, the more nervous I become, until finally we reach *her* house.

The Clown Lady.

"Can we skip this one?" I ask.

Marcus and Lindsey exchange a look, then they smile.

"What's wrong?" Lindsey asks. "Scared?"

"Maybe…a little."

Marcus steps closer to me. He's taller than both his sister and me, and he likes to stand close to kids shorter than him so he can intimidate them.

"You don't believe the stories, do you?" he asks.

"I don't know."

"Have you ever seen the Clown Lady before?" Lindsey asks.

"No."

Marcus takes a step back then bends down until his face is close to mine. His breath smells like potato chips. It's gross.

"Then you don't really know *what* she looks like, do you?"

"I guess not."

I heard my mom and dad talk about her once. They said she's a dentist who works out of her home. The dentist I go to works with other dentists, and their office has lots of rooms with white walls. I wonder if the inside of the Clown Lady's house is white too.

Marcus smiles. It's a mean smile, and I don't like it.

"Then there's no reason for you not to go ring her doorbell, is there?"

I glance at the house. The porchlight is on, but there are no Halloween decorations.

"I dare you," Lindsey says.

"*We* dare you," Marcus adds.

I do *not* want to go up to the Clown Lady's house, but I also don't want Lindsey to think I'm a scaredy-cat. I don't really care what Marcus thinks. He's a jerk.

I look over my shoulder to check if our parents are nearby. They are, but they're talking and laughing, not looking in our direction. I face forward.

"Okay," I say, and—gripping the handle of my pumpkin-shaped candy bucket tight—I walk toward the house.

There's nothing scary about it. It's a ranch house, red brick, black roof, shutters, and garage door. It doesn't look much different from my house, really. I think of the stories kids tell about the Clown Lady—that she pulls all the teeth out of her patients and makes jewelry from them. Necklaces, earrings, bracelets… They also say that she saves the very best teeth to eat, that she puts them in a bowl, pours milk on them, and eats them like cereal. Her own teeth are hard as rock, so she doesn't hurt them when she chews. At this point, whoever's telling the story will make loud chewing sounds, and I imagine I can hear them now. Crack-crack-*cruuuuuuuunch*… I need to pee—*bad*—and I wish I'd gone one more time before we left my house.

I step up onto the porch, and I reach for the doorbell with a trembling hand. But before I can ring it, the door opens, and the Clown Lady is standing there. She's short, stout, and dressed in a blue suit jacket, skirt, and black heels. Her black hair is short, glossy, with severe edges, and it looks artificial, like a wig made of rubber. Her face is covered with some kind of thick white powder, and her small, pursed lips are a startling red. She looks at me, smiles, reveals teeth white as snow. I try to say *Trick or Treat*, but I can't speak. Instead, I hold my bag out.

She's holding a large wooden bowl, and she reaches in, takes out a small chocolate bar, and drops it into my bag.

"There you go," she says. She takes something else from the bowl, a toothbrush, still in its box. "And this is for *after* you eat the chocolate." She drops it in my bag too.

She's still smiling, but there's a strange coldness in her eyes. I'm shaking so hard now that my bag rattles, and suddenly I feel warmth spread across the crotch of my pink uniform, and I begin to cry.

AFTER KEITH'S BURIAL, I fall into a deep depression. I start drinking too much, contemplate suicide, and then one day, the idea comes to me that maybe I don't have to let Keith go. Maybe—just *maybe*—I can bring him back. Myths and legends are filled with stories of people returning from the dead. Those tales have to have some basis in fact, don't they?

I start researching on the Internet, tracking down and reading old books, meeting with people who claim to be experts in the supernatural, and six months later, I'm sitting at a small round table covered by a large crimson cloth, a woman on the other side who has no name that I'm aware of, but who's reputed to be a highly skilled medium, someone who exists between our world and the next. She tells me of an old, abandoned cemetery, of an entity who guards the gate between worlds, one who takes the form of a figure you find most frightening and who only appears on Halloween night. And she tells me of the terrible price this guardian requires for its assistance. I don't care, though. I'll do anything to have Keith back.

Anything.

NIGHT FALLS while I hold Keith, and I keep holding him as it grows darker and the temperature drops. A light drizzle starts to fall, and his body becomes colder, until it feels as if I'm hugging a block of ice. I don't let go, though. I squeeze even harder. The Clown Lady—her feast finished—stands and watches us as she licks blood from her fingers. She says nothing, and I wonder what she's thinking. Is she darkly amused by my need to hold onto my dead husband? Does she pity me? Does she think I'm pathetic?

I don't care. I have Keith back, and that's all that matters to me.

After a time, my legs ache from standing still so long, and after more time, they become tingly, then numb. Keith has not moved since I wrapped my arms around him, hasn't so much as blinked. Eventually, the rain ends, the clouds clear, and the sky in the east moves from black to dark blue to light blue. Halloween night is almost over. I don't know what will happen when the sun rises. Will Keith vanish like morning mist burned away by the day's first light? Is there any way I can possibly hold onto him hard enough to keep him with me?

The Guardian might know, but she'll likely demand a price for any additional help, a price even more terrible than the one I've already paid. But it doesn't matter. I'll do anything, *give* anything, to keep Keith in the world of the living. But before I can ask the Guardian, Keith speaks for the first time tonight. His voice is a raspy hiss, and blood dribbles from his mouth onto my shoulder as he talks.

"Sing...something...for me..."

Tears well in my eyes. I don't want to sing what I sang to him just before he died, that ballad of love and loss. But I can't think of anything else, so I begin. My voice is rough after a night of breathing cold, wet air, but I do my best. But I only get the first few words out when the first light of dawn touches us. I'm still holding onto Keith, and I can feel him becoming...*less*, and I know that's he's going back to wherever the Clown Lady pulled him from—and there's nothing I can do about it.

The Clown Lady speaks for the first time in hours.

"You can't keep him here, but you *can* go with him—if you choose. You must decide quickly, though."

I barely feel Keith now, and I know I have only seconds left.

I look at the Clown Lady. "I'll go."

She smiles. "Nice doing business with you."

Shadows rush in from all directions then, and the world is gone.

NOTHING in the sky but darkness, air bitingly cold, a flat hard surface like marble beneath my feet. Off in the distance are large black spires, towers, or mountains, or maybe something else entirely. I'm still holding onto Keith, and I'm relieved that he feels solid once again. We're not alone, though. There are shadowy forms around us, so many that they're impossible to count, billions upon billions, stretching in every direction, all the way to the horizons and beyond.

I don't know what this place is, and I don't care. As long as I'm with Keith.

I open my mouth to continue singing, ready to pick up where I left off, but when I begin, no sound comes out. That's when I realize I've heard nothing since coming here. This is a place of silence, where there's never been so much as a hint of sound, and never will be.

The shadows drift closer to us, and I sense their anger and hatred. This is a realm of the dead, and I don't belong here. I'm *wrong*, and they can't tolerate my presence. I was a fool to think that Keith and I could be together again. He's dead, and I'm still alive.

Keith doesn't speak, but I hear his voice in my mind.

I can fix that.

He gently pulls away from me, wraps cold, stiff fingers around my neck, and begins to squeeze. I see bright sparks of light in my vision, then—sooner than I expect—darkness creeps in. My consciousness slips away as death comes for me.

It feels like love.

THE GIRL WHO BLED IN THE TREE

Terri Marshall swings her Altima onto the street where she grew up, heart pounding, hands gripping the steering wheel tight. She looks up at the rearview mirror every few seconds, afraid she'll see a pair of headlights reflected in the glass, relieved when she sees only dark road behind her. She knows she hasn't lost Duane, knows he's still following, but she's managed to put some distance between them, and that's enough for now. When her car's headlights wash across the front lawn of her parents' house—illuminating the For Sale sign in the yard—she hits the brakes too hard, and her car fishtails, tires squealing in protest. It's late, after two in the morning according to the dashboard clock, and she fears the noise might wake some of the neighbors, prompt them to peer between cracked curtains to see what's going on, maybe place a worried call to 911. She isn't concerned the sound of her car skidding will wake her parents. They're both dead and buried.

She whips the Altima into the empty driveway, parks with the passenger side wheels on the grass, and cuts the engine. She gets out, the garage door a smear of garish white in the headlights' glare, and slams the door shut. *Too loud,* she tells herself, but really, what does it matter? If Duane catches her, it's going to get a hell of a lot louder.

She hasn't been here for six months, not since she and Duane got the place ready to sell. It's been on the market for a while, long enough for Duane to start losing patience. *I don't know what the hell's wrong. I've sold houses in that neighborhood before. Maybe it's got some kind of bad karma or something.*

Two stories, white siding, black shutters, new roof, new windows. The front yard is well-maintained—Duane pays a service to take care of it—and while the lawn isn't huge, it's big enough for a good-sized oak tree. The tree is close to the house, and Duane considered cutting it down. *An old tree like that makes people nervous, makes them think about it falling on their house during a bad storm.* The idea appalled her, but rather than make a big issue of it, she told him the tree was charming, and that it would look good on the photos for the brochure and the house's online listing. He agreed, one of the few times he actually listened to her, and the tree still stands where it has all her life.

She needs it now.

She hurries across the lawn, the night air cold on her exposed arms and legs, the grass cool beneath her bare feet. It's mid-August, temperature in the high seventies, but it feels more like early fall to her, and she shivers. She wishes she had on something more than a Queens of the Stone Age T-shirt and shorts, but she had no time to change, not if she wanted to get out of the house before Duane grabbed hold of her. She almost didn't escape as it was.

When she reaches the tree, she takes hold of its lowest limb and hauls herself up. When she was a child, she needed to jump to grab the limb, but while she's by no means tall, she grew enough during adolescence that she can reach it easily now. Once on the limb, she crouches, bare feet on corrugated bark, one hand pressed against the trunk to steady herself. She reaches up, wraps her fingers around the next highest limb, and begins climbing. How far can she get? She has no idea. She was twelve the last time she climbed the tree, and she was able to get two thirds of the way up then. She's bigger now, of course, and she doesn't know if she can get that high, fears the thinner limbs won't support her weight. She decides to go as far as she can and hopes it will be high enough to conceal her.

She hears the engine of Duane's SUV before she sees the headlights. She feels a deep chill that has nothing to do with the temperature, and with it comes a mental flash of him standing in the open doorway of their master bathroom, a home-pregnancy test gripped in his hand, held up as if it were evidence at a trial and he the prosecuting attorney. *When were you going to tell me, Terri? When?*

The Altima's automatic headlights have switched off, but the vehicle is clearly visible from the street, and her less-than-stellar parking job makes it even more noticeable. She hopes the oak's leaves will provide cover, but they're sparse this low. She's tempted to climb higher to where the leaves are thicker, but she fears the movement will attract Duane's attention. There are no streetlights in this neighborhood—the residents think they spoil the area's aesthetics—and the SUV's headlights won't reach this far. Her clothes are dark, and if she remains still, the shadows might conceal her and he'll drive past without noticing her. She presses herself close to the trunk. If there was a limb on the side opposite the road, she would move onto it to better hide herself, but there isn't. She watches the SUV approach. If Duane drives on, she'll wait several minutes to make sure he isn't coming back, then she'll climb down, hop in her car, and get the hell out of here. She won't need the tree then.

But as the SUV draws near the house, the vehicle slows,

and Terri imagines Duane peering through the driver's side window to get a good look at her car. This is her parents' house, and he's been here many times over the years—and he's the goddamn realtor selling it. He *knows* there shouldn't be a car parked here this time of night, and of course he'd recognize her Altima. A second later, he guns the engine and turns into the driveway.

The limb she's crouched on has smaller branches coming off it. She takes hold of one of these, snaps it off, and drops it to the ground. She then raises her hand and brings it down fast and hard onto the jagged stub she's created. Pain flares bright and hot in her palm, and she can't stop herself from crying out.

The SUV door slams, and she hears Duane shout, "Where the *fuck* are you, Terri?"

She looks down, sees him standing in the driveway, sees that he's holding a gun.

She pulls her hand off the broken branch-end, biting her lip hard to keep from crying out again. She turns the palm upward, sees the blood welling forth, watches it begin to spill over the edges of her hand, run between her fingers.

Help me, she thinks. *Please...*

"*I* BRING ALL the money into this house, and that means *I* get to spend it anyway *I* want!"

Terri sits at the top of the stairs, listening to her father yell. She's twelve years old and wearing her favorite pajamas, the ones with little Eeyores on them, feet bare, legs drawn up to her chest, arms wrapped around them, chin resting on her knees. Her mother says something, but she speaks so softly that Terri can't make out the words. She's always quiet, and the louder Dad gets, the quieter she becomes. *Yell back!* Terri thinks. She knows it won't happen, though.

From where she sits, she can't see her parents. She hears water running in the kitchen sink, knows Mom is rinsing dishes so she doesn't have look at Dad. When he yells, his face turns a deep red. When this happens, Terri always hopes he'll have a heart attack, collapse to the floor, and die. So far he hasn't, though. Maybe tonight she and Mom will get lucky.

Dad bought a new car today—a Lexus—without consulting Terri's mother. Dad may make money, but he's terrible at managing it, so he leaves that job to his wife. But he's an impulsive spender, which puts her in the impossible position of trying to budget around his splurges.

"Carl, we can't afford a new car now, especially one so expensive." Mom's voice is whisper-soft, her tone apologetic.

A harsh smack of flesh on flesh, followed by a gasp then a sob tells Terri Dad has slapped Mom. She's seen him hit her—and worse—many times before. Her insides go cold and tears well, though they do not fall. She won't let them.

A moment of silence, and Terri expects Mom to say she's sorry, that of course he's right, what was she thinking? But when she speaks there's a thread of steel her voice. Just a thread, but it's there.

"If we keep the Lexus, we won't be able to afford Terri's dance class. You know how much it means to her."

Terri's gut knots with tension. Dance class is *everything* to her right now. It's her whole world, and she's good at it—her teacher says so—maybe good enough to become a professional one day. She'd like that. She wants to rush down the stairs, go into the living room, and beg her father to allow her to continue with her class. She could help pay for it. She's only twelve, but that's old enough to start babysitting, isn't it? Or maybe she could rake leaves and mow yards. She's willing to do whatever it takes. She doesn't move, though, just sits and listens and tries not to cry. Tries *hard*.

"What did you say?" Dad practically roars these words, and another slap follows them. "That girl is so goddamn uncoordinated, I'm surprised she can take more than three steps without tripping over her own damn feet. Sending her to dance class is like sending a three-legged hippo—a waste of time and money!"

Terri feels as if she's been slapped now, and the tears finally come. Before she realizes it, she's halfway down the stairs, then she's at the front door, then she's outside, the world a shimmering blur seen through her tears. It's a late Saturday afternoon in October, the air crisp and cool, but even though Terri isn't wearing a jacket, she doesn't feel the cold, doesn't feel anything except hurt and shame and anger—so much anger. Without thinking, she runs toward the oak tree in their front yard, her stocking feet crunching dead leaves beneath them. She reaches the tree and starts climbing it as easily as if it was a ladder, her young, strong body moving with speed and grace. This is where she goes when her father's cruelty becomes too much to bear, high above the world, surrounded by branches and leaves, alone, secluded, safe. She's spent countless hours up here, hiding and crying and wishing things were different than they are. In a way, the tree's her friend, her guardian, her protector, and she desperately needs it now. The tree's leaves have turned brown and orange with the season, and only two thirds of them remain on the branches to provide cover for her. She climbs as high as she can, does her best to conceal herself, and hopes it's enough.

She waits.

She hopes that Dad's too angry at her mother to have noticed her running out of the house, and she's ashamed to hope this, for it means that her mother is still bearing the brunt of Dad's anger, drawing it to herself and away from Terri. She shouldn't wish more pain on her mother, should take her fair share of it, give her mother some relief, but she's too scared. The front door flies open then and Dad storms outside.

"Terri! Where the hell are you?"

She doesn't answer, holds her breath. She can see him through gaps in the leaves, face red, eyes burning, hands clenched into fists… And then the tension drains from his body, and he smiles.

"Sweetie? Honey? Everything's okay. Your mother and I just had a little misunderstanding, that's all."

He glances toward the Lexus parked in their driveway, and his brow furrows, as if his anger is returning. But then he smiles wider and his brow smooths. She knows the smile isn't real, that he's putting on an act for her, trying to lure her out. He's done it before. But she wants the act to be real, wants him not to be mad at her, wants her kind, lovable Daddy back, even if he's an illusion. She shifts her position so she has a clearer view of him, but in doing so snags her left pajama sleeve on a broken branch. The sharp end pierces the fabric, bites into her skin, and the pain makes her wince. She draws in a hissing breath but doesn't cry out. She feels blood running down her forearm, fears she's seriously injured herself, but she won't call out to her father. Better to bleed to death in the tree than to let him get his hands on her. She wishes she understood where his anger comes from, why he is the way he is. Maybe if she understood it, she could do something about it, help him overcome it, or at least better know how to keep it at bay. She tried asking her mother once, but all her mother said was, *We are who we are.* She smiled grimly, then added, *Til death do us part.* Terri didn't understand her mother's response, but she felt the woman's despairing bitterness, and she's never asked her about Dad's temper again.

She will never know what prompted her father to look upward, some sixth sense, maybe. But look up he does, and when he sees her his Nice Daddy mask falls away, and Angry Daddy returns.

"Come down," he says, tone cold. "Now."

She doesn't move. Her pajama sleeve remains caught on the branch, the end embedded in her flesh, and she thinks she can feel a pulling, a draining, as if the tree is absorbing her blood. Dad's features darken, and he stabs an index finger toward the ground, as if he thinks she's lost the ability to comprehend English.

"*Now*," he repeats, like he's summoning a stubborn dog.

She stays where she is, lets the tree continue drinking her blood. Why not? It's been more a friend to her than her father ever was. It stands just outside her bedroom on the second floor, so close she can almost reach it when the window is open. How many times has she stood at the window looking out at the tree while her father yelled and hit her mother? Watched it change with the seasons, listened to the wind stirring its leaves and rustling its branches? How many times has she imagined jumping out the window in the middle of the night, catching hold of one of the limbs, shimmying down monkey-swift, until she reaches the lawn and starts running, never stopping, never looking back? There's no escape now, though. She knows that, but she can't bring herself to climb down and face her father. Instead, she wraps her free arm tight around the tree's trunk, and—gaze fixed on her father's face—almost imperceptibly shakes her head no.

Her father smiles, cold and cruel.

"If you're not going to come down on your own, I'll just have to come get you, won't I?"

He walks toward the tree, grabs a low-hanging branch,

pulls himself up with a soft *oomph* of effort. He climbs slowly, testing hand and footholds as he goes, angry but still in control. She wishes he climbed swiftly, recklessly, because then he might slip and fall, might hurt himself when he lands, giving her a chance to get down and run off before he can recover and grab hold of her. She wishes, wishes *hard...*

A dry brown leaf near her left shoulder detaches and falls, spiraling downward. It passes near her father's face, brushes his cheek, and he winces. A thin line of blood appears on his skin, and Terri realizes the leaf has cut him. He touches a hand to his small wound, frowns as he regards the blood on his fingers.

Another leaf breaks free, this one close to her right hip. Like the first, it spirals downward, and it slices the back of her father's left hand, which currently grips a branch not much wider than Terri's thin arms. This time the cut is deeper, and her father lets out a sharp cry of pain. There's more blood, too. A lot more.

Terri smiles. "Get him," she whispers.

All around her leaves quiver, and then they burst away from the tree in an explosion of red, brown, and yellow. They descend rapidly toward her father, so many that he's temporarily until lost to Terri's sight. They cut and cut and cut, and his screams are like sweet music to her. He tries to hold onto the tree, but he's in too much pain, and his hands are too slick with blood to maintain a solid grip. He slips, falls, hits the ground head first. There's a loud *crack*, like a branch breaking, and her father—a tattered, bloody thing—lies on the grass, not moving, eyes open and staring. Terri looks at him for a moment, and then she slowly pulls her left arm free of the broken branch that pierced her flesh. Blood trickles down her forearm, onto her wrist, then onto her hand and fingers. She presses those fingers gently against the tree's bark.

"Thank you," she says.

As Terri grew into adulthood, she promised herself that whatever else happened in her life, she wouldn't end up with a man like her father. But of course she did. She was cautious in her dating life, kept close watch for red flags—a quick temper, a lack of patience, simmering resentment, nurturing grudges... But she hadn't realized that people like her father didn't reveal their true selves right away. They were like carnivorous plants that create a sticky sweet substance to lure and trap their prey, and by the time you realize what's happening, it's too late. They've got you. Duane was like that, kind and attentive at first, but once he had his hooks into her, he dropped the act and reverted to the sadistic, controlling bastard he'd always been. Terri found herself living in the very hell she'd sworn to avoid, and she literally has the scars to show for it. Now here she is, clinging to an old oak tree in the middle of the night, her abusive spouse standing on the ground below, gun in hand. The gun—a 9mm Glock—surprises her. She knew he had one, but he's never threatened her with it. But then, she's never tried to escape him before, has she?

He walks up to the front door to check that it's still locked and finds it so. She wishes she had the presence of mind to unlock the door before climbing the tree. Duane might've gone inside then, giving her a chance to run off before he found her. A missed opportunity, hopefully not a fatal one. He thumps his fist on the door, as if to punish it for not granting him access to her, then he turns around and sweeps his gaze around the yard. This could go one of two ways, she thinks. He could decide to check the backyard, see if she's there, or if she's unlocked the rear door and entered the house that way. This *was* her parents' place, after all, and she has her own keys to it. Or it will occur to him—whether consciously or subconsciously—that she's up in the tree, just as it had to her father over two decades ago? One thing Duane won't go is give up and leave, not with her car parked in the driveway. He knows she's here somewhere.

She only has one option left.

She presses her bleeding hand to the trunk of the tree, hard, ignoring the pain, willing the tree to drink deep.

"Please," she whispers.

For a moment nothing happens, and she fears that the memory of how her father died has become cloaked in childish fantasy over the years. The tree didn't do anything to save her that day. Her father slipped all on his own, fell, and broke his neck. An accident, nothing more. She's an idiot for coming here hoping to find safety in the arms of her old friend. Years of enduring Duane's physical and psychological abuse has damaged her mind more than she realized. There's no other explanation for why she's come to believe that this tree is a sentient thing, and more, that it actually cares for her.

Does she move without knowing it? Is it the wind? Whatever the reason, the leaves around her rustle, drawing Duane's attention. He looks up, and despite the darkness and the foliage, he sees her. His eyes widen in surprise, and then his mouth stretches into a slow grin. He's been holding the gun down at his side, but now he raises it and aims it directly at her.

"Come down," he says. "*Now.*"

He speaks the words, but she hears them in her father's voice.

Can she shift position, put the tree trunk between her and the gun, shield herself from his bullets? That's assuming he'll even shoot. She *is* pregnant with his child, after all. But even if he empties the clip without hitting her, he'll simply climb up and get her, just as her father tried to do. The outcome is inevitable, and from Duane's darkly amused expression, he knows it too.

She lifts a foot from the branch she stands on, begins to lower it…

Then the tree starts to move. Gently at first, as if swaying in a light breeze, then faster, more violently, as if buffeted by gale-force winds. Sudden panic grips her, and she wraps her arms around the trunk to steady herself, presses her still-bleeding hand tight against the bark, and as she does this, she remembers Duane's words.

An old tree like that makes people nervous, makes them think about it falling down on their house during a bad storm.

Branches and leaves flail around her, blocking her view of Duane, but she imagines him standing frozen, gun raised, eyes wide, mouth open, as he watches her friend's increasingly wild gyrations. Branches curl around her then, enclose her in a sphere of leaves, as if to protect her. And then she feels the tree begin to fall. For a moment she's flying weightless, but then her flight comes to a jarring halt as the tree crashes into the house. She's bounced around some, but the leaf-sphere cushions the impact, and she's uninjured. She lies there a moment, heart racing, breathing heavily, and then the branches curl away from her, and she's able to crawl out and step onto the ground.

The top of the tree has smashed what was once her bedroom window and caved in a good portion of the house's façade. It snapped in the middle, and its lower half slammed into the ground, broken limbs burying themselves in the earth —and in Duane. He lies beneath the tree, thick branches impaling his chest and abdomen, pinning him like a dead, dried insect mounted for display. Blood courses from his wounds, runs from his mouth, and his unblinking eyes are glazed and sightless. His outstretched hand is empty, the gun lying some distance away.

She looks at him for a time, dimly aware of lights coming on in houses up and down the street. *I should hide the gun,* she thinks. *Before anyone gets here.* She walks toward it, but halfway there, her bare foot comes down on something hard. She bends down and picks up an acorn in her wounded hand. She holds it in front of her face, turns it this way and that, then she smiles, closes her bleeding palm around it, and continues toward the gun.

IN THE MONSTER'S MOUTH

Black water, black sky, strong wind.

A small wooden boat, no oars.

Faith's hands grip the gunwales for support as the craft rises and falls with the turbulent waves. She cries out in panicked desperation, but she can't hear her voice over the scream of the wind and the slap of water striking the boat's thin hull. She's dizzy, nauseated, and she wonders how much longer she can go on like this. Not very, she decides. Most likely she'll soon lose her grip on the gunwales and be thrown overboard, or the entire boat may capsize. She can think of worse ways for her life to end than drowning, but that doesn't mean she's in any hurry for it to happen.

The water stretches outward in all directions, and the air holds the sharp tang of salt. It doesn't smell like ocean water, though it's a familiar smell, one she can't place right now. This realm, whatever it is, is not completely dark, else how could she see anything? Precisely where the light—dim as it might be—is coming from, she doesn't know. Perhaps it's emitted by the air itself, a product of a trillion tiny glowing particles floating around her. Or maybe she's been adrift long enough that her eyes have adjusted to the dimness and now find it natural. Either way, she can make out certain shapes—cresting waves coming toward her, dark blurs in the sky she thinks might be clouds, a massive black shape gliding beneath the waves which she hopes is a product of her imagination, but which she fears is not. The shape bumps the starboard hull then, the impact so jarring that her right hand loses its grip on the gunwale. She grabs it again, steadies herself just in time for another bump, this one twice as strong. She's knocked back and forth, the boat tipping so far to the sides that it takes on water, enough to cover her feet up to the ankles. She wants to believe she's struck a piece of driftwood, but she knows better. A third strike, this one harder than the first two combined, and when the boat rights itself, she sees the portside hull is cracked in several places, and water is now streaming in. She has nothing with which to bail. She can't even use her hands—ineffective as they would be—since she can't risk letting go of the gunwales. The boat is taking on water fast, and there's nothing she can do about it.

She is, not to put too fine a point on it, fucked.

———

FAITH CLIMBED the last few rungs to the diving board, doing her best to keep her breathing even and relaxed. She was the youngest person on the team, and small for her age, besides, and she could feel everyone's eyes on her. Their dead-silent scrutiny made her nervous, not because they expected her to fail, but because they viewed her as a phenom and couldn't wait to see her dive. If she'd been a couple years older, they would've seen her as a good diver, but not as a rare oddity, like a zebra with purple stripes that could whistle. There was even talk of her trying out for the Olympic swim team, which she thought was ridiculous. Her coach didn't, though, and neither did her father.

She kept her gaze focused straight ahead. She knew Coach Swain was standing at the edge of the pool, and that the other members of the team were huddled around her, waiting to see how Faith performed. Her father was somewhere in the stands. Mom never came; she got too nervous watching Faith dive, always worried that she would end up getting hurt. If he could've, Dad would've been down there standing with Coach Swain, but family and friends were banned from being poolside, thank god.

Faith stepped onto the board, its wet warmth beneath her bare feet a familiar comfort. She stood there for a moment, eyes closed, breathing and visualizing the dive she was about to attempt—an inverse triple flip. In the space of a few seconds, she mentally performed the dive a dozen times flawlessly. When she was ready, she opened her eyes and started moving. When she reached the end of the board, she raised her hands over her head, jumped, came down—

"You got this, Faith!" Her father's voice, shattering the silence.

—and her right foot slipped.

She fell off the side of the board, spun through space, tried to contort her body so she would at least hit the water with a minimum amount of pain. She didn't succeed. There was a loud *smack*, and her entire nervous system lit up as if she'd struck concrete. Then she was beneath the water and slowly sinking.

Ow, she thought.

"WHAT THE HELL WAS *THAT*?"

Faith sat on the passenger seat of her dad's pickup. She'd

dried off after the competition and put on a T-shirt, shorts, and flipflops. Her hair was still a little wet, and Dad had the air conditioner blasting, so she'd wrapped a dry towel around herself.

She didn't answer her dad's question. She knew he didn't really want to hear what she had to say—especially about how *he* was the one who'd distracted her at a crucial moment. In his mind, he was always the star of the show, performer and audience all in one, and could do no wrong.

"Do you know how *embarrassing* that was for me? I could barely hold my head up as I slunk out of there."

"I want to quit the team," she said.

He kept on as if he hadn't heard her. "It's one thing to flub a dive. It happens sometimes. But to trip over your goddamned feet like that? There's no excuse for it, Faith!"

He went on like that for some time, and Faith gazed out the passenger window and tried to tune out his words. It wasn't easy. The man was *loud*. After a while, she felt a bead of moisture trace a line down her cheek. As she reached up to wipe away her tears, she remembered something she used to say when she was younger.

I'm not crying. My eyeballs are leaking.

<hr>

THAT SWIM meet had taken place Saturday morning, and by the afternoon, Faith was down in the basement, playing. At least, that's what she wanted her parents to think. Some old furniture of Grandma's was stored down here, stuff Mom couldn't bear to part with after Grandma had died, and sometimes Faith would rearrange it and pretend she was a grown-up who lived in her own house. There were two couches back to back, and she'd pushed them apart so she could use them like parallel bars, sometimes flipping up and over one of them and landing on the cushions. One end of the couches was near the unfinished basement wall. She climbed on top of the couches, straddled them, and regarded the wall. It looked solid. It looked *hard*.

It was just what she needed.

She was tired of performing, tired of competing, tired of the pressure, but most of all, she was tired of her father. She judged the distance, closed her eyes and visualized what she wanted to accomplish, and then she opened her eyes and flung herself at the wall, angling her left shoulder to take the brunt of the impact. When she connected with the wall, she felt as much as heard a harsh *crack*, and then she fell to the floor. She lay there, her shoulder burning like fire, but she had a smile on her face.

Let's see you try to make me swim now, Dad.

Tears rolled down her face, but these weren't tears of pain, even though her shoulder hurt like a motherfucker. These were tears of relief.

"It's hard having a narcissist for a parent. Did he ever..." The therapist trailed off, but Faith knew where she'd been headed.

"He never sexually abused me. He just used words. That was bad enough."

"How did he react when you broke your shoulder? Was he concerned?"

"He was disgusted. Before every competition he'd tell me that 'Pressure makes diamonds.' But while we were at the hospital waiting for X-ray results, he leaned over and whispered to me, 'I guess sometimes pressure crushes people. People like *you*.'"

SHE HEARS the crack of wood breaking, feels the boat fall apart beneath her. She plunges into the water, expects to find it freezing, but instead it's warm and salty, and as it floods her mouth, she realizes why the scent of it was so familiar to her. It's tears.

She doesn't swim as much as she used to, but the old reflexes are still there. Her body relaxes, she spreads her toes and allows her flip-flops to fall off, and then she kicks her legs to propel her upward. When her head breaks the surface, she looks around to orient herself. All she sees is water surging around her, rising and falling, and for now she lets it take her where it will. She sees dark shapes floating on the surface close by, and she feels a stab of fear. Are they what destroyed the boat? They don't appear large enough to have done the job, but maybe if they worked together... One of the shapes comes closer then, and she realizes it's a board, a fragment of the boat, and she almost laughs with relief. At least now she'll have something to hold onto while she bobs about in the water and tries to think of what she can do to get back to shore—assuming there still *is* a shore.

Something clamps down on her right hand, hard, and an instant later, she's yanked below the surface again. Her shoulder, the one she broke on that long-ago day in the basement, screams as something tears inside. She remembers the large shape she saw swimming underwater near the boat, and she knows this is the thing that destroyed the craft, that it did so purposefully in order to get at her. Whatever it is, it's heavy, and its weight drags her down rapidly into darkness. When she swam competitively, she trained herself to hold her breath for a long time, but she didn't have time to saturate her lungs with air before being pulled under, and she knows what's currently in her lungs won't last long. She needs to get away from whatever has hold of her or she will drown.

Fighting the force of water pushing against her as she's

dragged farther from the surface, she bends downward, reaches out, puts her hands on something big, scaled, slimy. For an instant, she's too stunned with disbelief to be scared. It's a creature of some kind, a fish, she thinks, but the goddamned thing is *huge*.

She hears a voice then, speaking inside her mind.

We're going to find out what pressure really does to you, Faith. Once and for all.

Her father. Of course. Who else could it be?

She continues sinking, shoulder on fire, her lungs beginning to burn.

"SHE WAS strong right up to the end. Unbelievably strong."

Faith sat in the front row, eyes raw and sore. They'd been leaking quite a lot over the last several days. Her father, wearing an expensive tailored suit, stood in front of her mother's open casket, blocking everyone's view of her face. A lectern with a microphone stood off to one side, surrounded by dozens of floral arrangements, but Dad had to be the center of attention. The fact that this was his wife's funeral instead of his had to be eating at him, and he was currently working hard to make this memorial service all about *him* and *his* pain. Faith's hands were clenched into fists, and if she hadn't known how much her mother hated to make a scene, she would've stood up, gone to her father, put her arms around him, and pretended she needed him to take care of her. He'd be irritated at having to cut his speech short, but he'd be forced to play the caring father in front of all the relatives and friends who'd gathered to say goodbye to Rita McCarthy. Faith didn't do it, though, feared that she'd only end up giving him more attention, and the thought of feeding his ego like that made her sick. So she suffered through his words, along with everyone else.

Dad spoke of how Mom's kidney disease progressed until she was on dialysis regularly. He talked about the wait for a donor kidney, the operation and recovery, and how Mom's body seemed to be adjusting well to the new organ. With each new part of the story he added, he stressed how he'd been at her side the whole time, taking care of her, marveling at her strength and resiliency. Him, him, him, him, him…

"But then the kidney began to fail…" He broke off with a choked sob so fake it wouldn't have impressed a child, let alone a room full of adults. "And then… And then… Oh *god.*"

His shoulders moved up and down, as if he was crying, but of course there were no tears. He had none for anyone but himself.

Brett McCarthy was a lawyer—a damn good one, to hear him tell it—but he prided himself at being good at anything he set his hand to, whether he was or not. He now walked over to the lectern, leaned over, and pulled an acoustic guitar from behind it.

*Oh no…*Faith thought.

Dad walked back to Mom's casket then lifted the instrument into playing position. He looked at his dead wife's face as he spoke.

"I thought I'd sing one of your favorite songs, dear. Is that all right?"

The only thing worse than Dad's guitar playing was his singing. Faith didn't want to do this, but it was an emergency. She closed her eyes, let her body go limp, and fell out of the chair and onto the floor. Noise broke out as people voiced their concern, asked if anyone present was a doctor, suggested someone call 911. Dad was kneeling at her side in an instant, holding her hand and patting it gently. She opened her eyes to see her father's face less than a foot away from hers.

"It's okay, sweetie. You're going to be all right."

His words were soft and loving, but his eyes were hard and cold as flint.

"WHAT'S the worst thing you can do to a narcissist?" Faith said. She smiled. "Upstage them."

"Has it ever occurred to you that by drawing attention to yourself like that, you were emulating him?"

She frowned. "What do you mean?"

"You wanted to beat him at his own game, so—at least for that moment—you had to become like him. And there are other parallels. You also became a lawyer, and the string of unsuccessful relationships you've had were all with narcissists like your father."

"Are you saying I'm searching for his approval?" She snorted. "Like that will ever happen."

"You've been seeing me for a while now, Faith, and I think it's time you come to terms with a fundamental truth. There's a hole in your heart labeled *Father's Love*, and it will never be filled."

Faith knew the therapist was right, but that didn't make her words hurt any less.

FAITH TRUDGED ALONG THE TRAIL, hands gripping the straps of her backpack. Its contents wouldn't weigh much if placed on a scale, but they were still a burden, one she was looking forward to being rid of. It was mid-July, the air hot, heavy, and oppressive. The mosquitoes were bad this close to the river, and she wished she'd thought to put on bug spray. She was wearing a tank top and shorts, and by the time she was finished here, she feared her arms and legs would be covered with bites. She could already imagine them itching, and she had to fight to keep from scratching at her skin. She'd expected this task to be miserable, and in a way she was glad she'd been right. It was only fitting.

Two weeks ago, her father had been in court, arguing a case for a client, the owner of a heating and cooling company who'd been charged with defrauding customers over the course of nearly twenty years. Faith had no doubt the man was guilty as hell. Dad loved defending the guilty. If he won, he got accolades, and if he lost, he received sympathy for having fought hard in what was ultimately an unwinnable case. That way, regardless of the verdict, he got the attention and recognition he craved. He'd been giving his closing statement to the jury when at one point he stopped speaking. According to what Faith was told later by the prosecuting attorney—one of those narcissists who she'd once dated—Dad seemed confused. He looked at the judge, then at his client, then his eyes widened, rolled white, and he collapsed to the floor. The heart attack was so massive, a doctor told her, that her father had most likely been dead before he'd started to fall. *At least it was fast,* the doctor said. Too fast, as far as Faith was concerned. Still, she knew Dad would've loved the theatricality of it, and she took grim satisfaction in knowing he'd died before realizing what was happening.

The trail angled downward, and before long, she reached a rocky bank on the edge of the river. She slipped off her backpack with a grateful sigh, placed it on the ground, and looked out at the water. She'd been ten years old the last time she'd been here, and the river seemed smaller than she remembered, the water muddy and sluggish. An old, weathered rowboat had been pulled onto the bank a hundred feet upriver, and she wondered who'd abandoned it and why. There was probably a story there, one she would never know.

She looked away from the boat and out at the water once more.

That's not how you bait a hook. Most of the worm isn't even on it. It'll fly off when you cast your line.

She drew the back of her hand across her forehead to wipe away the sweat, but all she managed to do was smear it.

That's too close to shore. You got to get your hook farther out into the water if you want to catch anything.

She knelt, got a bottle of water from the backpack, took a long drink.

Don't pull your line in too early! You've got to give the fish a chance to bite. God, you really are hopeless sometimes, you know that? Sometimes you make me ashamed to be your father.

She removed a hand spade from the backpack and began digging a hole in the rocky soil. When she judged it was big enough, she removed a cardboard box from the pack and set it on the ground next to the hole. She took off the lid to reveal a plastic bag filled with gray ashes. She lifted the bag, opened it, and poured its contents into the hole. Her father would've loved a large funeral, with him lying in state as dozens of mourners filed by his casket to tearfully say their goodbyes, followed by a service in which somber speakers enumerated his accomplishments and spoke warmly of him as a friend and colleague. Instead, Faith had him cremated and the only ceremony to mark his death would be the one she conducted now.

Once his ashes were deposited, Faith stood, pulled down her shorts, squatted over the hole, and pissed on his remains. When she was empty, she pulled up her shorts, shoveled dirt over the sodden mess that had been her father, then put the spade, box, and plastic bag into the pack. She then went to the water's edge and began to cry. Tears poured out of her, ran down her face, fell onto her tank top, continued falling until her shirt was soaked. And still the tears came, falling onto her shorts, running down her legs, forming a puddle at her feet. They joined with the river, fed it, caused it to rise. Black clouds rolled in to block the sun, and the air—so stifling only moments before—became chilly. Still she cried, her body racked by great heaving sobs, and the river overflowed the bank, the water level rising to her ankles, then halfway to her knees. The boat became dislodged from the shore and began drifting lazily toward her.

The ground beneath her feet trembled, and she looked back over her shoulder. The spot where she'd buried her father's ashes was underwater now, but the surface above it bubbled and roiled.

"No," she whispered.

Something hard bumped into her, and she turned to see the boat floating in the water in front of her. She took hold of the gunwale with both hands, more out of reflex than any conscious decision, and when the water exploded behind her, as if something large had burst upward, she flung herself into the craft. She was no longer crying, but the river continued to rise, flowing faster with each passing second, and the current carried the boat away from the rapidly disappearing shore. The sky grew even darker, the wind picked up speed, and Faith was borne away on the current. But something followed her—something big and angry.

<hr>

WHITE SPARKLES of light dance in Faith's vision, and she knows she's dangerously low on air. If she doesn't get away from this giant fish now, she'd a dead woman.

With her free hand, she feels around on the creature's surface, searching for... She finds an eye, the fucking thing as large as a soft ball, and she starts pounding on it. One, twice, three times... The fish still doesn't let her go, so she rakes her nails across the firm spongy substance. This does the trick. The fish-thing's mouth springs open, and Faith shoots upward like a rocket, arms stroking, legs kicking. Her right shoulder blazes with pain, and she knows she shouldn't be using that arm, but she has no choice. She needs air and she needs it *now*, so she swims toward the surface as fast as she can, giving it everything she's got, and to hell with her shoulder.

She feels her mouth begin to open of its own accord, her lungs so desperate that they're willing to attempt to breathe regardless of whether she's underwater or not. It's a physical imperative, instinctive and irresistible, and she knows she cannot hold it off any longer. But then her head breaks the surface, and she draws in a gasping breath, followed by another, and then another. Her vision grays out for a moment, and she fears she's going to pass out anyway, but then it clears, and she laughs.

"Fuck you, Dad! *Fuck you!*"

A board from the boat floats nearby, and she swims to it, using only her left arm. The board's not very big and one of the ends is jagged. She doubts it will be effective as a flotation device, but that's not the reason she wants it.

Just as she reaches it, the thing that is… was? …her father breaches the surface no more than five yards away from her. Its hide is a mottled gray—*Like ash*, she thinks—with staring black eyes set high atop the head, and a yawning mouth that looks large enough to swallow the world. Those inhuman eyes fix on her, and she hears her father's voice in her mind.

I'm making you swim now, aren't I, Faith? You're not doing too bad for someone so out of shape, but you're not going to win any trophies with that shoulder of yours—and you sure as hell aren't going to get away from me.

She remembers something her father told her when he brought her to the river when she was a kid.

You've got to give the fish a chance to bite.

And that's exactly what she intends to do.

The giant fish flips its tail and surges toward her, white froth churning in its wake. Faith angles the jagged end of the board upward, and as the fish's giant mouth closes on her, she rams the wood into the soft flesh of its upper palate. The creature tries to close its jaws on her, but the board prevents this, and she pulls herself out the mouth and, using her good arm, puts distance between herself and the fish. It thrashes its huge head back and forth in an attempt to dislodge the board, but the wood remains fixed in place, and then—with a loud wet *snap*—the jaws close. The sharp end of the board bursts through the top of the fish's head, the point emerging between its bulging eyes. Blood flows freely from the wound, and the fish floats there for a moment, empty gaze trained on her. She thinks her father will make some final cutting remark, but he says nothing. The fish slowly slips beneath the water and is gone.

Faith stares at the spot where the creature submerged, as if expecting it to rally its strength for one more attack, but it doesn't reappear. Now that her psychodrama has played itself out, she hopes the world will be restored to normal. Exhausted, shoulder blazing with white-hot pain, she scans the horizon, looking for any hint of shore, but she sees none. She treads water for several more minutes, but the world remains as it is, a seemingly endless expanse of dark water. She could pick a direction and start swimming, hope that she eventually finds land, but her shoulder is too badly injured for her to use the arm on that side. And even if she could use both arms, how can she hope to combat the water's currents? She can't. And without any point of reference, she'd have no way of maintaining a straight course anyway. She might swim around in circles until her strength is gone and she finds herself unable to remain afloat any longer. If she had any of the other boards from the boat…but she doesn't, and there are none in sight. For all she knows, they could have floated miles away by now. As far as she can see, she's left with only two options: continue treading water and hope some sort of rescue finds her before she descends into the deep to join her father, or she can give in to the inevitable—on her terms.

It really isn't much of a choice.

She takes in and releases several deep breaths, then she draws a final one, holds it, and allows herself to sink. The water is quiet, dark, and soothing, and as she descends she thinks of what her father told her after she broke her shoulder.

I guess sometimes pressure crushes people. People like you.

We'll see about that, she thinks.

She closes her eyes, curls up into a ball, and as she continues down, she waits to harden.

THE GARDEN OF LOVE IS GREEN

Brenton stands in moonlight, night air cool on his exposed skin, bare feet in grass. The blades gently stroke his flesh, and he smiles.

I love you too.

It's three a.m. in Ash Creek, Ohio, and he's standing in the middle of his backyard, wearing only a pair of gray satin shorts—they're all he ever sleeps in, regardless of the season. He's looking down, marveling at how the moon makes the separate blades seem like thousands of tiny silver sculptures. The six-foot tall white wood fence that encloses the yard glows in the moonlight, a frame, he imagines, for a work of art titled *Night and Silence*. Except the grass isn't silent, is it? It never has been, not for him.

He hears a multitude of small voices, speaking as one. To anyone else, it would sound like an almost inaudible breath of wind, if they heard it at all. Brenton has no trouble hearing it, of course. He closes his eyes and listens, opening himself to the meaning contained within those strange soft syllables. He has no idea how long he stands like this, waiting for some sense of meaning to make itself known to him, but at last it does, and his eyes open.

He knows what he needs to do.

He walks to the gate, unlatches it—the ground is slightly sloped here, and the door swings open by itself—and steps through. He heads for the wooden shed where the lawn equipment is stored. It's less than twenty feet from the gate, and he reaches it within seconds. There's a padlock on the door, although it isn't necessary. He lives in a safe neighborhood, and besides, who would want to steal weed trimmers, edgers, leaf blowers, and wheelbarrows? Still, better safe than sorry.

He has a pair of objects in the pockets of his shorts, one of which is the key to the shed. He uses it to unlock the padlock and then opens the door. It creaks, and as he always does, he tells himself to remember to oil the hinges next time he comes here. Not that there will be a next time. Moonlight spills into the shed, illuminating the reason for the padlock. Now *this* is worth stealing. The push mower—Brenton would never resort to something as gauche and impersonal as a riding mower, not on *his* grass—cost him in excess of five hundred dollars, and it was worth every penny. It has a powerful easy-to-start motor, optimized air flow for superior mulching, four cutting surfaces that create extra-fine clippings, and a smart drive system that matches the user's stride. Only the best for his lawn.

He tucks the key back into his pocket, wheels the mower outside, and checks to make sure it's gassed up. He keeps the tank topped off, but he always checks anyway. Satisfied, he replaces the gas cap and pushes the mower through the gate and into the backyard. He stops then, regards the grass, frowns. For the first time since he and Charlene moved into this house, well over forty years ago now, someone besides him has mowed the lawn—a service that Charlene hired—and while they didn't do a terrible job, they were, by Brenton's standards, sloppy. The blades are uneven, the cut pieces only partially mulched, and there are several spots that they missed mowing altogether. Disgraceful.

He hears the voice-that-is-many-voices speak once more, and this time he has no trouble understanding its meaning. *We do not blame you. Now begin.*

He primes the gas, pushes the power button, and the motor roars to life. The sound cuts through the night's quiet like a chorus of angry chainsaws, but he finds the noise sweet, soothing even. He then removes the second object from the pocket of his shorts: a roll of black electrical tape. He wraps the tape around the mower's safety shut-off lever to hold it down, so that the motor won't cut out while he does what he needs to do next. He carefully tilts the mower onto its side, exposing its whirling blades. He watches them for a moment, transfixed by their wavering blur of motion, then he kneels. The grass speaks once more.

Come to us.

Brenton leans his head forward.

"Stop moping."

Brenton responded to his wife without looking at her. "I'm not."

He stood on the wooden deck at the back of his house, arms crossed over his chest, scowling. The yard was only half-mown, and the sight of it filled him with a level of anger approaching rage. He didn't like to leave a job unfinished, and he'd *never* abandoned his yard like this before. He could feel his heart attempt to beat faster, but the new beta blocker he was on kept it restrained.

"You should be inside resting," Charlene said.

Three days ago, he'd been out there, pushing the mower, listening to the grass sigh in contentment as he trimmed it, when he suddenly felt short of breath and his pulse skyrocketed. Less than an hour later, he was in a hospital bed, hooked up to a heart monitor, and waiting to get an MRI.

Minor tachycardia, the doctor had pronounced once the test was over. She prescribed the beta blocker and told him to follow up with his family physician in a few days. *And no more mowing the yard,* she'd said. *Not with a push mower, anyway. You're too old for that shit.*

Old? He was only sixty-six, for Christ's sake.

As soon as he'd come home from the hospital, he'd wanted to go into the backyard and finish mowing.

If you're determined to make your heart explode, I won't stop you, Charlene had said. *Just don't expect me to call an ambulance this time.*

Had she meant it? Maybe. Probably.

Charlene went back inside, to call a lawn service to finish the task he could no longer perform. He continued standing on the deck until they arrived, and then he retreated into the house and didn't come back out until they were done.

<hr>

WHEN BRENTON WAS A CHILD, his family lived on a farm. Brenton, along with his five siblings, was expected to do chores, and a lot of them, but whenever he got a chance—which wasn't often—he liked to lie on the grass in the backyard, gaze up at the clouds, and relax.

He was eleven when he first heard the grass speak to him.

It was a hot August afternoon. He'd just finished helping his dad fix the tractor—mostly he handed tools to Dad whenever he asked for them—and he was drenched with sweat. Drops rolled off his skin, fell to the grass, were absorbed. He could feel the dampness being leeched from his shirt and jeans, pulled into the ground, greedily swallowed. It was an odd sensation, one which he supposed should've been disturbing but which he found strangely comforting, almost intimate.

He listened to the whispering's rising and falling cadence, found it so soothing he had to fight to keep from drifting off to sleep. There were no words, none that he could discern anyway, but there *were* emotions, and these created pictures in his mind. He saw the god-demon sun blasting down its unrelenting heat for days, weeks, without a single drop of rain falling from the sky. He saw the grass's green fade, become yellow, then almost entirely bleached of color. Lastly, he saw himself, lying on the ground, watering the grass with the moisture from his own body. When the images faded, he was left with a warm, almost loving sensation inside which his mind translated as *Thank you.*

THE NEXT TIME the family went into town, Brenton visited the library and checked out a book on plant life. He read the chapter on grass and ignored the rest of it. That night at dinner, he attempted to share what he'd learned.

Did you know that grass developed 60 million years ago, during the Cretaceous period? It's one of the strongest, most versatile plants, and it can live in rain forests, deserts, and cold climates. It even lives in some parts of Antarctica!

His family was usually silent while they ate, and they barely looked at him as he spoke.

His mother gave him a quick glance and a half smile. *That's nice, dear.*

He wanted to tell them more about what he'd learned, but

there was no point. They might hear him, but they wouldn't *listen* to him.

That night, he had a dream. He stood in the middle of a sea of grass, an endless field stretching outward in all directions, blades almost as tall as he was. The sun hung high above, huge and hot, and warm winds stirred the grass, made it ripple and sway like currents of green water. This time when the grass spoke, he understood every word.

We've been waiting a long time for someone to hear us, Brenton. Someone like you.

Then the grass closed in around him, wrapped him tight in its embrace, and squeezed until he could no longer breathe. The sensation was alarming at first, but he calmed as his mind began to shut down, and then he knew no more.

Brenton would have no memory of this dream once he woke, but it remained with him the rest of his life, always just below the level of conscious thought.

JULY FOURTH, a couple years later.

Every Independence Day, Brenton's family had a big meal outside to celebrate. Afterward, they'd play games and, when the sun went down, shoot off illegal fireworks. Brenton liked holidays because they were the only times his family really interacted. The rest of the time they kept to themselves, and at thirteen, he was starting to do it too. What was the point of spending time with people who didn't want you around, who didn't want *anyone* around?

One of the games his family played after dinner was lawn darts. These weren't the safe, soft-headed lawn darts of later years, oh no. These things were murderously dangerous, with thick metal spikes at one end and a plastic handle at the other, with a trio of flared-out flat plastic "feathers" to help control the flight. The object of the game was to hurl a dart into the air and attempt to land it in the middle of the other team's circle, which was defined by a thin round plastic hoop placed on the ground. Brenton was more than a little intimidated by the darts—especially by how fast his older siblings threw them—so he tended to stay on the sidelines and watch. This year, when it was his older brother Martin's turn to throw, their sister Dora shoved him as a joke. Off-balance, he released the dart and it flew high up into the air...

...and it came down straight toward Brenton.

Panicked, he ran, hoping to outdistance the dart, but when he glanced back over his shoulder, he realized he was instead running directly into its path. He tried to veer to the left, but his foot caught in a small depression in the ground, his ankle twisted, and he fell face-forward onto the grass. He lay there an instant, expecting the feel the metal tip of the dart pierce the back of his skull any moment, but then he felt pressure beneath him, as if a large hand raised up from the ground and gave him a hard shove. He flipped over onto his back a split second before the dart *thunked* into the ground exactly where his head had been. He stared at the dart for a moment, heart pounding, breath caught in his chest. His parents and his siblings were looking at him, none of them speaking or moving. He had the feeling that it wouldn't have mattered much to them which way his race against the dart had turned out. Then their paralysis broke and they came running toward him, shouting *Are you Okay?* and *Goddamn, boy, you were lucky!* But Brenton knew luck had nothing to do with it.

He reached down and patted the grass, felt its blades brush his palm.

HE MET Charlene when he was twenty and she was eighteen. She graduated from high school the same year Dora did, and the two of them were friends. He didn't know that, of course. He barely knew his siblings, let alone the people they hung out with at school, and Dora had been two years behind him. After the ceremony—which had taken place on the football field—Dora and Charlene were posing for pictures together, and she caught Brenton's eye and he caught hers. He wanted to ask her out, but he was too shy, but then he heard the grass urging him to be brave, and when the picture-taking was completed, he walked up to her, introduced himself, and asked if she would like to go with him to see a movie in town sometime. She shocked him when she said yes. He didn't know that her family's farm was failing, and that—in the back of her mind, at least—she feared being poor and hoped to find a spouse who would help her become financially secure. He had no money of course, and eventually his brother Stan would inherit their farm, not that Brenton wanted the damn thing. But Brenton had *potential*, or so Charlene hoped, and that movie date led to many more.

It was almost two months before they had sex for the first time. It was a late June, and they were down by the lake, hidden in the woods, blanket spread out on a small clearing that local kids called Lover's Lawn instead of Lover's Lane. Was the pun purposeful or accidental? No one knew, nor did they care, as long as they had a place to fuck. Brenton and Charlene had fooled around before, of course, and had made each other come in a variety of ways, but they hadn't gone all the way, hadn't done *it*. Brenton was as nervous as he was excited, and when he entered Charlene for the first time, he expected to feel a closeness, a joining, a merging as the two of them became one. It felt good—great even—but he didn't feel anything inside. No, that wasn't quite right. He didn't feel anything coming from inside *her*.

He leaned his head close to hers, kissed her, looked deep into her eyes, searched for any sign that there was *something* in there, but all he saw was another human being enjoying the sensations her body produced. He could've been anyone, could've been a goddamn dildo for that matter, and she would've reacted the same. He tried to pull out of her then, but she grabbed hold of his shoulders, twisted her hips, and flipped him over onto his back and straddled him. The maneuver moved them off the blanket, and Brenton's bare back, ass, and legs were pressed against the grass. Charlene rode him hard, shouting her enthusiasm so loud it caused nearby birds to take to the air in alarm. Brenton remained quiet and listened to the grass whisper its love as it undulated beneath him.

BRENTON MARRIED CHARLENE, more because it was expected than out of any real desire to do so. They moved to a new town in Ohio that wasn't significantly different than the one they'd grown up in, and Brenton found work as a tool and die maker. The job was dull and repetitive, much like farming, but at least he didn't end up with shit-covered shoes at the end of the day. He and Charlene never had children. They never even discussed the matter.

One spring day, when he'd been working as a machinist with the same company for thirteen years, he decided to take his lunch break outside. It was a beautiful, sun warm but not too hot, wind blowing but not too hard. He sat on the lawn in front of the building and took off his shoes and socks so he could feel the grass beneath his feet. As he was eating a ham sandwich, Glenn Siler exited the building. Glenn was his immediate supervisor, a hard, humorless man who had been with the company almost as long as Brenton had been alive.

Glenn's upper lip curled into a sneer when he saw Brenton sitting on the grass barefoot.

"What the hell is wrong with you, Dowling? You some kind of nature freak or something?"

Brenton felt the grass stir beneath his feet.

It's okay, he thought. The grass stilled, but he could feel its anger toward Glenn burning hot.

"I like the grass," Brenton said.

Glenn snorted. "You are a fucking weirdo, Dowling. I'm going to be watching your ass, so shape the fuck up."

Glenn walked off, the grass's furious whispers following him.

That weekend, Glenn was working in his front yard, edging the grass near the curb. Somehow he tripped, fell, and cracked his head on the curb's concrete surface. He died less than two hours later in the hospital. When Brenton heard about the man's death at work Monday morning, he smiled.

As Brenton leans closer to the mower's whirling blades, he digs his fingers into the cool grass.

Will this hurt? he thinks.

Yes. Very much so.

That's what I figured.

Brenton takes a deep breath, then shoves his face the rest of the way forward. The grass was right. It does hurt.

Very, *very* much.

"No, I don't know why he did it, and I don't care. I'm just glad he's gone. Yes, I know that sounds terrible, but we were married close to fifty years. That's more than enough time for a woman to put up with any man, don't you think? Especially one that's as…empty as Brenton was."

Charlene stands on the deck of their—*her*—house, phone to her ear. She's talking to Brenton's sister Dora. They've remained close ever since high school, and Dora's long been aware of how dissatisfied Charlene was with her marriage to Brenton.

"I mean, there just wasn't anything *there*, you know?"

Charlene looks at the spot where Brenton shoved his face into the spinning blades of his precious $500 mower. The lawn is still dark there, and she imagines his blood soaking the earth, feeding the grass. *Nurturing* it. A fitting end, really. He cared more about the goddamn grass than anything else in his life.

Charlene and Dora talk for a while longer, and when the sun begins to go down, Charlene ends the call and goes inside. A few moments later, Brenton—truly *in* the grass now—stretches forth new fingers. Blades of grass lengthen, slither up onto the deck like thin green snakes, move toward the patio door and find it unlocked. Brenton isn't surprised. Charlene never remembers to lock the damn thing. His new fingers reach into the kitchen and continue to grow as they feel their way through the house in search of Charlene. Maybe Brenton was empty during his life, or maybe no one ever bothered to take notice of what he did have inside him. Either way, he's full now, full to fucking *bursting*, and he's going to teach Charlene—and everyone else on the goddamn planet—an important lesson.

The future is green.

GOD SPELLED BACKWARD

ovement in the dark, shadows shifting among
shadows, forms emerging, taking shape, solidifying.
A half dozen figures, maybe more, crammed into your small
bedroom, shoulder to shoulder, front to back. You feel heat
radiating from their bodies, smell the nauseating tang of their
rank scent, hear their rough, eager breathing. They tower
over you—seven, eight feet tall—and as they gather around
your bed, foot claws *tkk-tkk-tkking* on your hardwood floor,
you sit up, press yourself back against the headboard, heart
pounding so hard your head thrums in response to each rapid
beat.

"Go away. You-you're not *real*."

Terrified as you are, you feel ridiculous saying this. If
they're not real, why ask them to leave? Why speak to them
at all?

There's a small lamp on the nightstand next to your bed.
You stretch your right hand toward it, fingers trembling so
hard that at first they can't grip the plastic switch. When they
finally do, you hesitate. If you can't see them, maybe they can't
see you. A child's logic, desperate, pathetic.

You turn on the light.

You see eight of them, three standing at the left side of your bed, three at the right, two at the foot. They're human-shaped, fur-covered, with canine heads—eyes blazing feral yellow, mouths open wide to reveal sharp white teeth and lolling pink tongues. Their colors vary, jet black, brown, a mix, muzzles and chests matted with blood that's still wet. They have hands instead of paws, clawed fingers coated crimson. They reach up, place these hands on the sides of their heads and lift.

You scream.

———

MALCOLM HUDSON IS DRIVING down State Route 32, roughly ten miles outside Hadleigh, Ohio, when a woman steps into the road in front of his car, turns to face him, and—illuminated in the bright wash of his headlights—raises her arms to get his attention. As if stepping in front of a moving car isn't enough of an attention-getter in itself. Malcolm grips the steering wheel tight, slams his foot down on the brake pedal, and his white Toyota Prius skids to a halt, bumper only a couple feet from the woman. He was going forty-five miles an hour, and if he'd been going any faster—a lot of people go sixty, even seventy on back country roads like this one—he wouldn't have been able to stop in time. She hurries to the driver's side door and motions for him to lower his window. He does, but only a couple inches. He doesn't know this woman, and he has no reason to trust her. Better safe than sorry.

She leans close, as if afraid he won't be able to hear her otherwise.

"Thank god you stopped!"

She's in her forties, not much older than him, with short

brown hair and glasses. There's a gash on her forehead, a line of blood running down the left side of her nose. Some of the blood has dripped onto her white blouse, the splotches a bright, startling red in the reflected illumination of his headlights. He looks to the right, sees a blue Ford Explorer in the ditch, headlights off, engine not running, its front end pressed against a wooden telephone pole. The pole lists to the side somewhat, as if the vehicle's impact knocked it askew—assuming there *was* an impact. The Explorer doesn't look damaged from what he can see, and the "blood" on the woman's face could easily have been faked.

"They forced me off the road," she says, voice strained, eyes darting back and forth, a frightened animal alert for danger. "They came out of the fields and rushed toward me. I swerved and..." She frowns, reaches up to touch the wound on her forehead, winces, pulls her fingers away, examines the blood on them, a bemused expression on her face. "I must've hit my head on the windshield."

Malcolm looks at the field beyond the Explorer. It's fenced in, the ground flat, grass low, pastureland for cows or sheep, maybe, or land for horses to run on and graze. The field on the other side of the road is the same. Both are empty. Whoever or whatever *they* are, there's no sign of them...if there ever was a *they* in the first place.

"Let me in your car. *Please*. They could be back any moment!"

Malcolm isn't about to let a stranger into his Prius, not without asking a few questions first.

"What ran you off the road?"

"I'm not sure. They were like dogs, except they were bigger —a *lot* bigger—and they...they..."

He knows what she'll say next. He hopes he's wrong, but he isn't.

"...walked on their hind legs, like a human."

"Dogmen." He barely whispers the word.

He looks deeply into the woman's eyes, searching for any hint of deception. It would be an easy thing to pull your vehicle into a ditch to make it seem it had been in an accident. Squirt fake blood onto your forehead, give it a moment to run down your face, and then—when you see a pair of headlights approaching—step onto the road and frantically wave your arms. Time for the show to begin: a prank played on a hapless driver, to be recorded and uploaded to the Internet or a ploy to get people to stop so the woman's friends can rush out from wherever they're hiding and rob the driver. In other words, a *trap*, of one kind or another. Malcolm's too smart to fall for it, though. He intends to raise his window, drive off, and let the woman wait for the next potential victim to come along—while he calls 911, of course—but before he can do this, shadowy figures rise from the ditch around the Explorer and start moving toward his car.

He knows these figures, has seen them many times over the years, felt the baleful intensity of their yellow eyes, inhaled their thick, musky-sour scent, heard the low threatening rumble of their growls.

He takes his foot off the brake, jams it onto the gas. The Prius lurches forward, the woman jumps back, afraid she might get knocked down, and the dark figures start running, clawed hands outstretched. As Malcolm roars away from the scene of the "accident," he keeps his gaze focused on the road in front of him, refuses to look up at the rearview mirror, doesn't want to witness the scene spotlighted in the red glow of his departing taillights. He hears the woman scream, the dogmen howl with savage delight, and he turns on the radio, cranks the volume as high as it will go, drives on.

MALCOLM IS SIX. He's sitting on the floor of his family's living room, playing a video game—Mega Man 4—his back against the couch, legs crossed, tongue sticking partway out of his mouth, brow furrowed in concentration as he works the controller. Bear, the family dog, is lying on the couch behind him. Bear isn't supposed to be on the couch. He's a big dog, an Airedale, and Mom doesn't want him scratching the fabric. Bear is Malcolm's buddy, though, so when no one else is around, he lets him sneak onto the couch where Bear always stretches out with a contented sigh.

On the TV screen, a Gachappon appears and attacks Mega Man, but Malcolm isn't worried. He knows a Drill Bomb will stop it easily. But before he can use the weapon, he senses sudden movement behind him, hears Bear snarl—a sound he's never heard the dog make before—then feels points of pressure on both the front and back of his head. Pressure becomes fire as Bear bites down, teeth piercing thin, tender flesh, and Malcolm releases a high-pitched shriek that is as much a cry of surprise and betrayal as it is pain.

THIRTY-SEVEN STITCHES IN ALL.

Boy's lucky, the doctor tells Malcolm's parents. *His hair will hide the worst of the scarring.*

Malcolm doesn't feel lucky, but he says nothing. On the ride home from the hospital, Mom and Dad debate what to do about Bear.

"Thank god he's had his rabies shots," Mom says.

"Malcolm must've done something," Dad says. "Bear's a gentle dog. He'd never do something like that unless he was provoked."

"Are you saying Malcolm *made* Bear bite him?"

Mom and Dad continue arguing once they're home. Mom

thinks they should rehome Bear, but Dad thinks she's overreacting. There's something about that word—*overreacting*—that sends Mom into a fury, and the two of them go to their bedroom so Malcolm won't have to hear them yell at each other, but of course he still can. Malcolm's alone in the living room. Bear's tied to a stake in the backyard, and Malcolm's glad. He wouldn't feel safe with Bear in the house, especially when Mom and Dad aren't around. He's scared of Bear now, sure, but it's more than that. He doesn't *trust* Bear anymore.

One good thing about his parents fighting: There's no one around to tell him what he can and can't watch on cable. He sits on the floor—he doesn't want to sit on the couch, not yet, maybe not ever—grabs the remote and turns on the television. If he was a teenager, he might have gone looking for R-rated movies in hope of seeing naked breasts, but he's six, so he scrolls through the on-screen menu until he comes to a movie called *Night Scream*. He loves horror movies, the scarier, the better. Who cares if they give him nightmares? They're totally worth it.

He selects the movie, which has already started, but he hasn't missed much, maybe five minutes or so. He didn't pay attention to the description on the menu, so when one of the characters—a hunter walking around in the woods at night with a shotgun—is attacked by a hairy monster with a canine face, Malcolm's shocked. *It's a dog,* he thinks. *A monster dog. Just like Bear.* He can't take his eyes off the screen as the creature rakes the hunter's face with its claws, and then sinks its teeth into the man's neck and tears out his throat. At least, that's what Malcolm thinks is supposed to happen. But the monster dog costume is so cheap that none of its features move. Its face is clearly a plastic mask—eyes that don't blink, mouth that remains frozen open—so the actor inside can only pretend to bite the other actor's throat. The effect isn't any more convincing than the creature costume, but despite that —okay, for some weird reason because of that—the scene is scary, *really* scary, like something out of a nightmare. Malcolm continues watching, transfixed, not realizing that he's trembling.

As the movie progresses, Malcolm learns the monster is called a dogman, and that this story takes place in Ohio, which is extra creepy because that's where Malcolm lives. He doesn't pay attention to the movie's plot much, but in his defense, the script isn't that great and the story's hard to follow. At first, it seems like there's only one dogman, but then it turns out there's a pack of them. The dogmen aren't shown much throughout most of the movie, which makes sense given their truly awful costumes, but at the film's climax, when the hero of the movie—a local veterinarian— teams up with a retired sheriff to battle the monsters, all the dogmen are clearly visible. Malcolm scoots close to the screen so he can examine their suits. He can easily see the lines where the masks, gloves, and boots end, and there are easy-to-spot zippers running down their backs.

After the battle, the sheriff is dead, as are all the dogmen. The vet's badly injured, and on the way to the hospital, he turns into a dogman—complete with a terrible mask covering his head—in the back of the paramedic van. The medics scream as he attacks, and that's The End. Roll credits.

As names scroll by on the screen, Malcolm sits silently, trying to process what he's watched. He doesn't hear his parents yelling anymore, but they're still in their bedroom. Maybe they've stopped fighting and are having what Mom calls *Mommy-Daddy Time*. He thinks about something the sheriff said in the movie.

No one knows where dogmen come from. Maybe they were human once, like you and me. Maybe they were dogs or wolves.

Maybe they are dogs most of the time, living with us until they're ready to kill...and when that happens, they change.

"MALCOLM, do you know where Bear is?"

Malcolm is sitting on the floor, playing Mega Man 4. He doesn't look up as he answers Mom's question.

"He's in the back yard."

"No, he's not. Someone untied the rope around his neck and let him loose. That same someone left the fence door open."

Now Malcolm looks at her, concern in his voice as he asks, "He'll come back, won't he?"

But inside, he smiles.

Bear never returns.

HE DREAMS of the dogmen that night. It's the first of many such dreams, and they're always the same—except for their ending. The first time when they remove their masks, they're all real dogmen underneath. The second time they have Bear's head. The third time they have Malcolm's. The fourth time there's only empty space beneath their masks. Those four endings cycle over and over, in no specific sequence, and Malcolm never knows which he's going to get. It doesn't matter. He hates them all.

THE SCARS ON HIS HEAD—WHICH *are* hidden by his hair, the doctor was right—itch sometimes, and when they do, he scratches them without thinking. Some of the kids tease him about having dandruff when that happens. He doesn't care. He doesn't have friends, doesn't want them. People only pretend to be your friend until they decide they want to hurt you, just like bear.

Fuck 'em.

———

HE'S THIRTY-SIX NOW, and he works as a health inspector. Too many businesses don't give a shit about regulations, try to cut corners to save a buck. He's happy to expose the bastards. He's never been married, never had a serious relationship. He's been told by more than one person that he has *trust issues*.

Fuck 'em.

———

HE SHOULDN'T HAVE LEFT the woman alone with the dogmen. He should've let her get in his car and driven her away from those things. He doesn't question whether the creatures are real. He learned a long time ago not to trust anything, and that includes what most people think of as reality. He should go back, try to help her. He turns off the radio, and the resulting silence seems as loud as the music was.

"She's probably dead," he says.

But how could they kill her? Their teeth and claws are plastic, and not particularly sharp.

"They could've taken off their costumes. Whatever is underneath could've killed her."

They're your *dogmen. You* dream *them. That makes* you *responsible for them.*

He doesn't buy that logic, but he turns around in the next farmer's driveway he comes to and heads back, driving fast, the scars where Bear bit him burning like acid.

He finds blood-slick bones with only a few meager scraps of flesh left on them scattered across the road. She wasn't lying. It wasn't a trap.

He frowns then. The closest bone to him is a femur—at least, that's what he thinks it is. It's been a long time since he took anatomy in college. Something about it doesn't look right, but he's not sure what. He nudges it with his foot. He expects it to make a clattering sound on the asphalt, but it's softer, almost like...

He crouches, reaches out to touch the bone.

It's plastic.

There's blood on his fingers now, and he raises them to his face, sniffs, licks.

Corn syrup and red food coloring.

He hears laughter then, made by multiple voices. Eight of them, he guesses. He stands, looks around, sees no one. The laughter continues, grows louder.

He realizes that he's made a mistake. He trusted *himself*—his perceptions, his intuition. If he'd just kept driving and gone home, he would've been fine. He could've continued to live his life as an untrusting sonofabitch and died a bitter old man. But now...

The woman's Ford Explorer is still there, and for the first time since returning, he notices there's something on the hood. He climbs down into the ditch, walks to the front of the vehicle, and finds a mask waiting for him. Like the dogmen's, this mask is cheaply made. Unlike the others, it was made to resemble a specific breed of dog. An Airedale, in fact. He gazes at it for a long time, and then he realizes the laughter has stopped. There's a hush in the air, a tense atmosphere of anticipation.

"Everything's fake," he says to the mask, "isn't it? Including me."

The mask doesn't reply, but does Malcolm see an approving glint in its plastic eyes? Maybe.

He slips the mask over his head, and his brothers step out of the shadows to congratulate him.

FOREVER

I'm sitting in my car, looking at a grassy field with a wooden sign rising from the ground that says *Townsend Park*. This is the place where my best friend Alison disappeared when we were both nine years old, and it's the first time I've been back in thirty years. I'm not sure how I expected to feel—nervous, maybe even a little scared—but all I feel is a distant sadness, more like a memory of emotion, a fading echo, than any real feeling.

I get out of my car, lock the doors, then start walking toward the sign. It's mid-December, but the temperature is in the high forties. It tends not to get too cold in Virginia this time of year, not like in Ohio where I live now. There's no snow on the ground and the grass is a dull, washed-out green, not the vibrant color I remember from my last time here. It was spring then, April 23rd, to be precise. The date's seared into my memory.

The park doesn't have an actual entrance, just this sign at the end of a cul-de-sac in a suburban neighborhood. The houses here are upper middle-class dwellings—two stories, with nicely landscaped yards and pools in the back. This town is a bedroom community for people who work in D.C., and while they aren't starving, they don't exactly qualify as wealthy. My parents lived a couple blocks from here, and Alison's lived across the street from us. I don't know if her parents are still there, don't know if they're still alive. I drove past their house before coming here, but I didn't stop. If they are still there, what could I possibly say to them? *Remember me? I'm the girl who was with your daughter when she disappeared. I'm all grown up and have lived the life Alison never got to. How are you doing these days?*

The wind is coming from the east, and although this town is an hour's drive from the ocean, I detect a hint of saltwater in the air, and it makes me smile. Alison's and my parents used to take us to the beach in summer, and we would splash in the water and play in the sand for hours. It's been years since I've seen the ocean, and I really should get back there some day.

I walk past the wooden sign and into the empty field. Alison and I used to run back and forth across the grass, racing each other. Although she was smaller than me, she was always faster, and I never could keep up. Sometimes we'd lie on our back and look up at the clouds, tell each other what shapes we saw in them. I saw things like cats and dogs, ordinary even banal shapes. But Alison saw things like a T-Rex riding a unicycle or a five-headed space alien. She was all imagination and boundless energy that girl, and I wonder what she would be like today if…

If.

If you keep walking straight across the field, you end up in another neighborhood. On the other side of that is a convenience store, and Alison and I used to take a short cut across the field and through that neighborhood so we could go to the store and get slushies. Grape for me, cherry for her. If you head left, though, you'll reach a stretch of woods that fill the park's west side, and I head in that direction now. The woods are a mix of trees—elm, cedar, oak, maple, pine. Most have shed their leaves, but some remain, stubborn holdouts that refuse to acknowledge the reality of the season. I admire their defiance. The sky's overcast, gray without being too gloomy. It's a balanced sky, one with an equal chance of bringing sun or rain, depending on which way the scales tip. I'm not sure which would suit my mood better, but I'll have to take what I can get. Life's like that, isn't it?

I didn't return to town specifically to visit the park. One of my cousins died in a car accident, and I attended the funeral this morning. My mom and dad stayed in Ohio, though. Both are in ill health—Mom's diabetic, Dad has heart trouble—but the truth is they fell out of touch with the rest of the family when we moved from Virginia. And since I'm an only child, and all my grandparents are dead, I was my immediate family's sole representative at the service. It was nice, as nice as a funeral can be, that is, but I spent most of the service thinking about Alison, which felt disrespectful to my cousin, but I couldn't help it. People are gathering at my cousin's house now, to tell her husband and parents how sorry they are as they nibble on finger food and drink warm soda. I know I should be there, but I couldn't make myself go. I've had enough of death for one morning, and the lure of the park, of *Alison*, was too strong.

When I reach the edge of the woods, I expect to hesitate, to have to muster my courage and force myself to keep going, but I don't slow down. If anything, I pick up speed as I walk past the first tree, dry leaves crunching beneath my shoes, and I continue on.

"I WIN, I WIN!"

"Not fair!"

We stop outside the woods, breathing hard, faces flushed, sweat gleaming on our skin. We're both wearing T-shirts, shorts, and sneakers, the day gloriously warm, more like summer than spring. It's the kind of day that kids wish would last forever, and neither Alison and I know that, in a very real sense, it will, at least for me.

I'm eleven and Alison is nine. She the annoying little sister I never had, and while she drives me crazy at times, I'm drawn to her boundless energy and enthusiasm for life, as if she's a miniature sun, blazing bright, her power feeding me—older, quieter, introverted—making me, at least for the time we're together, more like her. Bold and unafraid. We have a kind of symbiosis. She acts as the devil on my shoulder, tempting me into delicious mischief, while I'm the angel on her shoulder, trying to keep her from taking too many risks. I tether her to reality; she gives me wings to soar.

"We're not supposed to go in there," I say.

She bares her teeth in a wide smile.

"That's why it's *fun*."

She turns away from me and continues on into the woods. This is the moment when I still have a choice. I could stay here and wait for Alison to return, or I could leave the park and go home, secure in the knowledge that I won't get in trouble for disobeying my parents. But there's always a moment like this for me when it comes to Alison, standing at the precipice of a new adventure, trying to work up the courage to jump, never knowing what will happen when I land. Who am I kidding? I always follow her, and I do so now.

She's not very far ahead of me, and I know she went slow to give me time to catch up. I do, and then we're walking together, Alison in the lead as usual, forging a patch through the undergrowth. There are established paths in these woods, but Alison prefers to make her own way. Our bare legs are scratched by the thin branches of small trees as we go. The scratches sting, but I try to ignore the sensation. I doubt Alison even feels it. Her mind is too preoccupied with imagining all the wondrous things that might lie ahead of us. An enchanted castle, a fairy village, a dragon's lair… I look at the back of Alison's legs and see bruises. Most are minor, not so dark, but there's a larger one on the back of her left thigh, a purple splotch on her smooth, pink skin. I tell myself she got those bruises from her usual reckless play. She'd tried to perform some ill-advised maneuver—jumping over a lawn chair, riding a skateboard with her eyes closed—and she'd fallen and hurt herself. She was always trying stunts like that, and it was a wonder to me that she wasn't perpetually wearing a cast on one part of her body or another. And while it was quite possible these bruises were the result of another of her misadventures, I know how she got them. Or rather, who gave them to her. Her mother had a temper, and she lost patience with Alison, her wild child, easily. I wonder what other marks Alison's clothes are hiding, and I feel a deep sense of sadness coupled with helplessness. I wish there was something I could do to help her, to fix things for her, but I know there isn't. It's no surprise to me that she doesn't feel the pain of the scratches on her legs. She's felt worse in her short life. Far worse.

There's a light breeze blowing, and the leaves on the trees above us rustle softly, making a sound like a rushing river. I imagine I hear voices as well, whispering words that I can't quite make out. These voices aren't sinister, though. Their tone is soothing, comforting, a balm for the spirit. I wish that time could stand still and I could live in this moment, with Alison, forever.

I TRY to retrace the steps Alison and I took that day, but it was so long ago, and I can't remember exactly where we entered the woods or what route we took. I decide to do what Alison would, and I move forward confidently, no hesitation, as if I know precisely where I'm going. The trees are larger—they've had thirty years to grow, after all—and the undergrowth is sparser than I remember. Most likely the tree canopy blocks the sunlight during the other seasons, stunting the growth of the vegetation below. It strikes me that this is a perfect metaphor for growing older—age hindering new growth— and I think of how different I am from the child that followed Alison into these woods on that long-ago day. I was all potential then, my whole life lying before me. Now I'm a barely adequate literature professor at an unremarkable college, divorced and childless. I used to tell myself that there's still time to start over, that as long as there's life, there's hope, all the platitudes that we fall back on at three in the morning when the existential angst becomes too much and we can't sleep. I don't tell myself these things anymore because they're not true. Not for me, at least. I feel like an empty shell of the girl I once was, a ghost haunting my own life, and attending my cousin's funeral didn't exactly cheer me up. I suppose I've come to greet whatever lonely spirits might linger in the park. Like calls to like, after all.

A couple months ago, I was watching a true crime program on television called *Suburban Nightmare*. I was shocked to realize the episode focused on Alison's disappearance. There were interviews with her family, police officers who investigated, neighbors who joined in the search for her... I was glad the show's producers hadn't tracked me down. I couldn't imagine talking about that day on camera. I wanted to turn off the program, but despite myself, I was captivated and couldn't stop watching. There was no new information presented on the program, but it was difficult to hear people talk about Alison as if they knew her when *I* was her best friend, practically a big sister to her. Worst of all was having to watch Alison's mother get teary-eyed as she spoke of the last time she saw her darling daughter. Perhaps on some level her grief was genuine, but I remembered the bruises on the backs of her legs that day, and all I could feel for her mother was hatred.

It was so bizarre, seeing one of the pivotal events of my life turned into a thirty-minute (with commercials) show, complete with cheesy reenactments. I suppose that's one of the reasons why I've come here—to purge the emotional residue left behind from watching that program. *A walk through the woods is cheaper than therapy,* I think, and I manage a small smile.

As I move through the woods, I navigate by instinct, following an inner pull that guides me towards my destination. I haven't been here for thirty years, yet there is no floundering, no going about in circles, no turning back and retracting my steps because I've gone in the wrong direction. My soul knows the way, and it leads me there, straight and true.

The trees are older here, taller, set closer together, forming a barrier that's difficult to see through. I slip between a pair of elms and am immediately confronted by a fenced-in area. The fence is chain link, and it's a head taller than me, making it six feet in height, maybe more. There's a door built into the fence, but it's closed and sealed by a rusty padlock. The area is square, the ground covered with dead leaves, and in the middle is a tall stone monument, perhaps ten feet in height. The white stone is tinged with the gray of age, but its edges are still sharp, its details clear. The top of the monument was carved to look as if a vase rests atop it, with a cloth draped over it and a garland of flowers looped across. The design is meant to look classical, like Greek or Roman architecture, and there's a beauty and elegance to it that takes my breath away for a moment. When I was a child, I wondered what the stone vase was supposed to contain? Water? Wine?

Despite the fence, someone has gotten inside and spray-painted graffiti on the stone's surface in black. A peace sign, and below it four words in capital letters: THEY WILL LIVE FOREVER. This last word is hyphenated, *for* above *ever*, because of the monument's narrow width. The words send a chill rippling down my back, and I look away from them. There's a metal sign bolted to the fence near the door. I've seen it before, read its word, but I walk over to it to refresh my memory.

Townsend Family Cemetery
Burgess, Virginia

Below this, a pair of names and dates.

Thomas Townsend (1821-1892)
Marie Townsend (1826-1887)

The sign goes on to tell the Townsends' story, a childless couple who lived here during the Civil War and who left their land to the town after they died, with the stipulation that it be turned into a park. *For the children,* the sign says. Relatives commission this monument and erected it here, presumably where the couple was buried, to commemorate their generous gift. The entire park was once their property, and the park itself is as much a monument to their legacy as this stone pillar, maybe more so. Alison and I came here many times, and although we were tempted to climb the fence and go inside so we could inspect the monument up close, lay our hands upon the cold stone and think about the people buried there, we never tried. It seemed so disrespectful. Even Alison, as curious and impulsive as she was, didn't attempt to scale the fence.

I look at the monument and once more read the words—THEY WILL LIVE FOREVER—and I think back to the true crime show about Alison's disappearance. At the end, the narrator discussed various theories about what might've happened to her. The most prominent was that she'd been abducted by a stranger, taken somewhere and killed, her body disposed of and never found. Another popular theory was that her mother had something to do with her disappearance. The rumor was that Alison hadn't vanished in the park at all, that she'd gotten separated from me and eventually wandered home. Her mother, upset for some reason—Alison had been gone too long, she'd returned with mud on her shoes—punished her, perhaps beating her so severely she died. Panicked and facing arrest, her mother, with her father's help, hid her body somewhere and made up the story about Alison's disappearance. Local police had their suspicions, as did the community, but nothing had ever been proven. My parents didn't know what to believe. They were simply relieved that whatever happened to Alison didn't happen to me. Best case scenario, everyone figured, she ran away from her abusive home. Although a young girl on her own would be easy prey, people whispered darkly. Regardless of whatever happened to Alison, no one ever expected to see her again.

And they never did.

***

"Do you think they're *really* buried here?" Alison asks.

She holds onto the fence, fingers grasping metal links, forehead pressed to the chain link, as if she wants to get as close to the monument as she possibly can, maybe even hoping to push her body through the fence if she just tries hard enough.

The monument's stone is a bit whiter than it will be thirty years hence, and its surface is clean, unmarred by graffiti.

I didn't know the answer to Alison's question, but I knew what she wanted me to say.

"Of course they are. They wouldn't put a monument here if they weren't."

She grins and shivers with delicious fear.

"It must be nice." Her tone is wistful.

"What? Being dead?"

She shoots me a look.

"No." She pauses, considers. "Well, that might be okay. You'd get to sleep a lot and no one would bother you."

She puts a slight emphasis on the word *bother*, and I think of the bruises on her body.

"I mean being here all the time," she says. "Living in the words, trees all around, protected by a fence, peaceful and quiet…"

She falls silent and continues to stare at the monument. Tears begin to roll slowly down her cheeks, and I step closer to her and put my arm around her shoulder. I start crying too, and I stand next to my friend, looking at the monument with her, and for the first time in my young life, it occurs to me that being dead might be—just sometimes—better than being alive.

The padlock on the fence's door—which has only started to rust at this point—snicks open. Our attention is immediately drawn to the sound, and we watch as the door swings open of its own accord with a gentle creaking.

Alison and I look at each other, mouths open, eyes wide with fear. I want to run, run as fast as I can away from her, leave the park, and never come back. And if I was alone, that's precisely what I'd do. But I'm not alone. I'm with Alison, and while it's clear she's afraid, she shows no sign of wanting to leave. Quite the opposite.

She pulls away from me, does her best to wipe the tears from her face with her hands. Her smile is faint and unsteady, but it's there, accompanied by a glint in her eyes that I know only too well.

I shake my head.

"Come on," she says. "It's like we've been invited."

She reaches out to take my hand, but I step back and shake my head harder.

"Don't do it. It's not…" I don't know what to say. Not *right?* Not *safe?* Not *sane?*

Her smile becomes sad.

"I need to do this. I *have* to."

She's asking for my understanding, but I can't give it. After I remain silent for several moments, she leans forward, gives me a quick kiss on the cheek, then whirls about and sprints away from me. I try to grab hold of her to stop her, but she's already moved beyond my grasp. I run after her, chasing her around the fence.

"Stop!" I shout. "Please!"

She reaches the opening in the fence before I do, and she plunges through. I'm almost there when the gate slams shut and the padlock engages with a loud *snick*. I reach the door, grab hold of it, shake it hard, but of course it doesn't open.

Alison had stopped running. She stands inside the enclosure, looking upon the monument once more. Is she regretting her choice? Is she wary? Or is she excited by what's about to happen? Knowing Alison, I figure all three.

She turns to look at me one last time, then she starts walking slowly toward the monument. Shadow pools around its base, and from this darkness two figures begin to emerge, human silhouettes, and while they possess no distinguishing feature other than one being taller than the other, I know they are man and woman. A married couple. A *childless* couple. They raise their arms as they glide toward Alison, and I'm too terrified to watch anymore. I turn and run, run, run, and I don't stop running until I reach my house. I collapse into a sitting position on the porch, put my face into my hands and sob.

I NEVER TOLD anyone about what I saw that day. I made up a story, said that Alison and I had become separated in the woods. I called and called for her, I said, but she never answered. My parents called the police, and they came and questioned me. They began searching the park and people in the neighborhood volunteered to help, my parents included. I stayed home, fearing that I wouldn't be to pretend to look for Alison, wouldn't be able to deliver a convincing performance, so I stayed home. Alison wasn't found, of course, and she became officially missing, and she'd remain so for the next thirty years. I sometimes wondered what Alison's mother thought about her daughter's sudden disappearance. Was she upset? Scared? Relieved that the child she hated would no longer be a bother to her? I never found out, and I decided it didn't matter. All that was important was that Alison was behind her mother's reach.

Here I am, an adult, something that Alison never had the chance to become. An adult who returned to town for a funeral. An adult with a secret she didn't share with any of her relatives who attended the service.

"Hey, Alison," I say softly. "It's me, all grown up. I hope you found the peace you were looking for. You deserve it. I could use a little peace myself these days. I'm sick, Alison. I have a tumor inside my head, and it's inoperable. The doctors say I might have a year left, but maybe only six months. It depends on how fast the tumor grows from this point on. I haven't really started experiencing any symptoms yet, at least not serious ones. Sometimes I forget things, and sometimes I get dizzy, but that's it so far. It's going to get worse, though. A *lot* worse. And soon."

The leaves within the fence stir slightly. I might put it down to the wind, but at this moment, the air is still.

"You found a way to escape all those years ago. Could you help me do the same?" I pause, smile. "For an old friend?"

Nothing happens for several moments, and I begin to think the tumor has affected my brain more than I realized, that it's made me believe impossible things, and if I'm not exactly crazy, I'm not altogether sane, either. But then—just as I'm about to turn away—a pile of leaves near the monument leaps into the air and swirls around and around before adhering to one another and compacting into the shape a child. A *girl* child, I know, although there are no obvious feature to indicate gender. The figure comes walking toward me, the dried leaves that comprise its body making soft rasping and crunching sounds as it approaches. I should be afraid of this strange apparition coming toward me, but I'm not. How could I ever be scared of the best friend I've ever had?

When Alison reaches me, she stops and stretches out a leaf-covered hand, her "fingers" wooden twigs. *Nice touch,* I think. I take her hand, crying now, and the twig fingers feel surprisingly warm, as if I'm holding onto flesh-and-blood. She tugs me forward, pulling hard, and I feel my body trying to resist her. She pulls harder, and I experience a feeling of letting go, as if I've just shrugged off clothes that I'd been wearing too long, and ill-fitting ones at that. I feel light, feel free.

I look down at our clasped hands. Alison's is that of a young girl, bone covered by skin, and mine is smaller now, fingers slender, skin smoother. I look at Alison's face—we're the same height now—and see a little girl smiling at me. We're both dressed in T-shirts and shorts, as we were on that long-ago day. There are no bruises on her skin that I can see, no marks of any kind. This fills my heart with joy.

I glance back over my shoulder, expecting to see my adult body lying on the ground, dead, but nothing is there. I'm not exactly sure what's happened, but I know *why* it's happened. Alison has invited me to play with her, and I intend to do just that. I squeeze her hand in gratitude.

"Thank you," I say.

She squeezes back then lets go of my hand and gives me a huge grin.

"Race you to the park sign!" she says and before I can respond, she sprints past me toward the fence's open doorway. Laughing, I give chase. I don't think about the problems with my job or my failed message, and most of all I don't think about my tumor. All these things are unimportant now, so much so it's like they never really existed at all.

As I leave the enclosure, I catch a glimpse of two shadowy figures standing near the monument. The taller shadow has its arm around the smaller one, and the Townsends watch me as I face forward once more and pour on the speed. I know I won't catch up to Alison—she's too fast—but that's okay. I'm just happy to run, happy to feel alive…

…happy to be home.

OLD MONSTERS NEVER DIE

You sit cross-legged on the ground in front of a small fire. It's late January, and the flames do little to warm you, but that's okay. You don't mind the cold, barely feel it, in fact. You're wearing a thick jacket, but you haven't bothered to zip it up, and the top three buttons on the flannel shirt you have on beneath are undone. The clothes are a bit large on you. This is partly due to how thin you've become over the last several months, but you've always preferred your clothes loose and comfortable. They're easier to tear off that way, in case the change comes on you sudden and unexpected, which it sometimes does, especially these days.

It's after midnight—you don't have a watch on you so you don't know the exact time—and the sky is free of clouds, the stars clear, crisp points of light, bright jewels set in a vast curtain of black satin. The closest town is over twenty miles away, so there's no light pollution to spoil the view. No moon tonight, which is a shame. Your people don't need it in order to change, but their blood sings loudest when the moon is full and high. The scent of woodsmoke is thick in your nostrils, making it difficult to discern other smells, but not impossible.

Your senses might be dulled by age, but they're still far sharper than an ordinary human's, and you can detect the scents of trees all around you, of animals that have passed through this clearing over the last several days—squirrel, racoon, groundhog, possum, deer... Winter has been relatively mild this year, and the forest animals have been more active than they normally would be in January. *An easy winter makes for good hunting,* you think. For a moment, you're tempted to shuck off your clothes, change, and lope off in search of a deer. You salivate at the thought of fresh meat in your mouth and hot blood on your tongue, but you haven't come here to hunt.

You've come here to die.

You continue sitting in the middle of the clearing, surrounded by leafless oak and elm trees, branches stirred by the wind, rustling and clacking. You listen to the sound of night birds singing, gaze into the dancing flames before you, and wait. You should be relaxed, at peace with what is going to happen this night, but you aren't. You're on edge, right foot bouncing, fingers digging furrows into the dirt on either side of you. You don't want to be here, would rather be back in your cabin, sitting next to your woodstove, reading a book, listening to music, watching some mindless show on television, doing *anything* instead of sitting here waiting. But this is your people's way, and as much as you resent being bound by their traditions, bound you are—to some of them, anyway.

Later—a few minutes, an hour, it doesn't matter—the night birds fall silent. Your fire has grown low, but you don't put more wood on it. It has fulfilled its traditional purpose, to act like a beacon for whomever has come in search of you, a signal that you are not attempting to conceal your presence, that you are unafraid of them. You rise to your feet, joints that were once smooth and supple complaining at being forced to work in the cold.

A figure emerges between the trees and starts walking toward you. Five years ago—okay, maybe ten—your vision was strong enough that the clearing would have seemed bright as day to you. Not now. You can't discern the features of the one approaching until she's almost in range of the fire's light. But you know her scent as well as your own, for it *is* partially yours, just as it is partially her mother's.

She has come to you in human form, which is an insult, for it means she sees you as no threat, and she's come alone, which is an even greater insult. Among your kind, respect is shown by the number of those who attend one's Final Challenge, whether to participate or observe. But no one else in the pack has come to honor you, and no doubt Elena is here to perform what she sees as a distasteful duty, nothing more. You should've expected this, and you suppose you did deep down, but you're surprised by how much it still hurts.

She stops when she reaches the fire.

"Father."

Long brown hair, hard features, tall, garbed in a black shirt and old jeans, feet bare. She looks so much like Natalie—her mother—that the sight of her makes your heart ache.

"Elena."

You smile at her. She doesn't smile back. You speak the required words.

"Have you come to challenge me this night?"

She looks at you a moment, face impassive, eyes gleaming.

The traditional response to your question is *Prepare to defend yourself, Honored One.*

Instead, she says, "I haven't come to kill you." She smiles, displaying a mouth filled with sharp teeth.

"I've come to do something much worse."

"I DON'T THINK I can do it, Daddy," Elena whispers.

You and your daughter, who is ten years old, crouch behind a large oak. It's dusk in mid-April, and while the sky above the western horizon is a dark blue, the rest of the world is draped in shadow, and it will be full night soon. The oak lies at the edge of a stand of trees that form a half circle around the back of a small playground—swings, climbing equipment, monkey bars, slides, merry-go-round—beyond which is a soccer field, and then a suburban street. Cedar chips are scattered around the play equipment to absorb the impact if any children should fall, but there is only one child here this night. A girl, scarcely older than Elena, wearing a windbreaker over a T-shirt, along with jeans and sneakers. She sits on the middle swing, hands gripping the chains, tips of her shoes on cedar chips. She twists right, left, right, left, slowly, barely moving. You hear her soft whimpers, smell the salt of her tears. The girl's upset about something. She's too young to have had a fight with a lover. Maybe she had some sort of conflict with her parents, or perhaps a falling out with a friend. The specifics don't matter. Whatever has upset her has driven her to come to this small park as night falls, so she can sit on a swing and be alone with her sorrow. It couldn't be more perfect for Elena's first time.

You put a reassuring hand on your daughter's shoulder and speak, your words so soft only those with your people's keen hearing can detect them.

"Of course you can do this. You're an excellent hunter."

You squeeze her shoulder tighter, and without consciously willing it, your fingernails grow longer and sharper.

"I can hunt *animals*," Elena whispers, "but I don't think I can hunt a…a…"

"Human?"

"Person."

"We've been over this, sweetheart. Why do we hunt them?"

Elena hesitates. Your claws extend farther, points becoming sharp as needles, the tips piercing Elena's shirt and dimpling the young flesh beneath. Not quite drawing blood, not yet.

Elena begins to speak, but the words are without emotion, little more than rote memory.

"The Moonborn came into being at the same moment humans did. All things in nature exist in balance, and we were created to balance them. We are their greatest predator, and it is our sacred duty to thin their numbers, to keep their kind strong and healthy. To help them not only survive, but thrive. Humans don't know it—and if they did, they wouldn't believe it—but Moonborn are the best friends they've ever had."

"It's not enough to say the words. You have to *believe* them, too. Do you?"

You chose a night of a full moon for Elena's first human hunt, as is tradition, but moonrise is still an hour away. If the moon was up, she would feel it calling to her, filling her with strength, confidence, and desire. But you know your daughter can't afford to wait until then. The girl on the swing might leave at any moment, Elena needs to strike while the girl is wrapped up in her emotions and her guard is down.

Elena doesn't answer. You remember your first time, almost thirty years ago now. You felt much the same as Elena, and you remember what your mother did to help you get through it. You say the same words to your daughter that your mother spoke to you on that long-ago night.

"If you do not kill her, *I* will, and the death I give her will not be swift. I will make it hurt, and I will make it last."

Elena has kept her gaze focused on the girl the entire time you've been talking, but now she whips her head around, a shocked expression on her face. You've always taught her that it's a kindness to deliver the gift of death swiftly. She's never heard you talk like this before. Her nostrils flare as she inhales, drawing in your scent to determine if you're telling the truth. Her eyes widen as she realizes you are.

Images, sounds, and smells flash through your mind—a boy sitting on the edge of a creek holding a simple wooden fishing rod, your mother darting past you when you refused to kill him, the boy screaming as your mother began to slowly tear him apart… The next time she took you out, you killed the child she'd selected for you, and you did so without hesitation. A cruel lesson, perhaps, but a necessary one.

Moments pass as you and Elena look at each other silently. Finally, she breaks eye contact, turns away from you, starts to move toward the girl, her bare feet making no sound as she goes. The girl senses something, though, and she looks over her shoulder. Elena shifts form in less time than it takes a human to blink, and she rushes forward, wraps a fur-clad arm around the girl's chest, grabs her chin with her opposite hand —claws digging into soft flesh—and then with a single sharp motion, she breaks the girl's neck. The crack of snapping bone is loud as a gunshot to your ears, but you doubt if anyone else hears it. Elena pulls the dead girl off the swing before she can fall and quickly drags her back into the trees. She drops the girl onto the ground near you, and then she crouches over the body and begins to feed.

She starts slowly, gingerly tearing small pieces of flesh and chewing them with a grimace. She's eaten human meat since she was a toddler, but it's always been procured for her by her parents. She's never had to feed herself like this before, and she finds the process distasteful. But instinct takes over, and soon her head is buried in the girl's abdomen as she seeks out her most tender organs, making snuffling-growling sounds of satisfaction all the while. The rich smell of fresh blood makes your mouth water, but you do not join your daughter in this feast. This is her first kill, and no one may share it with her. You're so very proud of her, and you're about to tell her so when you see the dead girl's face for the first time. You rarely look upon the features of prey. Why would you? They're just meat. But something about this girl catches your attention, and you realize it's her hair—long, straight, and brown, just like Elena's. *Exactly* like. Their faces are different, though. The girl's is broader, and she has a small scattering of freckles on her cheeks. Her wide, staring eyes are blue, not green like Elena's, but the girls are the same basic height and weight, and nearly the same age, and for the first time in your life, you see not a prey animal but—as Elena said—a person. And not just any person. You see someone's daughter, and you think about how it would feel to you if some beast killed Elena and savaged her corpse like this, swallowing bloody gobbets of meat and making throaty *mmmmmm* sounds of pleasure.

You experience a sudden urge to backhand Elena and knock her off the girl, but you don't do it. You fight the revulsion you feel, tell yourself it's temporary, merely the result of seeing your sweet, innocent child become a blooded hunter for the first time. Elena is growing up, and it's only natural for a parent to have mixed emotions about this, right?

As enthusiastically as Elena eats, her small belly can hold only so much, and when she's full and draws away from the corpse, the body still has plenty of meat on it. It's the parent's duty to finish off whatever remains of a young one's first kill, but your gut roils with nausea, and you fear that if you get your face too close to the girl's body, you'll vomit. You don't want Elena to see this.

Elena is still in wolf form, and she looks at you with her green eyes, as if seeking your approval. You force a smile.

"Good job," you say.

But your tone is flat, your words without life, and Elena's

eyes narrow. She knows you're lying, but she doesn't know why. Neither do you, really.

AFTER THAT NIGHT, you found it a struggle to eat human meat, and you were no longer able to kill any of them. Gender, age, race, social position, state of health, none of it mattered. You viewed them all as people now, and you could not raise your claws against them. At first your wife feared you might be sick, and she said nothing when you went out hunting for animal meat, although she would not allow you to bring that *filth* into her house. The two of you tried to hide your… problem from the rest of the pack, but word got out eventually, and the pack elders asked to speak with you. The meeting did not last long. They offered you a human liver to eat, you refused, and you were a member of the pack no longer.

Your excommunication didn't extend to Natalie and Elena, but it brought great shame on them both. You wished that could've been avoided, but you knew that was impossible. You moved out of your home—your wife wouldn't allow you to say goodbye to Elena—and moved into a cramped trailer on the edge of the woods, and you've lived there ever since, thirty-one years now, and in all that time, you haven't tasted human blood or meat. You haven't seen your wife or daughter, either, and you've come to believe that you'll go to your grave without looking upon their faces again.

It turns out you were wrong.

YOU EXAMINE your daughter's features. She's forty-one now, but you can still see the ten-year-old girl in her middle-aged face, especially in her eyes, which look as green and vibrant as they did when you last saw her.

"You look weak," Elena says, "and I can smell death on you."

Your arms and legs are thin, your cheeks sunken in. Beneath your shirt, your stomach is concave, ribs prominent. You tremble, but not from fear. Well, not *only* from fear.

Elena continues. "What's wrong? Your special diet not agree with you?"

It's true. Your kind needs human meat to survive, and you've been slowly starving yourself for three decades, becoming weaker with each passing year. This is why you've chosen the Final Challenge—better to die on your feet, fighting, than to continue wasting away.

"Have you come to taunt me?" you ask.

She smiles. "I've come to offer you a choice."

She looks over her shoulder, and as if this is a signal, another figure emerges from the trees on the far side of the clearing. The wind is coming from that direction, blowing stronger now, and you pick up the newcomer's scent sooner than you did Elena's. It's not one scent, though, but two: Elena's mother—Natalie—and another scent, this one human. You don't understand at first, see only Natalie walking toward you, but as she comes closer, you realize that she's carrying a human child, a boy from the smell of him.

Natalie joins Elena, and you see the years have been kind to your wife. Ex-wife, you suppose, although you've never been officially divorced. Then again, you were never legally married, not as humans understand the process. Her long hair is gray, but her face looks much the same as the last day you saw her. A few wrinkles here and there, but you have far more. Her lips are pressed together in a tight, disapproving line, and her eyes fix on yours, and you see contempt in them, along with a small measure of pity. She's wearing an unzipped hoodie, a T-shirt, and jeans. Like Elena's, her feet are bare. The boy she holds is around ten years old—the same age as the girl who was your daughter's first kill, a girl whose name you never learned—and he's awake. Duct tape covers his mouth to keep him silent, but his eyes are wide with terror. He wriggles, trying to squirm free, but Natalie, even in this form, is far stronger than a human, and when she squeezes him against her, he moans behind the tape and stops struggling. When he's still, she drops him to the ground. He lands on his belly, and before he can attempt to rise, she places a foot on his back to hold him down. His face is lit by the dim orange glow of the dying fire as he looks at you, eyes pleading. *Please don't do this*, they say. *Let me go, I won't say anything!*

You're surprised your wife and daughter have come. As required by tradition, you found one of the pack—a middle-aged man who works at a feedstore in town—drinking alone in a bar and told him you were ready for your Final Challenge. You told him where you would be and when, and the man simply nodded and went back to his drink. You left, knowing that he would spread the word to the rest of the pack, and then, if the pack had any love left for you at all, someone would come to challenge you this night. But Elena and Natalie surely must hate you for the shame you've brought upon them, and you cannot imagine either possessing the merest scrap of affection for you. But they *have* come, although to offer you a far more terrible challenge than combat.

Elena's smile broadens, displaying her sharp teeth.

"Kill this boy, eat his flesh and drink his blood. Prove to us that you are still worthy of being Moonborn, and I will give you your Final Challenge."

Hearing these words, the boy starts screaming behind the tape. He thrashes, arms and legs flailing, but Natalie's foot holds him firm to the ground. You look at the boy, and you wonder where Elena and Natalie found him. Is his family aware that he's missing? Are they frantically calling friends and neighbors, hoping that someone—anyone—knows where he is?

"I told you he wouldn't do it," Natalie says, mouth curled into a sneer. "He's nothing but a simpering dog, afraid to follow his instincts, too afraid to be what nature made him."

"I am what I choose to be," you say.

"You're a coward." Natalie practically spits this last word.

"If you *choose* not to kill the boy," Elena says, "I'll kill him here, in front of you, and leave his corpse to keep you company. Mother and I will go, and no one in the pack will ever offer to challenge you. You will continue to weaken until you die, alone, and no one will sing your death-song."

"Although if you want to hurry up the process, you could always kill yourself," Natalie says. "It would be a fitting end for you."

Your people can heal any wound—even those caused by silver, despite what the legends claim—but an injury caused by the teeth and claws of one of your kind will prove fatal if it's serious enough. This includes self-inflicted injuries. One swipe of your claws across your throat, and you'd bleed to death in moments. Suicide is considered the ultimate expression of weakness among the Moonborn, and if you take this route, you will be reviled by the pack for generations. You tell yourself you don't care what they think, but you know it's a lie.

Elena's face softens then. "We're giving you a chance to reclaim your honor and restore ours. Take it. *Please.*"

You understand then that Elena and Natalie haven't brought the boy to you as a taunt or punishment, at least that's not their only reason. Elena is doing for you what you once did for her. You wanted to usher her into the full life of the Moonborn, and now she wants to bring you back to it.

She sees the boy as a gift, not as a person with his own life to live, his own destiny to fulfill.

You look at the boy once more. You've saved hundreds of lives by not killing humans these last three decades. It wasn't easy to abstain, for despite your desire to cause no harm to humans, the temptation—the *craving*—for their meat was always there. You learned to live with the hunger, but it was a struggle to keep it in check. You deserve a proper end to your life, just as any Moonborn does, and it's only *one* boy…

You feel the change come upon you, so swift there's barely any transition between your two forms. You gain height and mass, gray fur sprouts across your entire body, your hands become large and clawed, your face lengthens, teeth sharpen, ears become pointed. Your coat and shirt are too tight now, and you tear them off and drop them next to the fire. A corner of your shirt catches flame and the cloth begins to burn.

The boy absolutely loses his shit at the sight of your true form. His eyes grow so wide it looks as if they might pop out of his head, and a corner of the tape over his mouth has come loose, and when he screams, the sound is loud and shrill and echoes throughout the clearing. Natalie looks stunned, as if she thought you didn't have it in you, while Elena cries happy tears, believing her father is about to reclaim his place in the pack and redeem himself.

You snarl, leap over the fire, and attack.

WHEN IT'S OVER, you take human form again. You're covered in blood, some of it yours, most of it not. Elena and Natalie lie on the ground, bodies savaged beyond recognition. The wounds they inflicted upon you burn like hell, but during the battle you swallowed some of their meat and blood—more out of reflex than anything else—and you feel stronger than you have in years, alive and vital.

The boy is gone. Once Natalie's foot was off his back, he sprang to his feet and ran for the trees, screaming the whole way. You don't know where he is right now, but you'll find him. You'll do your best to calm him, and then you will lead him to town, where hopefully he will be able to find his way back to his family. You can't really show up on their doorstep to deliver him, shirtless and covered with blood. After this, you'll return to your trailer to clean yourself, get fresh clothes, and then you'll set out again. You've realized something this night. You may have saved some humans by refusing to eat their flesh, but that didn't stop the rest of the pack from continuing to prey on them. You could have—*should* have—done more these last thirty years, and while there's nothing you can do about that now, there is something you can do moving forward. You will hunt the Moonborn and make sure they never hurt anyone ever again. And when you're finished killing your pack, you'll move on to another, and another after that. You will become a greater monster than any of them could ever be—a monster's monster—and Moonborn parents will tell their cubs stories about you to frighten them into behaving. *Be good, or the Gray Hunter will get you.*

You smile at the thought.

You gaze upon the bodies of your wife and daughter one last time.

"Thanks," you say, breath misting on the cold night air, and then you begin walking.

THE ASHES OF OUR FATHERS

"Don't fall, Brenda. The last thing you want to do is break open Dad's urn," Theresa says.

"Yeah." Ira smirks. "We didn't bring a hand vac to hoover him up."

A rock rolled out from under your left foot a moment ago, causing you to list to the side. You adjust the backpack containing your father's urn, making sure it's strapped tight to your body. Your sister and brother might be joking. But you know how the universe works, how every moment we court disaster, how everything—even time itself—is always falling apart.

You imagine you hear your father's voice. *You think too much, Brenda.*

You can't argue with that.

It's late March in Arizona, and even though you're wearing a T-shirt and shorts, you feel overheated. You're not sweating, though. The dry desert air sucks the moisture from your body without you realizing it's happening. You've been warned that you need to keep drinking water as you hike, that it's all too easy to become dehydrated without being aware that it's happening. But you don't reach for the metal water bottle clipped to your belt.

Heat aside, it's beautiful here. The sun is out, the sky a vibrant blue dotted with cotton-ball clouds, almost no humidity. You haven't been to the desert since you were five, almost fifty years ago, and you'd forgotten—or hadn't been aware of—its stark, minimalistic grandeur. Featureless hard soil, stoic rock outcroppings, sparse vegetation... It's a place perpetually on the verge, always dying but never quite dead.

Your siblings are dressed much the same as you, and they carry backpacks as well, although theirs hold supplies and not human remains. They're both older than you by a decade or more—you were what your family euphemistically refers to as a "whoops baby"—but while they move slower than you, they're steady and sure. Solid, like the landscape around you. Physically, they're a study in opposites. Theresa is tall and bird-thin, with a brittle manner that makes her seem as if she's always judging the world and finding it wanting. Ira is shorter, round-faced and round-bellied, and he always seems amused by everything around him, although his amusement has a dark edge to it. One important way they're alike, though, is their eyes. There's a shared awareness there, a *We know something you don't know* slyness.

They look their age. Skin lined, leathery, and sagging. Eyes receded into their skulls rendering the outlines of their sockets prominent. Liver spots on the backs of their hands, teeth yellowed from decades of coffee consumption. Lips thin and dry, barely there at all, really. Theresa's hands shake all the time, not Parkinson's, but some neurological condition you can't remember the name of. Ira has acid reflux, and he's always swallowing stomach acid that's bubbled up in his throat. He has gas too, and his farts smell like days-old rotten meat.

They're like a pair of ambulatory corpses, you think, or

close enough to make little difference. You adjust the backpack again, although there's no need. You feel the urn shift, almost as if the ashes stir inside, and you keep walking.

YOU'RE four years old when you see a dead body for the first time. Your grandfather had a pacemaker installed several months earlier—although you aren't sure what it is—and Something Went Wrong with it. That's how the grown-ups say it, emphasizing the words in low, soft voices. *Something Went Wrong.*

The room in the funeral home where your grandfather's coffin rests is crowded with people, almost all of them adults you don't know, all wearing suits or dresses. Many of them are old—hair white, skin corrugated, hands bony and thick-knuckled. More like claws, really. This is a *viewing*, your father told you, although you don't understand why anyone would want to look at a dead person. Dead people are scary. In stories, they come back as ghosts, skeletons, or zombies. But people keep walking up to the coffin as if they aren't afraid. They stand there, looking down at your dead grandfather, not speaking, sometimes shaking their heads as if in denial, sometimes crying, before moving on to make room for someone else to *view.*

When it's your family's turn to go up, your mother puts her hands on Ira and Theresa's shoulders to steer them. They're teenagers, though, and while they seemed shook up, you can tell by the way their bodies stiffen at your mother's touch that they think they're too old to need physical reassurance. You, however, are not, so when you father reaches down to pick you up, you go into his arms gratefully. He carries you to the coffin and you hug him tight, looking over his shoulder so you won't have to see your dead grandfather. You hear your mother crying, and this makes you turn your head to look at her. She stands in front of the coffin —which is white, not black like the one cartoon vampires slept in—hands still on your siblings' shoulders. You can't see Ira and Brenda's faces, but you don't think they're crying. They're big kids, after all. Almost grown-ups themselves

Your gaze falls upon your grandfather then. He looks more like a giant doll than a person—still and quiet, like a toy resting on a shelf, waiting for someone to pick it up and play with it. The skin on his face and hands looks hard like plastic, and someone put makeup on him, which is weird, since as far as you know, only girls wear makeup. His gossamer-fine hair seems extra white, almost as if it's glowing, and you imagine that it emerges in tufts from regularly spaced holes in his scalp, just like a doll.

You look back over your father's shoulder then, and you see the old people gathered in small groups, talking to each other in hushed tones. Some look as old as your grandfather, others look even older. Several of them notice you looking at them, and they smile in a way that, if you were an adult, you'd recognize as sympathetic and sorrowful. But you're a child, and their smiles strike you as horribly wrong. Who smiles at a funeral?

At that moment, on a subconscious level at least, you come to a profound insight. The old people smiling at you look like Grandfather. He's dead, so that meant they're *almost* dead. They're like ghosts, but still solid and visible. Death isn't something that comes for you, like a cartoon Grim Reaper. It's *inside* you, growing from the moment you're born until it replaces all the life you have until only it is left.

Death isn't an interruption of life. It's the end product.

YOUR FATHER WANTED to be cremated, which was fine with you. You hated the idea of seeing him embalmed, dressed in a suit, and laid out for people to inspect and whisper, *He looks so lifelike.* He also requested that his ashes be scattered in a canyon in Arizona, one of his favorite places in the word, where he loved to hike alone and enjoy the solitude. You lived in Arizona for the first few years of your life, until your father —a civilian contractor with the military—was transferred to an Air Force base in Ohio. You moved there, and it's where you've lived ever since. Ira eventually moved to Colorado Springs, and Theresa settled in St. Louis.

So this morning the three of you—four, if you count your father's ashes—set out from the hotel where you're staying and came to this park. Only so many people are allowed to hike it at a time, and you and your siblings had to make reservations months in advance. But now you're here, several miles from the park entrance, heading toward the canyon your father loved so much. You don't feel good about this trip, though. It feels pointless. And it doesn't help that Ira and Theresa are talking to each other, voices so soft you can't make out their words, their tone secretive, conspiratorial.

"What are you two gabbing about back there?"

The back-and-forth whispering continues for several more seconds before Ira responds.

"You seem in a hurry to get this over with."

You don't look back. "Aren't you?"

"You should take your time," he says. "Really *live* the experience. After all, it's not every day that you get to fulfill your dad's last wish."

"This isn't exactly fun for me," you say.

"I didn't say you should *enjoy* it. I said you should *live* it. Life moves fast enough as it is. No need to make it move any faster."

"You miss the important things that way," Theresa adds. "A

place like this, a time like this… It's a perfect opportunity to face certain truths."

"Gain a new perspective," Ira says.

You change the subject.

"If you're both having trouble keeping up, I can slow down."

"No need," Theresa says. "We might be older than you, but we're not dead."

"Yet," Ira puts in, and they both laugh, voices dry and brittle as old bone.

You keep walking.

———

You're in your mid-thirties, and you're standing in front of a bathroom mirror, examining your reflection. Your eyes are red, the flesh beneath dark and swollen. You see the beginnings of crow's feet, of a vertical line between your eyebrows caused by too much frowning. You found—and immediately removed—a white hair among the black last week, and you've been obsessively checking for more ever since. Theresa is mostly gray now, and she doesn't bother to color her hair. You remember something she said to you several Thanksgivings ago. *Each one of these white hairs is a spot where Death tiptoed up and gently touched me.* She laughed then, but you'd never heard anything more horrifying.

You don't see any white hairs, and you're relieved. But you know more will be coming, and sooner than you think.

With a heavy sigh you exit the bathroom and walk down the hall, heading back to your mother's room. You pass old people, women mostly. They're all wearing robes over hospital gowns and need assistance to get around, whether it's a walker, a wheelchair, or a younger staff member holding onto one of their arms to provide support. Their faces are expressionless, cheeks sagging, mouths open... But their gazes flick toward you as you pass, and they seem to be laughing darkly at you.

We know something you don't know...

You walk faster, doing your best to ignore them, until you reach your mother's room. She's lying in bed, eyes closed, white blanket drawn up to her chin, just as she was when you left her a few minutes ago. The safety rails are up on both sides of the bed to prevent her from falling out. The small TV atop her dresser is on, but the volume is so slow it's barely audible. It's tuned to a Christian broadcasting station, and a man with too-perfect hair, an expensive suit, and a $10,000 smile stands before an audience, microphone in one hand, black leather bible in the other. He paces back and forth on the stage, mouth moving rapidly, but you can't hear what he's saying. You don't know why your mother watches this shit. Neither she nor your father were especially religious while you were growing up, but it's all she watches these days. Then again, living here day after day, knowing this is a place where people come to die...who wouldn't want whatever comfort they could get, even if it came from a third-rate televangelist?

The facility smells of disinfectant—gallons of it—but it can't completely mask the other odors. Urine, feces, vomit, and a sweet tang that makes you think of decaying flowers. You take shallow breaths, but it doesn't help much. Your mother's room has its own bathroom, but you didn't want to disturb her while she was sleeping, so you used the one in the hall. You wish you'd thought to step outside for some fresh air before returning.

You sit in the padded chair next to the bed, and you reach toward your purse on the floor to retrieve the book you'd been reading, a cheesy paperback romance called *The Billionaire's Secret Lover,* when your mother opens her eyes for the first time since you got here two hours ago. You forget about your book and sit up straight.

"Mom?"

She doesn't respond right away, and you wonder if she's aware that you're here, but finally she speaks.

"Brenda? Is that you?"

You want to say, *Who else would it be? I'm the only one of your kids still living in Ohio.* Your father comes by a few times a week, but he's started putting in overtime at the base to make some extra money to help pay your mother's medical bills, and sometimes—a lot of times—he's too tired to come sit with her.

"Yeah, Mom. It's me."

Her head swivels slowly on the pillow as she turns to look at you. Her rheumy eyes have trouble focusing, but she smiles.

"How are you, dear? How's Matthew and Kristin?"

You and Matthew divorced three years ago, and your daughter is attending grad school in Massachusetts. There's no point in telling her this, though. It'll only confuse her, and she won't remember anyway.

"They're fine. We're all fine. How are *you* feeling?"

"Oh, the same as always. Tired." Her smile falters but then strengthens once more. "Won't be long now."

You reach beneath the blanket and take your mother's hand. The thin flesh feels cool and rubbery, the bones beneath fragile as papier-mâché. The sensation turns your stomach, but you don't let go.

"Don't talk like that."

"Why not? What's true is true. Has anyone told you yet?"

The abrupt change in topic catches you off guard, although it shouldn't. Your mother does this all the time. *Dementia's a bitch*, you think. Aloud, you say, "Tell me what?"

"No one has, have they? I can hear it in your voice. You're

still a bit young, but what the hell. None of us are getting any younger, are we?"

She pauses a moment, gathering scattered, partially formed thoughts. Then she begins.

"You know how when you're a young child, there are things adults don't tell you? Not until you're ready?"

"You mean like sex?"

A weak nod. "That's a big one. There are others. Like what a soul-draining grind work can be, and how every relationship—with family, friends, lovers—eventually ends up disappointing you somehow. Or you end up disappointing yourself."

Now it's your turn to nod.

"By the time you're in your thirties, you think you know what it means to be an adult. But there are things old folks know that we won't tell you until you're ready to understand. Things passed down from one generation to the next, things that aren't written down in any book."

You fear your mother's going to tell you about some new delusion, and you remind yourself to smile and nod, whatever it is.

"We don't talk about it much, even among ourselves. But we all *know*. And when the time is right, we tell our children, just as you'll tell Kristin one day."

Despite your best efforts not to react, you're starting to get scared. You think of the way the facility's other residents looked at you on your way back from the bathroom. You think of how the old people at your grandfather's funeral kept to one another's company, conversing in low tones. Part of you thinks your mother is talking crazy, but another, deeper part realizes she's about to clear up a mystery that's been bothering you for almost thirty years. You grip her hand tighter and lean in.

"What do you want to tell me, Mom?"

"About death…and the true meaning of life."

You feel a tingle travel down your spine. Even if this is just her dementia talking, you're excited. You're also scared, and you're not sure if you're ready to hear whatever it is she has to tell you. But what if there really *is* a secret, something old people know and only pass on to their middle-ages descendants? Don't you have a right to know? Isn't it your heritage?

"Okay, Mom. What is it?"

She locks gazes with you. She seems fully present and aware for the first time in a long while. Then she blinks several times.

"What is what, dear?"

WHEN YOUR MOTHER DIES, she's cremated, and your father scatters her ashes in the backyard flower garden that she tended lovingly for many years. It's overgrown with weeds now, and you consider taking it over for her, clearing it up, getting it back in shape, but you can't bring yourself to do it. At her memorial service, the old people keep to themselves, talking quietly and occasionally watching the younger ones, including you, and smiling in way that makes your skin crawl. You keep thinking of what your mother said.

We don't talk about it much, even among ourselves. But we all know.

You've never been especially health conscious, but the next day you join a gym, buy books on eating right and staying youthful. You begin dating younger men and, eventually, dying your hair. You get your teeth whitened, use creams to preserve your skin's elasticity. And when junk mail from AARP, retirement savings programs, and even funeral homes begins arriving at your home, you turn to plastic surgery.

Nothing drastic. Some eye work, tightening the sagging skin on your neck, that sort of thing. You consider a tummy tuck, maybe an ass lift and boob work. But you read how too much surgery—even minor procedures—can put a strain on one's body, and you decide against any more procedures. You do yoga and tai chi, put yourself through fasts, juice cleanses, and coffee enemas. Anything to try and hold onto whatever scraps of youth you can, to stave off becoming one of *them.*

Years pass.

Eventually your father is diagnosed with liver cancer nine months. The doctors go through the motions. Surgery. Chemo. But it's obvious they don't hold out much hope. Your father is in his eighties after all. Once again, as the only child in the area, you get the duty of taking your father to his various medical appointments and caring for him at home, although he tries to discourage you from doing too much of the latter. He grins, a trifle weakly, and says, *I'm a big boy. I can take care of myself.*

The chemo takes its toll on him, as it does for so many. He loses hair, weight, energy, the very spark of life. He becomes a flesh puppet, a thing of stick-bones and paper-skin, and the worst of it is that after everything he's been through, the cancer is still in him, still spreading. Still eating.

One afternoon, after you bring him home from the latest round of useless poison being pumped into his body, the two of you sit in the family room watching a nature documentary on TV, a show about the longest-lived creatures in the animal kingdom, ironically enough. Your father sits in his chair, and you sit in your mother's, although it always makes you uncomfortable to do so. You both watch the program in silence for a time, not really paying much attention to it. Eventually, during a commercial, you work up the courage to ask him a question.

"Dad, one time, not long before Mom passed, she tried to

tell me something. Something about a…I guess you could it a secret that older people keep. One that they pass on to their adult children. Do you know what she was talking about?"

Your father doesn't answer you right away. The commercial ends and the program comes back on. You watch a segment on the ocean quahog, a clam that can live more than 400 years.

Lucky fucker, you think.

Just when you begin to feel foolish for bringing up the subject, your father starts speaking. He doesn't take his gaze off the TV, and his tone is calm, almost empty of feeling.

"You're not ready. Not yet. You will be soon, though."

His words hit you like a punch to the gut. It's true, what you've suspected for almost fifty years. The old know something, something they don't want the young to know. How long has this conspiracy of silence been going on? Decades? Centuries? Longer? A thought occurs to you then.

"Do Theresa and Ira know?" You're surprised to feel a pang of jealousy at the idea that your siblings might have been granted knowledge that has been denied you for so long.

"Yes. They'll tell you when the time is right. Don't ask me again, okay?"

He turns to look at you then. His voice has softened and his tone is almost pleading. His eyes are moist, but tears don't come. It's almost as if his ravaged body can't produce enough fluid to cry.

Feeling you own tears threatening, you answer. "I won't, Dad."

Five months later, your father is dead.

THE THREE OF you come to an overhang, and by unspoken agreement, you stop there. You step to the edge and look over.

You can't really call this a cliff. The drop to the rocky ground is twenty, maybe thirty feet. You might well survive a fall from here. If you don't crack open your skull, snap your neck, or injure any internal organs.

This is the place.

"I can't believe Dad used to come here and sit," you say. He brought you with him once or twice, but you were young then, and you have only hazy memories of being here.

"He liked the solitude," Ira says.

"He said it was a great place to watch the sunrise," Theresa adds.

Both of them remain several feet back from the overhang's edge, and you feel their gazes on the back of your head. They're watching you. Measuring. Judging. You slip off your backpack and put it on the ground. It feels good to have the weight off you, literally and figuratively. You undo the straps and withdraw the urn containing what's left of your father. Despite the heat of the day, its smooth metal surface feels cold beneath your hands. You stand, holding the urn tight, then turn and face your siblings.

"It's time," you tell them. "Say what you have to say."

Ira glances at Theresa, and she nods.

"They say that you don't truly become an adult until you've had your first real experience with death," Theresa says. "But that's not true."

"You don't become a *real* adult until this moment," Ian says. "When you learn the truth."

"No one knows who was the first to figure it out," Theresa says. "Maybe it happened due to some primitive instinct or intuition. Whichever the case, the knowledge has been passed down from generation to generation long before recorded history."

"There's a reason why every living thing ages and dies," Ira says. "And it's not a biological one. You know how in the bible the paradise of Adam and Eve is referred to as the Garden?"

"Yeah," you say.

"That's because the world *is* a garden," Theresa says. "It always has been. And *we're* the crop."

"All life is, actually," Ian says. "God—or whatever passes for God in the universe—created life for a reason. God needs sustenance like any other creature, but he grows his own food."

"He doesn't harvest us all at once, though," Theresa says. "We're like dairy cows. He milks us throughout our lives, draining our energy drop by drop until we're all used up."

Theresa spreads her hands as if offering her septuagenarian self as an example.

"Some people last longer than others," Ira says. "But we all end up the same way, like empty fruit rinds, all our juice drained."

"We're nothing but food, and that's all we've ever been," Theresa says. "All *anyone* has ever been."

"You're probably wondering why people pass this knowledge along," Ira says, "why we don't keep our mouths shut and let people live their lives in ignorance. After all, wouldn't that be kinder? But think about how Mom ended up. How Dad withered away to nothing. When you're old and dying, when you look back on your life and wonder if it was worth it, if you really made a difference, at least you know you fulfilled the purpose you were made for. Thanks to your contribution, the Gardener will continue."

"In a way, we become part of him," Theresa says. "You are what you eat, right? Well, you're also what eats *you*."

"Once they learn the truth, some people kill themselves, out of despair or in the hope of denying the Gardener what's left of their life force," Ian says. "Others enter into a deep depression, withdrawing from the world and everyone they love. Still others decide to make the most of whatever life remains to them. They travel, take up hobbies, and generally try to enjoy themselves. That's what Dad tried to do—until the cancer took hold of him—and that's my philosophy as well."

"And mine," Theresa echoes.

"Well…we promised Dad that we'd tell you, and we have," Ian says. "Now it's up to you to decide what to do with the knowledge."

You look at them for a moment, then smile. "But I already know what to do."

Your siblings frown. This isn't what they expected you to say.

"I first sensed the truth at Grandfather's funeral. That's when I realized that something—Time? Entropy? Call it what you will—was nibbling away at every one of us, devouring us bit by bit. I felt the truth of it down to a cellular level. *Deeper.* And that awareness became stronger as I grew, accompanying me wherever I went, like a tumorous growth that couldn't be removed. Every day I wondered how much of me was left, and how much longer I'd last.

"When Dad wouldn't tell me the secret, I decided to try and learn it on my own. I started volunteering at an assisted-living facility, the same one Mom was in, as a matter of fact. Lots of old people there. It didn't take long for me to befriend a woman who'd never had children, and she told me since she didn't have anyone else to pass on the knowledge to. I didn't believe her at first, but like I said, I could *feel* the truth of it in the core of my being. I guess the older you get—the closer to death—the more you're aware of it. But even though I came to acknowledge the truth, I refused to accept my place in the cosmic food chain. There had to be something else I could do other than meekly accepting my fate. It took a couple more months of talking to old people, in person and through the

Internet, hinting for what I was searching for since no one would talk about it openly, but I finally found a group—or rather *they* found *me*. They showed me there was another path, and they taught me how to walk it."

Ira and Theresa look confused, afraid even. You suppose they find your icy-calm demeanor off-putting. This is not how they intended the day to go. But they also seem intrigued.

"What path?" Ira asks.

You smile wider—more like bare your teeth, really—and both of your siblings flinch. Your teeth are whiter than they used to be. Sharper, too.

"Simply put, if you can't beat 'em, join 'em."

You remove the lid from your father's urn and toss it to the ground. You turn the urn over and gray ash pours out, and as it falls, it curves abruptly upward, as if caught by a strong wind. But the air is still. The cremains begin to swirl around you, enclosing you within a spinning gray helix. Theresa and Ira are horrified, but they stand where they are, frozen to the spot. You drop the empty urn. It makes a soft clang as it hits the ground, bounces, and then comes to a stop.

"I appreciate you both wanting to tell me the truth. I know you thought it was a mercy. But there's only one mercy in this world."

You make no motion, give no command, but the cremains fly toward your siblings, splitting into two separate streams. Before either Theresa or Ira can react, ashes fly into their noses, plunge into their mouths and down their throats. Their eyes roll white and their bodies jerk spasmodically, as if their nervous systems have been short-circuited. This only lasts a few moments, and then the spasms cease and your siblings collapse to the ground, as lifeless as the soil beneath them. A moment later, the cremains drift out of their corpses and fly toward you, and you open your mouth and inhale deeply.

When the ashes are inside you, they settle and become still, waiting patiently for your next summons.

You gaze upon the bodies of your brother and sister. You feel no sorrow at their loss, no horror at what you've become. You feel only satisfaction at having done your job. Your siblings had it wrong. God isn't a gardener. He's a farmer. And you are one of his field hands.

You walk away from the overhang, the empty urn, and your dead siblings. It's time to start your chores.

THE WHITE ROAD

It didn't happen the way the stories said it would. He didn't experience a sensation of formless floating, wasn't gazing down at his own body lying on the operating table as the surgical team worked to save his life. One moment he was unconscious, the next he was wide awake, standing several feet away from the table, the doctors and nurses, and what presumably was his own body. He felt disoriented, disconnected, and he raised his hands to look at them, as if trying to assure himself of his own reality. His hands looked completely normal, but his forearms were bare—which only made sense because he was naked. It was at that moment he became aware of how cold it was in the operating room, and he began to shiver.

A dream, he thought desperately. *Please let this be a dream.*

He took a bit of excess belly flesh between thumb and forefinger and pinched hard, giving the flab a twist for good measure. He felt the pain, but the sensation didn't jolt him out of the dream. He breathed, could still smell the scents of the operating room: the tang of bleach combined with a harsh medicinal odor. He could feel his abdominal muscles tighten with anxiety, heard his stomach gurgle as it produced excess acid. This couldn't be real, but all his senses insisted that it was.

He remained standing, bare feet on cold blue tile, surgical team working with swift, economical motions. The atmosphere in the room was tense, and he could see beads of sweat forming on the head surgeon's brow. He waited for another member of the team to wipe away his sweat, but no one did. They were too focused on their patient—on him.

People who claimed to have near-death experiences reported feeling a calm sense of peace during the time their spirits were separated from their bodies. But he felt a mounting sense of panic that was swiftly becoming overpowering. Not because he appeared to be dying. He had no fear of death. He was afraid he would *survive* death, that his consciousness would continue to exist in some form after his body had long fallen away to dust. He could not imagine anything more terrifying. He screamed, the sound coming from deep inside his being. The noise filled the room, but no one heard, no one turned to look at him, and he began to weep. Tears fell from his eyes, as solid and real as he was, and struck the floor with tiny, inaudible splashes. But they didn't land on blue tile. Instead, they hit white brick. He could feel the hard, uneven surface of stone beneath his feet now, and he knew he no longer stood on tile but on the—

Road, his mind supplied, and while the notion of a road inside an operating room was ridiculous, he knew that's exactly what it was: a white road. Although *road* did seem too big a word. *Path* might have been better. It was only four feet across, and it stretched from one wall to another, seeming to lead nowhere in either direction.

Phillip Price—fifty-six, overweight, poor eater and non-exerciser—had come to the hospital for a triple bypass. Technically coronary artery bypass graft surgery. His surgeon, who right now had his gloved hands inside Phillip's chest, had told him during their initial consult three weeks, two days, and four hours earlier that the procedure, while not without risks, was almost routine these days.

Doesn't look so routine from where I'm standing, Phillip thought.

He'd read an article on ScienceNewz.com one hundred and twenty-seven days ago that theorized the human brain retains consciousness for up to ten minutes after death. Maybe that was happening to him now. Maybe he was dead, or dying, and his mind was imagining he was outside his own body, maybe as part of some last-ditch but ultimately futile attempt at survival. He'd read—eighteen years, ten months, and six days ago—that men ejaculate at the moment of death, as if their bodies want to make one last longshot attempt to fertilize a woman's egg, life desperately trying to continue itself, regardless of how astronomical the odds were. His mind in a sense was projecting his consciousness outside of itself, like forcing a passenger off a sinking ship onto a lifeboat and pushing them away so they wouldn't be pulled down with the vessel when it sank. If so, this projection— regardless of how real it seemed—would be no more successful than all those dying men shooting semen into nothing. All he had to do was endure this for another few minutes until his mind shut down for good, and then he would wink off as swiftly and easily as he'd winked on. He would be gone at last—and everything in his mind would go with him. It was what he wanted more than anything in the world. What he *didn't* want was something like what happened next.

Cracks appeared in the wall where one end of the "road" disappeared, jagged fissures that made harsh cracking sounds as they grew longer and wider. Chunks of plaster began to dislodge and fall to the floor—the pieces hit with loud *thunks,* but none of the doctors or nurses turned to see what was happening. Phillip watched the wall break apart, telling himself it was proof of his hypothesis, an indication that his mind was experiencing the first signs of its demise.

But then the wall burst inward and a large shape thrust its way through and into the operating room. It was twice Phillip's size and fashioned entirely from bone. Skulls, to be precise. Big ones, little ones, human, animal, and ones whose origins Phillip couldn't identify, all fused together to approximate a humanoid form—head, torso, trunk, arms, legs. It paused for a moment, bone feet comprised of tiny bird and rodent skulls on white brick. Except the brick didn't remain white where the creature's feet touched it. Black stains spread outward from the two points of contact, as if the thing's feet were leaking thick black ink.

Its overlarge head was made of what Phillip believed were the skulls of infants, and that head oriented on him now. There were no eyes in the sockets—on any of the hundreds its skull body possessed—but Phillip nevertheless felt the weight of its regard settle on him. It looked at him for several long seconds, conglomerate body shaking with rage, anticipation, or hunger—maybe all three—skulls *clack-clack-clacking* together like an orchestra composed entirely of castanet players. It was a cartoonish sound, and it should've been ridiculous, but Phillip had never heard anything so horrible in his life. But then, this *wasn't* his life anymore, was it? It was his death, and who knew what dark wonders lay in store for him as he faded from existence?

The lower jaws of the skullbeast's head dropped in unison, as if the creature bellowed a warning or a challenge, but no sound emerged. Instead, Phillip was struck by an utterly cold wind which tore at his naked flesh like knives of ice. The skullbeast started toward him then, hands raised, skull fingers curled into claws, feet rapping dryly on brick as it came.

Phillip did not question the skullbeast's reality, nor did he question its intentions. His body—whatever its current nature —acted entirely on instinct. He spun around and began running in the opposite direction, down the White Road and toward the unbroken surface of the other wall. Fat rolls bounced and his cock and balls jiggled as he went. He saw the wall rushing toward him, and he fully anticipated slamming into it. With any luck, he'd hit his head hard enough to render him unconscious before the skullbeast could catch hold of him and begin tearing him apart. He didn't mind dying, but he didn't want to do it in searing agony if he could avoid it. But when he reached the wall, it gave before him, almost as if it were made of thin rubber no thicker than the surgical team's disposable gloves. For an instant he thought the wall would snap back into place, sending him flying backward into the skullbeast's less-than-tender embrace. But the rubber wall tore and Phillip stumbled forward, the wall closing up behind him like a giant soap bubble. He was through! He was safe!

And he was someplace else.

PHILLIP FIRST BECAME aware that other people forgot things when he was a toddler. His mother was in the kitchen making lunch—tomato soup and grilled cheese—and she was frustrated. She'd bought a fresh package of cheese slices at the grocery three days, four hours, and twenty-two minutes ago. Phillip had been with her at the time, and he could've told her every item she'd bought in the order she'd pulled it from the shelves, as well as the order in which the woman working the cash register had rung them up, including the price of each item. He didn't even need to concentrate to summon all this information. His mind did it all by itself. Up to this point, he'd assumed everyone was like him, that they remembered every second of every day in perfect detail, and they could retrieve any of those memories with ease. But if that was true, why couldn't Mommy remember that she'd put the cheese slices on the refrigerator's middle shelf behind a carton of eggs, instead of in the meat compartment on the bottom of the refrigerator as she usually did?

He watched her standing in front of the open fridge, holding the door with one hand, the other resting on her hip while she glared at the fridge's contents, as if they'd somehow conspired to hide the cheese from her. Then he walked over to her, took hold of the egg carton, and slid it off the shelf, revealing the cheese slices. Mommy looked at him a moment, frowning, but then she smiled.

"Thanks, sweetie."

She grabbed the package of cheese, Phillip returned the eggs to their place, and Mommy closed the refrigerator door. She stepped to a counter and resumed making Phillip's lunch, and he watched her, wondering if there was something wrong with her, if she was sick. He would eventually learn that there was indeed something wrong with her, the same thing that was wrong with the whole damned human race. They forgot while Phillip remembered.

AFTER PUSHING THROUGH THE WALL, Phillip experienced an instant of darkness which he hoped was the advent of death. He was sorely disappointed when his vision cleared and he found himself standing in the middle of a street festival. Booths and food trucks lined both sides of the street, and the crowd was so thick that people were forced to walk shoulder to shoulder at a snail's pace. The sun was high overhead, the day blisteringly hot. Everyone was sweating and most wore sunglasses to protect their eyes. Still, they seemed happy enough.

At first Phillip had no idea where he was, but then it hit him: The Freedom Festival, the July 4th celebration that his hometown put on every year. He'd come annually, up until he'd moved away when he was twenty-seven, and while he hadn't been back since, he'd heard the festival was still going strong. Given his inhumanly perfect memory, it only took him several seconds of looking around—at the booths, the people's hairstyles, their clothing—for him to know that this particular festival was the one he'd attended the summer before his senior year of high school. Which meant—

He looked to his right and saw Tricia Cole walking at his side. She was seventeen, also a soon-to-be senior, with curly brown hair and a round face that a lot of guys thought unattractive, but which he'd always found cute. She wore a yellow tank top, white shorts, and sandals. She didn't have sunglasses, and he could see her warm chocolate eyes. Even if he hadn't possessed a perfect memory, he could never forget those eyes.

He remembered that he was a middle-aged man—and worse, *naked*—but when he looked down at his body, he saw he was clothed in a *Star Wars* T-shirt, shorts, and sneakers. He wasn't skinny, but he was much thinner—he'd weighed 168 pounds that summer—and he realized, with more than a little astonishment, that he was seventeen again. Someone else might've been thrilled to find themselves reliving a scene from their adolescence—*The best years of your life*, his father used to say—but these people didn't have his memory. He knew exactly what was going to happen next, and he dreaded it.

Tricia reached for his hand, her fingers hot and sticky from the heat, and when her flesh came in contact with his, he jerked away. She gave him a surprised, hurt look.

"Sorry," he said and made himself take her hand. His stomach gave a sick twist, but he did his best to ignore it.

Philip—the middle-aged version inside the teenager's body—did not choose to do or say these things. They happened automatically, repeating exactly what he'd done on that day. *I'm not living this,* he thought. *I'm reliving it.*

Tricia stiffened when he took her hand, but she forced a smile and relaxed a little. They'd dated for most of their junior year but had broken up a month before school let out. They'd only recently begun seeing one another again—six days, five hours, and twenty-seven minutes ago—but things were still not back to normal between them.

Tricia had starred in the high school theater production last year, *The Phantom of the Opera*—the play, not the musical. She'd played Christine, the object of the Phantom's obsessive desire. Daryl Burke had played her boyfriend, Raoul. In one of the scenes, Christine and Raoul kissed, and while Phillip knew Tricia and Daryl were only acting—and additionally there were rumors around the school that Daryl was gay— Phillip hadn't been able to keep from feeling furious jealousy whenever he saw them kiss on stage. The problem was that, with his memory, he never *stopped* seeing them kiss. And his memories didn't merely extend to sight and sound. He remembered his emotions just as vividly. When he recalled an emotion, it hit him with the same force as when he first felt it. There was nothing between Tricia and Daryl—he sincerely believed that—but he could not stop remembering their kissing in the play. And the worst of it was when he and Tricia kissed. He saw her kissing *Daryl,* then experienced the same resentful jealousy. He would break off their kiss, they would argue, and before long she broke up with him, unable to stand his jealousy any longer. He'd tried to explain to her what it was like having a memory like his. But of course she couldn't understand, not fully. Who could?

Maybe you have perfect recall, she'd said. *But it's your choice whether or not you think about that memory, isn't it?*

So they'd split up. But partway through the summer, Tricia began having second thoughts, and she called and said she wanted to give "them" another try. Phillip feared the same thing—or something similar—would happen. It was why he didn't have friends, why his relationship with his parents was distant. Because he could not forget anger and sadness, could feel them anew at any time, and because of this he could not forgive. With a memory like his, everything was *now*, and how could you move on if everything you ever experienced was happening inside you all the time?

But when Tricia asked him if they could start dating again, he wanted so badly to make it work that he could learn to control his memory instead of letting it control him. If he worked at it, worked *hard*. But so far it didn't seem to be working, and Tricia seemed to be aware of it. Like him, she was going through the motions, but—

Out of the crowd, Daryl came walking toward them, a perfect smile on his perfect face. He wore a short-sleeved button shirt, top two buttons undone to show part of his chest, along with khaki pants and bowling shoes. Phillip had no idea why Daryl wore those shoes, but—with the exception of play performances—he had never seen Daryl without them.

Walking beside Daryl was Franklin Hoffstetter, equally handsome, equally well-dressed, but wearing regular shoes. Franklin was also in drama club, but he did behind-the-scenes stuff, such as makeup and set design. Maybe they were a couple, maybe they weren't. Phillip didn't know, and he was glad. With his memory, it was a relief not to know something.

When this incident occurred in real life, Daryl had greeted Tricia with a hug, they'd exchanged a few pleasantries, then Daryl had said hi to him, and he and Franklin had continued on their way. The whole time Daryl had spoken with Tricia,

Phillip had been watching them kiss in his mind, over and over, jealousy boiling over inside him. He'd tried to ignore his feelings, but they refused to go away, and before long, Tricia and he ended up fighting again—for the last time.

But that's not what happened now. Before Daryl could speak, screams filled the air behind them, and Phillip—now able to command his body instead of just being along for the ride—turned to see people pushing toward him, expressions of absolute terror on their faces. Farther back, people flew through the air, hurled this way and that, faces, arms, and hands covered with ragged wounds.

Bite marks, Phillip thought. *Hundreds of them.*

People slammed into him, but Phillip managed to keep from being knocked down, and soon he saw the skullbeast. The thing had followed him from the operating room, and it appeared determined to reach him, regardless of who stood in the way. He turned back toward Tricia. There was no sign of Daryl or Franklin, and he assumed they'd fled with the rest of the people in the area. But Tricia was still there, watching with horrified fascination as the skullbeast tore its way through the crowd.

Phillip knew that Tricia wasn't *really* Tricia. Last he heard, she was a lawyer working in Milwaukee with a husband and two kids in college. But he still couldn't stand by and let this Tricia, the memory of a girl he'd once loved, be hurt. He was still holding onto her hand, and he pulled her toward the sidewalk, passing between a shaken lemonade stand and a booth where a woman was selling knitted hats and scarves. There was no way they could run in this frenzied crowd, but once they were on the sidewalk, they could—

Tricia's hand was yanked out of his, and he spun around in time to see the skullbeast wrap its arms made of skulls, all of which possessed teeth, and pull her into a deadly hug. Tricia screamed as dozens of skull mouths began tearing into her flesh. She thrashed in the creature's embrace, shrieking in agony, blood spilling from her wounds onto the ground. Phillip was overwhelmed by the awful sight, and his earlier resolve to save her melted away. He had a thought then. A terrible, selfish thought. Every detail of this awful moment would be recorded in his memory, and he would never be free from Tricia's blood and pain.

He tore his gaze away from Tricia, looked down, and saw he stood less than a foot away from the sidewalk—a sidewalk made from white bricks.

As he turned and ran toward the sidewalk, which in reality was the White Road, he felt like a complete shitheel for leaving Tricia to be chewed to death by the skullbeast. He told himself that she wasn't real, was nothing more than an especially vivid memory, but it didn't help. He still felt like a coward for abandoning her, but he didn't turn back around. If anything, he ran faster, as if desperate to get away from her screams.

The White Road ran parallel to the street for a dozen feet or so before curving into the yard of a small building containing offices for a realtor and a massage therapist. The road terminated at the base of a large oak tree at the side of the building, but Phillip followed the road without question or hesitation. The road had taken him away from the operating room, and it would take him away from here. It *had* to.

Tricia's screams cut off, and he heard a loud *thud* that he assumed was the sound of the skullbeast slamming her body to the ground. This was followed by the *clack-clack-clack* of the creature's bony feet as it resumed its pursuit of him. Sweat poured off Phillip, and the hot air burned his lungs. What the hell *was* that thing? An emissary of Death, perhaps the Grim Reaper himself, albeit with a slightly altered appearance? Or was it a natural creature, a thing that appeared when someone died to devour their soul, kind of like an afterlife version of a vulture? Or was the skullbeast simply a metaphor, an image his dying mind had conjured to process what was happening to him? If the latter was true, his brain was way more screwed up than he'd thought.

Then again, he *was* running straight for a tree, so how sane could he be?

The skullbeast caught up to him when he was three feet from the oak. The creature swiped one of its skull-fingered hands toward him, and he felt the tiny mouths of those fingers rake his shoulder, teeth tearing the cloth of his shirt and biting divots into his flesh. He cried out in pain and stumbled, but he didn't fall. He covered the last few feet to the tree and, unable to stop himself doing so, he closed his eyes in anticipation of hitting the trunk while running flat out. If he was lucky, the impact would knock him out, and he wouldn't feel the skullbeast savage his unconscious body.

But instead he felt the same rubbery resistance as he passed through the operating room wall, and then he was through.

AFTER TRICIA and he broke up for good, he never dated again, and he didn't forge any friendships. Why bother? He knew his memory would eventually destroy any relationships he managed to develop.

With his gift (curse) he could've studied any field in college. Medicine, law, engineering, business... But money wasn't his primary concern in life. Living like a normal person, at least as normal as he could manage, was his goal. For him, that meant finding a job where he could work, a place where he would come into contact with as few people as possible. So he passed on college and took a job in data entry.

He sat in front of a computer console in an office all day, inputting meaningless streams of random numbers. Later, when the technology was there, he did the same work, but now he did it at home, making the job even better. Without anyone around to interact with, his new memories weren't of hurt feelings—sadness, rage, betrayal, jealousy, envy—but rather calm, tranquil memories of typing at a computer all day. It was as close to bliss as a person like him could ever find.

When he thought about dying—which he did increasingly as the years passed—and considered the possibility of an afterlife, he hoped that, assuming there was one, it would be that of the ancient Greeks. Before the spirits of the dead could enter the paradise of the Elysian Fields, they first had to drink from the River Lethe, whose waters erased all memory of their mortal lives. Then, unburdened by the cares of their time on Earth, they could fully enjoy eternity. That sounded like Heaven to him.

A thousand hurts—a thousand thousand—all of them as fresh in his mind as the moment he experienced them, all of them *present* twenty-four seven. It was a kind of living hell, and while he didn't have the guts to commit suicide—he'd made a couple half-hearted attempts before admitting to himself that he could never go through with it—he looked forward to death, to the extinction, the *obliteration* of his consciousness. It was why he ate so badly, why he was so slothful. He didn't want to extend his life by as much as a single second. And when he died, all his memories would perish with him, and then—and *only* then—would he be free at last.

The worst thing he could imagine was surviving death with all his memories intact, a million small ghosts that would haunt him for all time. It was his greatest fear and worst nightmare combined, and he was experiencing it now.

THE SKULLBEAST PURSUED Phillip across an ever-changing landscape of memories. The funerals of his parents after they'd died in a collision with a semi when he was twenty-six. The burst appendix that nearly killed him when he was thirty-four. The heroin-addicted younger sister who'd continually hit him up for money, and who'd died from an overdose behind a Goodwill Store when he was forty-three. And more, so many more, all of them as alive and painful as when he'd first experienced them.

The further he ran, the wearier he became, until it was all he could do to keep putting one foot ahead of the other. He wanted to stop running, wanted to turn around and let the skullbeast have him, tear him apart, and in the process grant him the oblivion he so desperately craved. But he couldn't bring himself to do it. Maybe because he feared the agony of hundreds of ancient dry teeth piercing his flesh. Or maybe because he feared that, as bad as this endless pursuit was, something infinitely worse than mere mutilation might be in store for him if he allowed himself to be caught. Whichever the case, he forced himself to keep going. And then—after finding himself in a memory from last year in which he sat in his car after being rear-ended by a man in an SUV, a man who stood outside his window screaming at Phillip as if the accident had been his fault—the White Road veered away from his car toward a carpet store on the corner called We Got You Covered. He got out of his car, pushed past the red-faced screaming man, and followed the white brick over to the curb and to a section of the store's outer wall—less than ten feet from the entrance—where it didn't disappear but instead continued through a huge hole that looked as if it had been made by an exploding bomb.

When he saw what lay on the other side of the hole, he

almost fell to his knees and began sobbing. It was the operating room where this mad chase through his memories began, and this hole was where the skullbeast had broken through the wall originally. The White Road, for all its twists and turns through his past, was a closed loop. He had gone nowhere, and he was exhausted.

Some last shred of survival instinct remained to him, though, and he jumped through the opening and into the operating room. The Road here was no longer white, but rather a black so cold that it burned his bare feet. He was naked again and back in his normal body. He stepped off what he supposed was now the Black Road, bent over, put his hand on his knees, and gulped air. Was the Road—*his* road, he realized—entirely black now? The skullbeast had pursued him across its entire length, spreading its corruption with every step, so yes, it was most likely entirely black now. He had no idea what that meant, but whatever it was, he doubted it was good. Still breathing hard, he turned to look back at the huge hole in the wall. The skullbeast had slowed as it approached the hole, and now it stood on the other side, watching him but making no move to join him in the operating room. His shoulder throbbed from where the skullbeast's claws had raked him, but the pain was the least of his worries now.

The surgical team had gone quiet and still. After a moment, the lead surgeon said, "I'm going to call it." He glanced at the digital wall clock. "Death occurred at 1:37 pm."

The atmosphere in the room became heavy and somber, and the surgical team began shutting down monitors and putting away instruments. The doctors were the first to depart, leaving the rest of the team to finish the clean-up. No one spoke as they worked, and—as before—no one was aware of his presence. Phillip was too tired to feel anything other than mild melancholy at his own death. He'd wished for it so long, but now that it had happened, it was worse than an anticlimax: it was a non-event. His consciousness still persisted, and his perfect memory remained intact, only now his brain had added every instant of his flight from the skullbeast. People said your entire life flashed before you were about to die. *Looks like they were right,* he thought.

Your kind always makes this process more difficult than it has to be.

The voice—although that wasn't exactly what it was—sounded both amused and weary.

Phillip turned back toward the hole in the wall and watched as the skullbeast climbed through. It no longer seemed interested in attacking him and it moved slowly, almost casually toward him, arms at its sides. Phillip was still frightened of the creature, but that fear was a faint echo of what it had been, and his body didn't respond to it. He no longer felt an urge to run, no longer cared about preserving his existence on any level. Whatever was going to happen next, he just wanted to get it over with.

The skullbeast stopped directly in front of him, but it made no move to touch him.

Humans always react so poorly to the life review. We thought you might be different since you retain such complete and vivid memories of your experiences. We thought re-examining them would cause you no discomfort. Ah, well.

This was followed by a sound that was almost but not quite a sigh.

Still, it is complete now, and that's what's important, yes?

Phillip was so flabbergasted by the skullbeast's change in behavior that he had no idea how to respond. The skullbeast seemed to take his silence in stride and continued.

You were right earlier when you recalled the article you read, the one about human brains only surviving a brief time after death. You have no souls to continue on after your bodies cease functioning, and once your brains finally shut down, you are gone forever.

Phillip felt the first stirrings of hope since waking in the operating room. The pursuit through his memories, while had seemingly gone on for so long, had in reality taken place in the ten minutes or so his mind needed to close up shop. Only a few moments more and he would finally—*finally!*—be free.

When my people first became aware of yours—when we understood what happens to you when you die—we were filled with sorrow. You see, unlike you, we have no ending. We endure forever.

As the skullbeast spoke, the edges of its body began to soften, and the white of its bone grew darker, until what stood before Phillip was a faceless human-shaped shadow. Still twice as large as him and still scary, but not as terrifying as before.

When we first reveal ourselves to you, you see us through the lens of your fear, believe us to be demons come to steal your souls. Nothing could be further from the truth. We come to help.

The shadow man put a cool hand on Phillip's shoulder, and the bite wounds healed instantly.

Another willful misperception. I never tried to hurt you. As I said, we wish only to help. We appear when humans are near death, and we make a...I suppose you could call it a copy of their memories. We preserve them inside us, giving you an immortality that you cannot obtain in any other way.

That was why the White Road turned black, Phillip realized. Once the skullbeast, shadow man, whatever-the-hell-it-was had recorded his memories, the white disappeared, indicating the road had shut down.

Phillip didn't like where the shadow man was going with all this. He tried to take a step backward, but the shadow man still had a hand on his shoulder, and his grip tightened, keeping Phillip where he was.

And then, once we contain your memories, we absorb your consciousness and allow it to dwell inside us. You can then experience whichever of your memories you wish whenever you like. In effect, you become your own Heaven.

"No," Phillip whispered. Then he shouted, "No!"

He tried desperately to free himself from the shadow man's grasp, but he couldn't. The shadow man took hold of Phillip's other shoulder, as if to make doubly sure he'd stay put. Phillip continued repeating no, shaking his head back and forth so rapidly that the shadow man became a black blur in his vision.

There's no need to fuss. This won't hurt a bit.

An opening appeared in the shadow man's face where a mouth would've been on a human. It expanded, growing larger and wider. The shadow man then inclined his head toward Phillip and lowered his great maw over the man's head. And as the shadow man took him into his darkness, Phillip screamed—a scream which would echo throughout his perfectly preserved memories for all eternity.

GOING HOME

*W*e *don't forgive to make those who've hurt us feel better or to excuse what they did. We forgive to help us heal.*

The words of Dr. Karnes echo in Emily's mind as she sits behind the wheel of her Ford Plymouth. The car is sixteen years old—nine years younger than she is—and they've both done a lot of hard traveling in their time. But this trip, the trip home, is the hardest of all.

As the exit for Ash Creek draws closer, she tells herself that she doesn't have to take it, that she can jam her foot down on the accelerator, fly past the exit, and keep going. She can drive the Plymouth until it runs out of gas—or until its ancient engine gives out—pull over, abandon the car, and start walking. She can walk until her feet bleed and then she can walk some more. She can walk until she forgets her name, forgets her past, forgets *him*.

She takes her foot off the accelerator, activates her turn signal, takes the exit.

There are no other cars on the exit ramp, but there's a man standing at the bottom holding a brown cardboard sign with four words written on it with black magic marker.

WILL KILL FOR FOOD.

Emily blinks, certain she's read the sign wrong, but when she looks again, the words remain the same. Despite her sunglasses, the light stabs her eyes, and she feels a migraine begin to stir inside her skull. She isn't surprised by the sudden onset of pain, only that it hasn't hit her before now.

There's a traffic light at the end of the ramp. The city put it here during Emily's freshman year of high school after a senior girl took the exit, failed to yield as she merged with the road it connected to, and was broadsided by a man in a pick-up truck. The man lived, but the girl didn't, and now there's a traffic signal here to prevent future tragedies from occurring. Emily doesn't know if something so simple as a light can do that, but she figures it's better than nothing.

The light's red, and she brakes as she comes down the ramp and stops. The man with the sign stands on her left, not more than ten feet away from her, and Emily does her best to keep her gaze focused straight ahead—she doesn't want the man to think she's staring at him, and she certainly doesn't want to encourage him to approach her—but she can't stop herself from sneaking several quick looks.

The sign still reads *WILL KILL FOR FOOD*, but now she can see the man's hands: thick-knuckled, hairy, black dirt beneath the nails. It's early November in southwest Ohio, sunny but chilly out, and the man wears a bulky green parka unzipped, a flannel shirt beneath. His jeans are dirty and torn over the left knee, and his sneakers are old and barely held together by strips of silver duct tape. She wonders if he's cold. It's windy out, and if she was the one standing there, she'd have the parka zipped, the hood up, and she'd still be shivering. She's rail-thin—*No meat on your bones*, her father used to say, and she's always cold.

The man's age is impossible to guess. He has a thick black beard peppered with gray, and shoulder-length hair the same color, and under all the hair he could be anywhere from late twenties to late thirties. His eyes are his most distinct feature. They're a deep dark blue, and they're the saddest eyes she's ever seen. It's those eyes which make her lower the Plymouth's driver's side window.

"That sign sure is an attention-getter."

The sound of her own voice intensifies the pain in her head, but she manages to smile.

The man doesn't react at first, and she thinks maybe he didn't hear her, or worse, that he might be crazy. But then his sad blue eyes lock onto hers and he returns her smile. Dry cracked lips pull away from jagged yellow teeth.

"Thank you," he says.

His voice is a deep rich baritone, perfect for radio announcing or recording audiobooks. It's liquid honey in her ears, and hearing it sends a delicious shiver down her back.

Emily reaches for her purse, which rests on the passenger seat beside her. She removes her wallet and takes out a twenty-dollar bill. She rarely carries cash these days—who does?—but before she left her apartment in Cincy, her roommate repaid her the twenty dollars she loaned him a couple weeks ago. Funny how things have a way of working out.

She turns back to the window and is startled to see the man has stepped over to her car and leaned forward until his face is just outside window. If he leans forward so much as another centimeter, he'll technically be *inside* the car. Certainly he's close enough to reach in and grab her if he wants, and suddenly his sign isn't so amusing anymore.

Her head throbs as he smiles apologetically.

"Sorry. I didn't mean to startle you."

She expects his breath to be foul, but it's actually rather pleasant. It smells like flowers after a rainstorm. She remembers reading somewhere that people's breath can smell sweet when they're sick—*bad* sick—and she wonders what might be wrong with him and how bad it is.

She holds up the twenty with a swift, nervous motion, almost shoves it in his face.

"Here." She forces a strained smile. "And you don't even have to kill anyone for it."

He draws back a few inches, reaches in to take the bill from Emily's hand—doing so gently—and then he crumples it in one hand and pops it into his mouth. He grins as he chews.

"It's good," he says. "Thank you."

Her breath catches in her throat, and she can't move. She imagines him reaching in with his hands—black dirt beneath the nails—wrapping them around her throat and squeezing until everything goes black. But he pulls back to where he was standing when Emily first saw him. He holds up his sign once more, his features now slack, and his strange blue eyes focus on some point far in the distance. He's still chewing.

Emily presses her foot to the gas and gets the hell out of there. Her head feels as if it's going to explode, and she resists the urge to glance in the rearview mirror, afraid of what she might see.

———

Emily PULLS into a convenience store parking lot and dry-swallows a couple migraine pills. Then she sits back in her seat, eyes closed, and waits for them to start working. After a while, the pounding in her head lessens, enough so that she can function, and she pulls back onto the road and continues heading home. No, not home. To her father's house. The encounter with the man at the end of the exit ramp still haunts her, but the memory is eclipsed by her anxiety about seeing her father again. It's been six years—and a lot of therapy—since she's stood in his presence, and she's scared.

Experiencing fear is normal. But don't let fear make decisions for you.

Emily doesn't know how many times Dr. Karnes has given her a variation on this advice, but it's good and she's determined to let it guide her.

Her father has a small ranch house on the east end of town, an ugly thing with banana-yellow siding and a small yard whose grass always seems to be perpetually on the verge of dying. It looks the same as it did on the day she drove away and didn't look back. There's some comfort in that sameness, and more than a little sorrow, too.

She pulls her Plymouth into the driveway, parks, turns off the engine. She sits there for several moments, eyes fixed on the front door, hands gripping the steering wheel tight.

"You can do this," she says.

She takes a deep breath, grimaces as the action sets off a fresh wave of pain in her head and gets out of the car. When she reaches the front door, she stops. She doesn't grasp the knob, doesn't knock, doesn't take her phone from her pants pocket and text her father that she's here. Until she does any of these things, she can still turn around and leave, drive her old beater of a car back to her apartment. Until she does one of those things, she isn't committed.

Putting this off won't make it any easier.

Dr. Karnes' voice again. Not a memory this time, but something she might say if she were here.

Steeling herself, Emily grips the knob. The metal is cold and she shudders, but she turns it. The door is unlocked. Her father often forgets to lock doors, even at night. After her mother's death, Emily took it upon herself to lock the doors before going to bed. She wonders if any of those doors has been locked even once since she moved out. Her father is lucky no one has entered the house in the middle of the night and slit his throat or put a bullet in his head. It would almost be a relief to her if someone had.

She thinks of the homeless man and his sign, *WILL KILL FOR FOOD*, and she feels suddenly queasy. *Just the headache meds*, she tells herself. *Should've eaten something when I took them.* Not that they've done much good so far. Her brain feels as if it's trying to break out of her skull.

When she tries to open the door, it only moves about a foot before being stopped by something inside. Something solid, heavy. She imagines that it's her father, trying to keep her from entering, and she says, "Dad? Is that you?" But there's no reply. She pushes harder, and whatever is on the other side of the door slides a few inches. She leans her shoulder against the door and shoves hard. The door moves several more inches, and she thinks it might be open wide enough for her to slip through. She's a small woman—short and petite—but even so, it's a tight fit. But she makes it inside, and she considers this a small victory.

Nice try, Dad, but you're not going to get out of this that easily.

The physical exertion of shoving the door has set her head to pounding again, but she does her best to ignore the pain. It's a near-constant companion these days, and she's had plenty of practice living with it.

It's dark inside, but enough light comes through the partially open doorway to reveal why she had such trouble getting in. The vestibule is crammed tight with boxes, paper sacks, and plastic garbage bags, all of them full. There are stacks of magazines and newspapers bound with twine as well, along with sloppily folded clothing. Much of the latter is women's clothing—her mother's—and seeing it fills Emily with a powerful emotion that's equal parts sorrow and rage. The smell hits her then, an odor of spoiled milk, rotting meat, and what she thinks might be urine. The throbbing in her head worsens, and she's grateful for the pain as it's a distraction from the stink. Is her father dead somewhere in the house? He's only in his early sixties, but that's old enough to have a heart attack, isn't it? She feels nothing at the prospect of her father's death, and she remembers something she once told Dr. Karnes.

I don't think I'll feel anything when my father dies. The sadness and relief will cancel each other out, leaving me feeling empty and tired.

She doesn't think he's dead. The stench isn't strong enough to be a decomposing body. This might be wishful thinking, though. She already found one parent dead, and she doesn't want to repeat the experience.

Before she can stop it, a series of still images flash though her mind like stuttering movie footage. She's thirteen, and she enters the upstairs bathroom. She needs to pee, has to go so bad her bladder aches, but she forgets all about pissing when she sees her mother's naked body in the tub, sees the bloody gashes in her wrists, sees the blood…

Emily squeezes her eyes shut and smacks a hand against the side of her head. White light explodes behind her eyes, and for an instant the pain in her head becomes so intense, it's almost as if she ceases to exist for several seconds. She returns to herself as the pain slowly ebbs to a manageable level, and the memory of finding her mother dead in the bathtub recedes once more, gone back into the cage where Emily keeps it locked away.

She doesn't close the front door. Leaving it open might not do much to air out the stink, but it's better than nothing. Feeling as if she's entering a toxic waste site and should be encased within a hazmat suit, she begins making her way around the piles of junk in the vestibule. The front hallway is equally as cluttered, and when she comes to the living room, she gasps in shock. Every surface, every inch, is covered with cardboard boxes and trash bags, more magazines and newspapers, to the point where none of the furniture is visible. There are only chair and couch-shaped mounds to hint at where furniture might be. The only items that remain visible are those hanging on the walls—the flat screen television and framed photographs of family, grandparents, and cousins, a couple of a beloved poodle who died when Emily was a child. There are no photos of Emily or her mother, and Emily wishes this surprised her, but it doesn't.

"Dad? Are you in here?"

She imagines him inside the room, buried somewhere beneath all this junk, maybe playing some demented game of hide and seek, stifling his laughter as he prepares to jump up and shout *Surprise!* But none of the junk stirs and her father doesn't appear. He's always been something of a pack rat, the kind of person who's reluctant to throw away anything, no matter how useless or broken it is. *What if we need it someday?* was always his excuse. Now, without his wife to curb his impulses, her father has become a full-on hoarder.

The man needs therapy more than I do, she thinks.

She doesn't want to see the state the kitchen is in—bad enough that she can smell it from where she's standing—so she avoids it and instead makes her way to the stairs. She feels her phone buzz in her pocket, and she pauses at the base of the stairs and looks at the screen. It's a text from her father.

I'm in my office. Come on up.

Office? As far as Emily knows, her father doesn't have a home office. Then again, since she hasn't been here for half a decade, who knows what changes he's made? After all, he's turned the inside of the house into a makeshift landfill, hasn't he?

The stairs are just as cluttered as the rest of the house, although the objects stacked and piled here are, by necessity, smaller. Columns of paperback books—true crime, mostly—a mound of haphazardly folded holiday sweaters, vacuum cleaner that stopped working when Emily was six, and so on. Like the vestibule and the living room, there is a narrow pathway up the stairs, but this one is even narrower and not straight. Emily is forced to go slowly, place her feet carefully, if she doesn't want to slip on something, twist an ankle and fall. She imagines herself doing just that, tumbling backward down the stairs, knocking over her father's carelessly placed junked, landing in a mound of cast-off clutter, one more forgotten piece of junk. She continues wending her way up the stairs, and she thinks of a mythology class she took in high school, remembers the story of the minotaur, a half-man, half-bull creature that dwelled at the center of a vast labyrinth. Is her father the monster at the heart of his maze of junk? If so, does that make her Theseus, come to slay him?

But she hasn't come to cause harm. She's come to make peace. Peace with the past, peace within herself. And so she does her best to ignore the stink that permeates the entire house, the stench seeming to come from everywhere at once —breathing through her mouth helps—and she tries not to contemplate the disordered nature of the mind which has turned her home into a huge, compartmentalized dumpster. She concentrates on moving onward, still unsure what she's going to say when she finally confronts her father. She's had five years to consider her words, has mentally drafted and revised them a thousand times, but even now she hasn't settled on the message she wishes to convey.

I love you, Daddy is too trite, and she's not sure it's true anymore. *Fuck you, bastard* is straightforward and to the point, but it doesn't communicate the complexity of what she feels about her father. *I love you, now fuck off.* Closer, but still not right. She hopes inspiration will strike when she sees him.

She reaches the upstairs landing, the next segment of the clutter-maze the house has become, and she stops. On her left is the upstairs bathroom where thirteen-year-old Emily found her mother's exsanguinated body in a crimson-slick tub. The bedroom she still thinks of as Mom's and Dad's lies beyond the hall bathroom, and while it has its own master bath, her mother rarely used it. The door to the hall bathroom is closed, and Emily is tempted to open it, but she doesn't want to see what her father has done to it. She doesn't think she can stand to see that he's filled the tub—the place where her mother's life literally went down the drain—with more of his random shit. Her headache intensifies as she looks at the closed door. It feels as if her brain has suddenly sprouted a mass of inward-facing spines, and her vision goes gray for a moment. Emily never used this bathroom after finding her mother dead, never even set foot in it. She used the master bathroom —her *father's* bathroom—exclusively.

The door to the master bedroom is open, and when she looks inside, she sees her father sitting at a card table where her mother's vanity—which had belonged to her grandmother —once stood. Emily wonders where the vanity is now. Down in the basement maybe, part of a vast reef-like structure formed from other forgotten objects. Or did her father sell it? Either possibility fills her with rage. When she was a child, back before her mother's migraines got bad, Emily used to sit at the vanity on her mother's lap and they looked through her collection of jewelry together. Now the card table sits in the vanity's place, along with a metal folding chair. A laptop sits upon the table's surface, the rest of which is covered with empty coffee mugs, fast-food soda cups, and crumpled hamburger wrappers. And, of course, her father's there, too. He sits in front of the computer, fingers tapping away at the keys. His "home office" is as cluttered as the rest of the house —even the bed is being used as storage, at least the left side of the mattress is. The side her mother used to sleep on. Her father has placed a mound of laundry—towels, shirts, socks, underwear—there, and Emily wonders if it's because he's too lazy to fold it and put it away, or if it's because he's filled the dresser drawers and linen closet with junk. Maybe both, she decides.

He's tall—six-and-a-half feet—and beefy. Big, but not fat. He's clean-shaven and his short brown hair is neatly combed. He's wearing a light blue polo shirt and navy slacks. His feet are bare, the toenails too long and yellow. His grotesque toenails are perfect symbols of her father, Emily thinks. His shaven face and combed hair indicate a man who is disciplined and orderly, at least on the surface, but underneath there is only chaotic, mindless neglect. His hands are surprisingly delicate. They seem smaller than they should be given the size of the rest of him, and the skin is soft and pink. He has a bad habit of biting his fingernails, and the skin around them is red and sore. This doesn't stop him from typing, though. If he feels any pain, he ignores it. She wonders what he's writing. Probably a rant on some message board dedicated to political debate, or maybe he's commenting on a science article he's just read. His interests are many and varied, and he considers himself an expert in just about everything.

This really is it—the very last moment that she can leave without talking to him. He hasn't noticed her standing in the doorway, and she can easily slip away before—

He stops typing then, straightens in his chair. His head turns toward her and at first his face is devoid of expression. Eyes empty, features slack. But then he recognizes her, and a broad grin splits the lower half of his face.

"Pumpkin! It's so good to see you!"

Now it's too late.

THE DINING ROOM is as cluttered as the rest of the house, but her father moves some things so they can sit and have a small space to set their coffee mugs down.

"I work from home these days. Consulting."

Emily doesn't ask what sort of consulting he does. Something to do with computers, she assumes. She doesn't really care.

The coffee he made for her is black. She takes it with cream and sugar, but he didn't offer either. Some kind of brown gunk is crusted to the rim of the mug, and there's some yellowish stuff—egg?—stuck to the handle. She's reluctant to bring the dirty mug to her lips, so she leaves the coffee on the table, untouched. Her father doesn't seem to notice. His mug is equally dirty, but he sips his coffee without hesitation.

Emily sits with her hands folded in her lap as her father drinks his coffee. He shows no sign of being uncomfortable with their silence, and if he's aware of it, it doesn't concern him. Eventually, he speaks.

"Sorry about the mugs. I tried to tidy up before you got here, but…" He trails off and shrugs.

She wants to ask him how he could let things get this bad, but instead she nods as if to say she understands.

"So…do you have a special guy in your life these days?"

Emily is bisexual. She told her father this before she moved out, but she isn't surprised he doesn't remember.

"I'm not seeing anyone right now," she says, which is true.

It's his turn to nod, and he takes another sip of his coffee.

"How's work?"

Emily drives for a rideshare service to pay the bills while she takes college art classes…when she can afford them. She doesn't want to tell her father this, doesn't want him to know too much about her, doesn't feel he has the right.

"It's good."

Another nod from him.

"I read this fascinating article yesterday about a termite colony in South America that's larger than Britain."

She's not surprised by this abrupt change in topic, and she listens as her father continues telling her about the termites, practically reciting the article from memory. She pays no attention to the specifics of what he says. Instead she tries to imagine her mother in her place, listening to her husband go on about whatever obscure subject has captured his imagination that day. What was it like for her to be talked *at* so many times, never being talked *to*? Emily thinks it must have been a slow erosion of her mother's spirit, a bit more of herself washed away with each mind-numbing syllable her father spoke. But Emily doesn't have to imagine. After her mother's death, her father still needed an audience, and so he'd turned to his daughter. She sat through hundreds of mini lectures on a vast array of random subjects, from the origins of jai alai to the proper way to forge a sword using Toledo steel to the history of progressive rock. There's no pattern to his enthusiasms, no connective tissue whatsoever. His mind is like the house—and vice versa—full of random, useless, meaningless junk. She wonders if there's any place in the gigantic trash heap of his brain for memories of her and her mother. Maybe a few, stored in some forgotten corner, buried beneath a mound of trivia.

Emily begins to lose patience with her father, and she interrupts him before he can finish telling her about the giant termite colony.

"I want to talk about something."

Her father stops speaking mid-sentence and stares at her as if she's just slapped him. He's not used to being interrupted, and she feels deep satisfaction at the almost shocked expression on his face.

Careful now, Dr. Karnes' voice says. *You've come here for closure, for healing. Not revenge.*

"It's about Mom. How… How could you not know how depressed she was? How come you couldn't see what was happening to her?"

"I did."

Those two words slam into her like a gut punch.

"I saw that she became quiet and withdrawn. I researched depression, sent her links to article I thought might help her. I don't know if she read them."

Emily remembers two things her mother told her, on two separate occasions. When Emily asked what had attracted her to her husband, she said, *It was because of how smart he was.* Several years later, after listening to her husband go on about Roman aqueducts for over an hour after she had informed him that her aunt had died, she said, *Your father is the most intelligent idiot I've ever met.*

Emily always assumed her father was unaware of his wife's depression, that he was as oblivious to it as he was to everything else in the real world. She hated him for that, for not being mentally and emotionally present enough to get her mother the help she needed, help that could've saved her life.

Emily supposes her father's research into depression, however ineffective, shows that he cared about her mother on some level, that he tried to help in the other way he knew how: by providing information. But people weren't machines to be programmed. You couldn't simply feed data into them and expect them to behave the way you wanted. She doesn't bother telling her father this. She knows he won't understand.

Her father continues.

"She grew more distant over the years. Kept to herself. Stayed in the bedroom and napped throughout the day. You know what she was like."

Emily remembers it very well. She visited Mom in her room from time to time. Mom talked to her, told her stories of when she was a kid. But no matter what Emily did, her mother's sadness remained—and worsened.

"Why didn't she see a doctor?"

"I don't know. She never mentioned wanting to."

Then you should've insisted she see one, should've carried her there if you had to! That's what you do when someone you love is sick and can't take care of themselves!

Anger flares strong and bright inside her, and she fights to keep it contained. Dr. Karnes stressed how important it is for her to remain as calm as possible during this confrontation.

If you start yelling and accusing him of being a terrible husband and father—which undoubtedly he was—he'll just shut down and quit listening.

Emily takes a deep breath and then releases it slowly. Her anger dims a bit but its fire doesn't go out. She has come to the Question.

"Do you ever feel guilty, Dad? Like you could've done more to help her?"

Do you blame yourself for her death like I do? Do you realize that your lack of anything even approximating human emotion killed her as surely as if you'd put a gun to her head and pulled the trigger? It just took longer.

Her father finishes the last of his coffee as he mulls over her question.

"No. I read a great deal about suicide after your mother's death, and I came to the conclusion that if someone is truly determined to kill themselves, no one can stop them. I can't say that I understand what she was going through, but at least her pain ended. Sometimes it's better that way."

Emily's anger rises once more, and she can't keep it out of her voice as she speaks. "Better for who? For her? Or for you?"

Instead of answering right away, he looks around at the junk piled on and around the dining table, and his eyes widen as if he's seeing it—*really* seeing it—for the first time.

"Yes," he says.

And just like that, Emily's anger—her white-hot blazing rage—is gone. A deep calm settles on her, and while she has more to say, has rehearsed her words during her drive home, she has no need to say anything else now. She's gotten what she's come here for. For the first time in hours, her head doesn't hurt and the relief from the pain is so strong she almost weeps. At least one good thing has come out of her visit.

She leaves her mug, still full, on the table and stands.

"Thanks for the coffee, but I have to go now."

She doesn't bother fabricating a reason, but she knows she doesn't need to offer one. She's sure her father will be relieved as she is once she's gone.

"Oh. Well, it was good to see you. Come back again." These last words are flat and toneless, and Emily knows he doesn't mean them.

"Goodbye, Dad."

She turns and begins making her way through her father's maze. He doesn't offer to accompany her, and she doesn't ask him to.

ON HER WAY out of town, she stops at the same convenience store where she took her migraine medicine earlier. Inside is an ATM. She withdraws twenty dollars, folds it neatly, places it in her front pants pocket, and leaves.

She drives to the exit ramp where she got off the highway, and the man with the sign reading WILL KILL FOR FOOD is still there, standing and looking off into the distance. Emily parks her Plymouth on the side of the road, gets out, and walks over to him. He turns to look at her as she approaches, his face without expression. She takes the twenty out of her pocket, unfolds it, and holds it out to the man. He takes the bill and, just as he did before, he crumples it in his hand, puts it in his mouth, and begins chewing. He looks at Emily with his strange blue eyes, as if waiting for her to say something.

She takes the ATM receipt from her pocket. She wrote on the back of it before leaving the gas station, and now she hands the receipt to the man, showing him the back so he can see what he's written. It's an address. Her father's.

Still chewing the twenty-dollar bill, the man takes the receipt. He looks at the address, and then he looks at Emily.

"I don't know if you like to eat anything besides money, but there's a ton of junk in my father's house. It would an absolute feast for—" She almost says *something*—"someone like you. You can have it all with my blessing, if you'll just do one thing for me."

The man swallows the twenty and then raises a questioning eyebrow. Emily reaches out and taps her index finger against his sign. The man smiles, revealing teeth stained green, and he nods. He looks down at the address once more as if to memorize it, then he crumples it and pops it into his mouth. He tucks his sign under his arm and starts walking.

As Emily watches him go, she says, "It's better this way."

Agreed, Dr. Karnes says.

Emily heads back to her car. Time to go home.

NEGATIVE SPACE

You're sitting on a couch in a home that's not yours. On the floor in front of you are three young children—two boys and a girl—playing with toys. In the corner of the room is a sparsely-decorated Christmas tree. On the wall to the left of the tree hangs a flatscreen TV displaying images of the kids' dead father. He looks at you, smiles, winks. No one else notices.

Your wife is in the kitchen, sitting in the breakfast nook with the children's mother. They've been friends since childhood, more like sisters, really. They even resemble each other, at least a little. They're both blonde, both fair-skinned. The mother is shorter than your wife and petite. Your wife is medium height and, while not heavy, has more meat on her bones. You wonder if the mother has always been this thin or if she's lost weight while grieving the loss of her husband. The Bereavement Diet.

No one else is looking at the screen. They don't even seem to realize it's on. The memorial video prepared by the funeral home has been playing on a loop for the last three hours. A procession of photos meant to encapsulate a life, set to a soundtrack of bad instrumental music that you suppose is meant to sound inspirational and uplifting. But it sounds obscene, a parody, a mockery.

The women huddle together, holding hands, talking quietly, sometimes crying together. You're not privy to their conversations, and there have been a lot of them over the last couple weeks. You're not really sure why you're here, but you know why your wife is. Her mother died not too long ago—the first family member she's ever lost—and she was wracked by grief and depression for the better part of a year. When she learned her friend's husband died unexpectedly—hello, middle-aged heart attack—she was determined to visit. Christmas was coming, and she didn't want her friend and her children going through the first major holiday since their husband and father's death without someone there to offer support. So the two of you left Ohio, drove to Virginia, and have stayed in the friend's house for the last thirteen days. Christmas is still a week away. You don't know if you can make it.

You're supposed to be watching the kids so the women can talk uninterrupted, but aside from needing a diaper change or a snack now and again, they don't require much from you. They play quietly, sitting on the floor or on the other crouch positioned at a right angle to the one you're on, each alone in his or her little world, subdued and expressionless.

On the screen, the parade of still photos continues. The father standing before a grill in summertime, cooking hamburgers. This grill is in the backyard right now, covered with an inch of snow. Sitting on a beach next to his wife, his arm around her, both in swimsuits and sunglasses, both smiling. You wonder who took the picture. You wonder if they smiled only for the camera or if they really were happy that day. The father in the hospital, gazing down at a swaddled newborn that he's holding carefully, as if it's made of glass and might shatter if he grips it too hard. You don't know which of his children this is. Does it matter?

The father turns toward you, holds out his child as if offering it to you, his teeth bared in what's supposed to be a smile.

You look away from the screen. The horrible music plays on. And on.

THERE ARE a number of strange coincidences—more like connections, really—between you and the dead man. You share the same birthday, only he was one year younger than you. Your wives were childhood friends, and they're both younger than the two of you by fifteen years. You've both been married before but were your new wives' first spouses. You both have children from your prior marriages, all grown and leading their own lives. But that's where the parallels end. Your current wife and you have no children together. It's not something you planned, just worked out that way. The dead man was an Airforce vet, with his own heating and cooling business, a MAGA type, an avid hunter, suspicious of anyone who isn't white or straight. You're far more interested in books and film than in killing animals for trophies. You're a liberal who thinks diversity is a strength, not a weakness, of a society. You doubt the two of you would've been friends if you'd known each other. You like to think you could have at least been civil to one another. Maybe, maybe not.

YOU AND YOUR wife sleep in the daughter's bedroom. The family has no guest bedroom, not with three children living in the house. The master bedroom is empty. The widow—it's so odd to think of someone so young as being a *widow*—won't sleep there. She hasn't so much as sat on the bed since her husband died. Logically, it would be the best place for you and your wife to sleep, but her friend has kept it as a kind of shrine to her husband, and you get that. The daughter's room is painted a stereotypical pink, with a mural of a pair of cartoonish owls sitting in a tree behind the headboard, gauzy white curtains over the single window. The bed is small. It's meant for a child, after all, and there's hardly any room for you and your wife to lie on it together. And once you do lie down, there's no room to move, not unless you want to roll off the mattress and onto the floor. On your first night here, your wife wanted to make love in this bed. You found the thought grotesque—Fuck in a little child's *bed?*—and you feared if you did, you'd break the damn thing to pieces. You declined, and the two of you haven't had sex since.

The girl sleeps downstairs with her mother, on one of the couches, the TV playing all night long. The boys sleep in their own rooms upstairs, usually waking once or twice during the night. Sometimes you go take care of them, sometimes your wife does. Their mother—physically and emotionally exhausted—often doesn't hear them cry and call out to her in the night. You haven't slept well since you got here. The small bed and the crying boys don't help, but the main reason you have trouble sleeping is that even on the second floor, you can hear the memorial video playing, over and over, all night long, each and every night.

YOU'VE NEVER WATCHED the video all the way through, have only paid attention to bits and pieces of it, the most you can stand at any one time. Sometimes everyone leaves the room, and the video continues playing for an audience of no one. A man's life reduced to a household fixture, an everyday object, unnoticed and ignored, like an end table in a corner where a decorative vase is displayed, hardly ever looked at, rarely dusted. You ask your wife that if you pre-decease her—which given your age difference is likely—to *please* not have a memorial video like this one made for you. Or if she does have one made, to please not turn it on and leave it running 24/7. The idea that you might become something that your family enjoys having on in the background, on the edge of life but not part of it, horrifies you. She promised. You hope she meant it.

ONE OF THE BOYS—THE older one who can walk—comes over to you. He walks well enough, although he has a tendency to wobble and is a little pigeon-toed. You're surprised that he doesn't fall more often. He's wearing blue pajamas with a cartoon dog on the front, and his feet are bare. They make soft *smack-smack-smack-smack* sounds as the boy comes over. He's holding the TV remote in his left hand, gripping it tight so he doesn't lose it.

The boy holds the remote out to you.

"Happy," he says.

The first time you heard him say this word, you had no idea what he wanted. Now you know that it's the boy's way of asking for *Sesame Street* to be turned on. You're not sure it's a good idea. He spends a lot of time playing games and watching video on a tablet computer, hogging it for himself and fussing if his siblings come near it. He doesn't have the tablet now, though. He wants to watch Happy on the big screen. You wonder if he sees any connection between the memorial video currently (still) playing and his father. The boy ignores the pictures of his father for the most part, but when he does look at the video, he displays no sign of recognition.

You take the remote from the boy and glance in the direction of the breakfast nook. Your wife and her friend are kissing now. Not a quick we're-friends-and-I-love-you peck. This kiss is long and deep, with plenty of tongue. You can't believe what you're seeing. You start to rise from the couch, intending to go into the kitchen and find out what the hell is going on. But then you blink and the two women are just sitting again, holding hands, not kissing.

"Happy!" the boy says, insistent.

Fuck it.

You look away from the breakfast nook, point the remote at the TV to switch it from video to cable so you can put on Happy. You see the husband-father on the screen pointing at you and laughing. You hit the button to switch to cable, and when the husband's face disappears and the hideous memorial music cuts off, your wife's friend screams.

THAT NIGHT, lying beside your wife in the too-small little girl bed, you wonder how much time *you* have left. Is there some hidden biological time bomb ticking away inside you, ready to explode at some unknown point in the future? A heart attack like the husband-father? Maybe a stroke? You hate going to the doctor's office, go only when you must, but now you wonder if it wouldn't be prudent to get a checkup, and soon.

Lying beside you, your wife lightly snores. You wonder if she's dreaming, and if so, if she's dreaming of kissing her friend. Did that really happen or was it your imagination? You really don't know. Everything has been so strange and dreamlike since you got here.

You think about sliding your hand beneath the sheets and

reaching out to cup your wife's breast, maybe put your other hand between her legs. You almost do it, but then you hear the music from the memorial video playing downstairs, and you keep your hands where they are. You feel tired. Old.

IT AMAZES you that someone can be such a presence by their absence. The husband-father has been dead for two months, and yet he's everywhere in this house. In the grief-haunted expressions of his wife and children. On the TV, of course, and in his home office. Your wife's friend hasn't touched the latter, and its surface is still cluttered with papers related to his business, bills and invoices, mostly. His computer is on, the background image a picture of him with his wife and kids. You wonder if your wife's friend has left his computer on and running since the day he died. Probably. On the wall next to the computer are two hunting trophies, a pair of mounted deer heads, stags with impressive antlers. They're disturbing enough in their own right—bristly dry fur, unseeing glass eyes —but to make them even more hideous, each has a pair of hooves mounted beneath, turned upward as if they're supposed to be hooks upon which you could hang jackets or hats. The sight of these hooves, the way they're turned upward, makes you queasy. You look away from the trophies, back to the computer screen on the desk. The image of the dead man, his wife, and their kids is still there, but now they all have deer heads, their hands upturned hooves.

You back away from the desk, unable to take your eyes off the screen. You hear your wife call out, asking for help changing the kids' diapers. You turn away from the desk, the trophies, the horrible image on the computer screen, and you hurry out of the room. The idea of dealing with piss and shit-soaked diapers infinitely preferable to remaining another moment here.

When you were a child, you were always picked last when it came time to choose teams for baseball, basketball, football… You would raise your hand in class whenever you knew the answer to a question, but teachers rarely called on you. You graduated in the middle of your class in high school, and your grades in college were far from spectacular, but you managed to graduate from there, too. Your dating life was equally unremarkable, but you still found a woman to marry. You were together for almost twenty years before you divorced. She was cheating on you and had been almost from the beginning or your marriage. She wasn't certain your two daughters were biologically yours. You decided to continue being their father, regardless, but the girls drifted away, and now they only talk with you on the phone once or twice a year, and even then, only briefly. You divorced your wife and you threw yourself into your work. You own a restaurant that always seems on the verge of closing, but you somehow keep it afloat year after year. Your current wife started out as one of your waitresses. It was love at first sight for you, but she didn't think much of you one way or another. You kept working on her, though, and eventually you wore her down and she agreed to go out with you. Your relationship was on again, off again for a long time, but after it finally seemed to settle down to mostly on, you proposed. You were shocked that she said yes. Your marriage has been okay. She never remembers anything about you—your work schedule, your birthday, your anniversary, your interests and enthusiasms. And often she goes about her business for days on end without interacting with you much. Once you confronted her about this, asked why she seems to ignore you so often.

She thought about it for several moments before answering.

"I guess some people are just more *there* than others."

YOUR WIFE'S friend works a forty-hour week. Usually she has to put her children in daycare, but since you and your wife came, you've been watching the kids during the day to help her save money. Her husband died without leaving a will, and without his salary or benefits, her finances have become tight. You like these times with the kids, primarily because you can turn off that goddamned video without your wife's friend freaking out.

One afternoon, your wife is sitting on the couch, the youngest boy in her lap, the older two children sitting next to her, one on either side. She's reading a Dr. Seuss book to them, one you remember from when you were a child, full of silly rhymes and sillier pictures. The kids really enjoy it, and when she finishes, the older boy shouts, "Read more, Mommy!"

You wife beams at the boy, not correcting him.

"Of course, sweetie."

She turns back to the beginning of the book and starts again while you sit on the other couch, doing nothing, just watching and listening.

WHEN YOUR WIFE told you she was going to visit her friend—with or without you—you asked her why she was adamant about going.

"Is this about your mother?" you asked.

The question angered her.

"*No*. Lori and I were both only children. We lived across the street from one another, and we became friends. We played together all the time, practically lived at one another's houses. She's the closest thing to a sister I've ever had, and she feels the same way about me. There's nothing I wouldn't do for her, or she for me."

You never heard your wife speak with such strong emotion before, such passion, such love, such determination. She's never spoken about you like that, and you're jealous of her friend, of the woman's prior claim on your wife's heart.

"She needs me, and I'm going, simple as that. You can come or you can stay. Your choice."

You went.

WHEN ALL THREE kids have gone down for naps, the two of you go to the basement, where the laundry room is. You would love to take a nap yourself. You forgot how draining taking care of little children is. There's always work around the house to do, usually cleaning of one sort or another. Kids never stop making messes. So your wife decided to do some laundry, and you came along to help. She prefers to do chores alone, doesn't like you getting in the way, so you "help" by standing to the side and watching her as she works. Once she gets a load of clothes started, you work up the courage to ask her a question.

"Why am I here?"

She looks at you, laughs.

"That's a bit existential, isn't it?"

"I mean, why am I here with you, now. In Virginia."

She frowns slightly. "You've come to help Lori."

"That's why *you* came. I've hardly done anything since we arrived. There doesn't seem to be much for me *to do*."

Your wife opens her mouth to respond, but then she hesitates, frowns deeply. You realize she doesn't have an answer to your question, and this saddens you.

She smiles, tries to lighten the moment by making a joke.

"It was a long drive from Ohio. I needed somebody to take the wheel when I got tired."

She smiles broadly, as if to say, *Funny, right?*

You try to smile back, but you can't quite manage it.

DINNER THAT NIGHT is McDonald's. Your wife's friend doesn't have the energy to cook after a long day at work. She's a manager of a physician's office, and you wonder how she gets through her day, dealing with sick, injured, and maybe even dying people. How could this possibly take her mind off her husband's death? But it's not that she doesn't want to cook tonight; she doesn't want you or your wife cooking, either.

She's very particular about what she eats, your wife told you on the drive here. *She wants what she wants when she wants it. Filet mignon one day, Chef Boyardee from a can the next.*

You guess this is one of those Chef Boyardee times.

The oldest boy and his sister both got chicken nuggets, fries, and soda. The younger boy—barely more than a baby, really—is strapped into a highchair and gets dry Cheerios to munch on. Your wife has a salad, as does her friend. Neither of them eats very much. You got a grilled chicken sandwich, but you don't eat much of it, either. You're all crammed into the breakfast nook, which barely has room for two people, let alone six. There's a dining table, but your wife's friend keeps it covered with junk—laundry that needs folding, boxes of clothes she's bought herself as retail therapy and never opened after bringing them home, piles of magazines she hasn't read...

She's complaining about how her family won't help her out with childcare, and neither will any of her friends. This segues into tearful fretting about what to do with her husband's business—Keep it going? Shut it down? He has employees, only a couple, but they have families of their own to feed. This in turn gives way to a discussion about whether she should get breast implants. According to your wife, her friend has always had body image issues, and while the friend insists she's not ready to even *think* about dating yet, might not *ever* be ready, she wants the implants so she can feel better about herself. Plus, she and her husband had talked it over, and he'd agreed, so getting the implants would be like heeding one of his last wishes, right?

You know different people grieve in different ways, but breast implants? Less than three months after her husband died? It sounds insane.

"I mean, *look* at these things."

Your wife's friend stands, removes her blouse, drapes it over the back of her chair, removes her bra, tosses it on top of the blouse. She steps back so both you and your wife can have a good view. She puts her hands on her hips, looks at you both, then says, "Well?"

Her breasts are on the small side, but she's petite and they seem perfectly suited to her body. You're shocked that she so casually disrobed in front of you, and that she's asking for your opinion on her tits.

"I think they look fine," your wife says. "If you really want implants, though, you should get them. I'm just not sure that this is the best time. It's hard enough recovering from surgery without having three little children around to jump on you and climb all over you." Your wife turns to face you. "What do you think?"

If she's uncomfortable that her friend is partially naked in front of you, she gives no sign.

You look to her for some clue how to react, but she just smiles and nods, as if to say, *Go ahead. Humor her.* You turn back to your wife's friend, try to think of something to say that won't come across wrong.

"They're perfect."

Instead of giving you a grateful smile for reassuring her, your wife's friend scowls.

"You're lying. It's obvious you like bigger boobs. Look at who you married."

She picks up her blouse, leaving the bra on the chair. She slips her arms into it and begins to button it once more. Her nipples are hard and quite visible beneath the blouse's fabric.

You look to your wife, hoping to get some sympathy, but she's started eating her salad. You look at the kids to see how they've reacted to the sight of their mother exposing herself to strangers. But they're all focused on their food and seem to have no clue what their mother just did.

Thank god for small favors, you think. At least the children won't be traumatized by what their mother did. But if they were older, it might be a different story.

"Eat your food," your wife says.

Not being able to finish all the food on her plate used to get her in big trouble with her parents, and she never leaves any food uneaten, not a crumb. To placate her, you always do your best to clean your plate when eating. You look down, expecting to see your chicken sandwich, but instead you see a long, bloody bone, one end terminating in a hoof. You glance back at the video, see the man on the screen dressed in full hunting regalia—camouflage shirt, camouflage pants, boots. He's kneeling next to a dead deer, holding its head up by its antlers, tongue lolling from one side of its mouth. Is this one of the two deer in the office? Maybe. You see the dead animal only has three legs.

Go on, the man says. *Try it; you might like it.*

You look at the bone. There's not a great deal of meat left on it, but there's some. You reach down, take hold of the ends of the bone with your fingers, and gingerly raise it to your mouth. You lick blood from its surface, find a dot of meat and pry it off with your teeth. You begin to chew.

It's the best damn thing you've ever tasted.

After dinner, all of you go into the family room. Your wife and her friend sit on one of the couches, so close their legs touch, talking again, always talking, pausing now and then to cry together. The memorial video is playing—of course—and the volume is, as usual, too loud. It's gotten to the point where even you have become used to it. More like numb, really. And that strikes you as a remarkably sad thing.

Something that's surprised you about this visit is how emotionally demonstrative your wife has been since you got here—to her friend and the children, that is. Not to you. She was like that with you when the two of first starting dating ten years ago, but it's been a long time since then, and now you're more like friends who have occasional sex. It's not a bad life, not exactly, but it's not how you hoped your relationship would be.

You're sitting cross-legged on the floor, the children playing around you with dolls, trucks, blocks, things that light up, make noise, play music. You keep trying to interact with them, to engage them, but they don't respond beyond a distracted glance in your direction now and again. It's almost as if they aren't fully aware of your presence.

You look to your wife and her friend. Their tops are off

now, their chests bare, and they're fondling each other's breasts, almost as if comparing them. This is too much. You're right *here*, damn it!

"What the hell are you two doing?"

They don't say anything, don't look at you, don't acknowledge that you've spoken in any way. Your wife leans in, presses her lips to one of her friend's nipples, begins to suck. The friend closes her eyes, tilts her head back. The kids look up, see what's happening, and they giggle and clap with delight.

"Mommies!" the little girl says.

The three laugh harder.

You stand and look around at all five of them, the kids, the women. None of them pay you the slightest bit of attention, and you wonder if you're really there at all. You look at the TV on the wall, and for a second you think something is wrong with your vision. It looks like the husband-father's hand is protruding from the screen, crossing the line dividing his two-dimensional world from your three-dimensional one.

You step past the children, walk up to the screen, and examine the hand. It looks so *real*. You wonder what would happen if you reached out and touched it. Would it feel real, too?

You hear a voice in your mind.

Go ahead. Try it. You—

"Might like it," you finish.

Your hand is surprisingly steady as you reach up to take the man's. He clenches his hand around yours, almost as if the two of you are shaking hello. And with a single powerful yank, he pulls you off your feet and lifts you toward him. Your vision blurs for a moment, and the world shifts vertiginously around you. When everything settles once more, you find yourself standing next to the husband-father. You're outside on a warm summer day, in his backyard, as a matter of fact.

He's standing next to his grill, which looks newer than it does in real life, cooking burgers. He's wearing a T-shirt, flip-flops, and an apron which says *Don't Blame Me, I Just Cook Here* on the front.

There's no one else in the yard. The two of you are alone.

You look behind you, expecting to see the house, but instead you see a gigantic IMAX-size screen where the house should be. Displayed on it is the family you just left. Kids on the floor, laughing and clapping, their mommies on the couch, loving each other. A tear rolls down your cheek, and the other man puts a hand on your shoulder. The cheesy music that seems to come from all directions in this place swells.

"It's okay," he says. "They don't need us anymore. I'm not sure they ever did. Burger?"

You look at the tableau one last time before turning your back on it. The tears are flowing freely now.

"Sure, why not?"

THE GRAY ROOM

You pull your beat-up Chevy Malibu into a parking space in front of an old two-story apartment building. You kill the engine and turn to Liza, sitting in the passenger seat beside you.

"This looks shady as fuck," you say. You try to sound cool, like you're amused, but you can't hide the nervousness in your voice.

She laughs, or at least tries to. It comes out more like a chuffing sound, a noise produced by the cancer-ridden throat of someone who's been smoking for decades. But Liza doesn't smoke. She has a far different addiction, one you've come here to feed.

"You can't buy this shit over the counter at your neighborhood pharmacy," she says. She pauses, thinks a moment. "I'm not sure you can buy it anywhere else."

Anywhere else in town? you wonder. Or does she mean anywhere else in the world?

She was beautiful once. At least, she looks like she might've been. There's a remnant of blue in her dull gray eyes, an echo of gold in her dingy straw-like hair, a touch of faded pink in her dry, cracked lips. You try to imagine what it would be like to kiss those lips, and you feel a shiver of disgust.

She opens the passenger door and steps outside. You hesitate a moment longer. Do you really want to do this?

It's beyond any high you've ever imagined. Beyond sex, love, life, death—and more.

That's what she told you at the bar last night, when you tried to match her shot for shot and ended up drunk off your ass while she seemed perfectly sober. It's the *more* that really caught your attention, the hook that sank deep in your flesh. What could be more than life and death? What would that *more* feel like?

She smacks the flat of her hand against the driver's side window, startling you.

"You coming or are you going to puss out?" she demands.

She's wearing a Rancid T-shirt and faded jeans that look at least two sizes too big for her. She's using an old piece of rope for a belt, and her bare feet are so dirty, at first glance it looks as if she's wearing a pair of black slippers.

You smile at her, trying to look like you do this kind of thing all the time, but it feels strained, and you fear all you've managed is an uneasy grimace. Still, she steps away from the door and you get out.

It should be dark, should be the dead of fucking night, but it's two in the afternoon. Although as much as you drank last night, it still feels way too early to be out of bed. The sunlight stabs your eyes, sets your head to thudding. A sudden dizziness hits you, and you put a hand on the car roof to steady yourself.

When you first pulled up in the front of the building, you thought it was old. But now that you take your first good look at it, you see it's downright ancient. The brick might've been red once, but the years have leeched away most of the color, leaving it almost white. It looks soft and porous, as if on the verge of crumbling to dust. The windows are cracked, the glass so grimy it looks as if it's been whitewashed from inside. Whatever color the shutters once were is impossible to tell. The paint flaked off them long ago, leaving behind only weathered gray wood. The roof is missing a good number of shingles, maybe as much as half. It's as if a huge storm blew through her recently, stripped the shingles away, and no one's got around to replacing them. There's a sidewalk in front of the building, and a small set of concrete steps that leads to a door. The sidewalk is cracked and broken, as are the steps, and the door—gray wood like the shutters—hangs slightly askew, its metal handle covered with rust. The ground surrounding the building is dotted with patches of dead grass but otherwise is bare, the soil hard and lifeless, the color of diseased bone.

An odor hangs heavy on the stale air, a rank foulness that reminds you of the time you were mowing your parents' back yard as a teenager and you ran over the flattened, desiccated corpse of some small animal—a squirrel, probably—that had died and remained out in the summer sun for days. As the chewed-up pieces of bone and leathery hide were ejected from the mower's discharge chute, a greasy stomach-turning stench had filled the air. The air around the building reminds you of that smell, only worse.

But all of this—the building's appearance, its smell—is nothing compared to how the place makes you *feel*. You're instantly on edge, jaw tight, teeth clamped together, eyes narrowed. It's as if there's a sound just outside your range of hearing, like the almost inaudible hum of electronic equipment. It worms its way into your ears, making you feel as if thousands of tiny insects are walking across the folds and ridges of your brain.

"Not much to look at, is it?" Liza says.

She tries to sound flippant, like she's aware of the effect

the place has and is unaffected by it. But you can hear how uncomfortable she is, and for some reason, this bolsters your courage. You suppose it's good to know Liza's not as tough as she pretends to be. It makes you feel less alone.

She starts toward the door, and as she mounts the steps, concrete crumbles to dust beneath her feet. You follow, and you feel the steps sag beneath you. You're slender and Liza is close to emaciated, but even so you expect the steps to collapse entirely beneath your combined weight. But they hold, and when Liza opens the door—which is surprisingly silent given its condition—and holds it open for you, she smiles, revealing sore, bleeding gums and soft gray teeth. You could turn around. It's not too late. You could run back to the car, get inside, and drive the hell away from Liza, this place, and whatever waits inside. Last chance. Going once... Going twice...

Gone.

SHE FINDS you in the parking lot of Bottoms Up, a dive bar on the west side of Ash Creek. You're sitting in your car, windows down, head back, eyes closed, listening to the heroin's sweet, sweet song. Except the song isn't as sweet these days, is it? It isn't as loud, either. More and more often, it seems to fade into the background, and sometimes it falls silent altogether. You've become habituated and need stronger doses to get you where you want to go. Problem is, you're not exactly raking in the dough working in the kitchen of a twenty-four-hour hamburger joint, the kind of place where the patties are small and square and taste like used condoms. So you buy the best you can afford, but it's not enough, not anymore.

"Enjoying the ride?"

You slowly open your eyes and find yourself looking into Liza's face, although you don't know her name yet. Her hands —small-fingered, nails bitten to the quick—grip the edge of the window, and she's crouched down so she can look inside.

The smack in your veins might not be hi-test, but it's made you mellow enough, so you don't make a face upon seeing her. Her skin is sallow and drawn so tight to her skull she almost looks like an animated skeleton. At first you were afraid she was a cop who thought you'd OD'd and was ready to give you a shot of Narcan. But you can see she's only another addict looking to whore herself out so she can afford her next fix. The town's full of them. You're not an addict, though. You're a *user*. Big difference.

Her breath is foul, like the stink from an open sewer, and you turn your head slightly to move your nose away from the stench, but it doesn't help.

"Not interested," you mumble, the words barely audible even to you. She has no trouble hearing you, though.

"How do you know? I haven't offered you anything yet."

You have to admit she has a point. But you just want to be left alone.

"Fuck off," you say, voice raised to show you mean it.

The woman doesn't go anywhere. She continues looking at you through the open window. She smiles, the movement making her dry lips crack and bleed in several places.

"You've got a problem. I've got a solution." She pauses, then adds, "If you've got the balls."

She hasn't said so directly, but you sense that she knows precisely what your problem is. Who knows? Maybe she can smell it on you. Takes one to know one, right?

"Come inside with me. We'll do some shots and talk about what we can do to get you where you want to go."

You look at her for a moment, considering. Then you say, "What the fuck?" and get out of the car.

THE ENTRYWAY IS short and narrow, two apartments on the top floor, two on the bottom, and four rusty metal mailboxes set into one wall. The baby-shit brown carpet is frayed, torn, and dotted with suspicious-looking stains. Dead insects line the baseboards, and at first you think they're cockroaches, and there *is* a superficial resemblance, but these insects have too many legs, each of which ends in clawed toes. Fliers plaster the walls, held in place by yellowed strips of tape. They're printed on different colors of paper—blue, pink, yellow, and, of course, white—and they advertise services or make announcements for things that you've never heard of, some of which are downright enigmatic.

HAVE YOU SEEN THE REST OF ME? CALL followed by a long string of symbols unlike any numbers you're familiar with.

TWO MINUTES OF DARKNESS! LOWEST PRICE IN
TOWN!
COME EXPERIENCE THE GREAT DISMAL.
DELICIOUS CANNIBALS—FIFTY PERCENT OFF!

The smell in here is even worse than outside. It's like an overfilled dumpster baking in August heat—spoiled fruit and rotten meat slathered in piss and shit. Your gut convulses and stomach acid sears the back of your throat. You don't throw up, though, even if your body wants to. You haven't put anything in your belly besides booze for days, and there's nothing to bring up. A small mercy.

Liza leads you to the ground floor apartment on the left. A few meager flakes of pale green paint cling to the door, and a symbol has been crudely carved into the wood in place of a number, a lopsided circle with an X over it. The door across the hall has a zig-zagging line running downward from left to right.

Liza doesn't bother to knock on the door with the circle and X on it. She takes hold of the rust-caked knob and turns it. She pushes the door open and grins at you, displaying her soft gray teeth once more.

"After you," she says, gesturing for you to precede her.

There's something seriously fucked up about this building, about the whole goddamned situation. How badly do you want this? You don't, you decide. You *need* it.

You enter and Liza follows, pulling the door shut behind her.

SOMETIME AFTER YOUR first couple shots, but way before your last, Liza asks you a question.

"Why do you do it?"

She doesn't specify what *it* is. She doesn't have to.

You shrug. "Because it feels good, I guess."

"Just good?"

You grin. "Okay, it feels goddamn fan-fucking-tastic."

"But not like it used to."

"No. I wish it did."

"What if I told you I can hook you up with something that's a hundred times better? Hell, a *million* times."

"I'd say you're full of shit."

She continues, taking no offense, "What do you imagine the ultimate sensation would be?"

You have to think about that for a time before answering.

"Dying," you say.

She purses her lips in disapproval. "Dying's no great trick. Everything dies, even the universe. It's just dying so slowly compared to us that we don't really notice."

She's starting to irritate you by this point, and you're thinking of leaving after one more shot. Or three.

"So what *is* the ultimate sensation?" you ask.

"To *feel* the universe dying." Her dull eyes seem to brighten a bit as she speaks these words. "To know what it's like to be in the throes of death for billions of years, with billions more yet to endure. It's..." She breaks off, searching for the right words. "Rapturous. And that's what you've been searching for, isn't it? The same thing we're all searching for. To escape these sacks of meat we're trapped in—" she slaps her chest for emphasis—"even if only for a short time. Doesn't that sound better than heroin?"

Until tonight, you haven't given much thought to the reasons why you use drugs. But Liza's words resonate with you. You're such a small person, living such a small life. To touch something so big...to know what it's like to be *everything*—even if that everything was dying... That would be the ultimate, wouldn't it?

"And there's a drug that can make you feel like this?" you ask.

She nods. "And I know where to get it."

THERE ARE no lights on in the apartment. There's a window on one wall and a glass patio door, but both are covered with sheets affixed to curtain rods with wooden clothespins. The sheets are thin, though, allowing enough light to filter through so you can see. The walls are the sickly gray color of diseased mucus, and the floor is covered with taped-together sheets of plastic that wrinkle with each step you take. There's no furniture, at least not in the main room—the gray room— which is all you can see at the moment. But the room is far from empty. The space is filled with some manner of bizarre sculpture made from bones lashed together with rusty barbed wire. Arm bones, leg bones, spines, ribcages, pelvises, skulls... all arranged in haphazard fashion, none of the pieces connected in anything remotely resembling a natural way. You recognize some of the bones as human—from both adults and children—but others appear to be from animals. Dogs, cats, birds, cows, horses, large reptiles like alligators or crocodiles... But some of the skeletal pieces are...different. Skulls with one eye socket, three, or even more. Two mouths, no mouth, a circular orifice where a mouth should be. Twisted spines with serrated fins protruding from them, pelvises which are all sharp angles, rib cages that are curved outward instead of inward, the ends of the ribs sharpened spear points. After the initial shock of seeing this lunatic construction, you realize it's made of more than just bone and wire. Thin plastic tubing runs throughout the thing, coiling around bones, running in and out of eye sockets and mouths, threading through ribs... The tubing isn't empty, though. Something thick and dark moves through it, and you can almost hear the moist sound of oozing sludge.

Like the outside of the building and the entryway, there's a strong smell inside the apartment, but it's different than the others. It's the smell of dead, lifeless earth, of a desert so barren it's incapable of sustaining even the hardiest form of life. With each breath you take, it feels as if you're losing moisture, drying up inside a little bit more, and you wonder what would happen to you if you stayed here too long. Would you become a shrunken, dried husk, nothing but parchment skin draped over dusty bones?

"Oh, hello, Liza. I didn't hear you come in."

You turn toward the voice—a mild and not unpleasant tenor—and see a man enter the gray room from small hallway that presumably leads back to an equally gray bedroom.

Although from what you've seen of the apartment so far, it might be best to avoid making such assumptions.

You expect the man to look strange, perhaps even inhuman, but he appears perfectly normal. Middle-aged, balding, medium height, clean-shaven, dressed in a long-sleeved white shirt with the collar buttoned, black slacks and black shoes. But then you notice that what hair he does have looks as if it's been painted onto his head, and his shirt is preternaturally white, so much so that it almost glows in the room's dimness. And his pants and shoes are so black it's as if they're a void, drawing in the surrounding light and snuffing it out.

He smiles as he sees you and makes his way carefully around the bone-and-wire construction to greet you. He's still smiling when he gets there, and you see his teeth are as white as his shirt, so white it hurts to look at them directly. You also notice that every tooth is exactly the same size and shape—perfect little squares aligned in twin rows. His eyes look normal enough, except that they give the impression that they have no pupils, but rather small openings that, if you wished, you could fit the tip of your pinkies into them.

He extends his hand for you to shake, and you hesitate a few seconds before doing so. His flesh is cool and rubbery, and the feel of it causes you to shiver with disgust. He gives no sign that he notices. Instead he releases your hand, smile still in place.

"Please forgive the plastic," he says. "The Spiritus Mori leaks sometimes. You are...?"

You give him your name. He nods, continuing to smile, as if it's a very fine name indeed.

"I'd give you mine, but I'm afraid I don't have a name. Never had any use for one, I suppose." He claps his hands together and rubs them vigorously. They make a sound like two snakes sliding against one another. "Let's get down to business. You've come to sample my wares, yes?"

You nod. "How much?"

The man looks offended. "I don't charge!" Then his expression turns sly, and he adds, "Not the first time."

He turns to Liza.

"And you wish to partake as well, my dear?"

Up to this point, Liza has seemed confident and relaxed, completely in control. But now she bows her head, almost in supplication, and when she speaks her voice is plaintive, as if she's begging.

"Yes. I've brought the first half of my payment." She gives you a quick glance before turning back to the man in the too-white shirt.

"So I see. Are you prepared to pay the remainder?"

"Yes." She whispers the word.

"Excellent!" Another hand clap followed by more sliding snakeskin. The man walks over to the Spiritus Mori and taps the head of a tiny bird skull, once, twice. He then holds his right index finger up to the skull's beak and a single drop of a thick, tarry substance emerges and falls onto his finger. He quickly switches hands and catches the second drop on his left index finger. He then returns to the two of you. Whatever the substance on his fingers is, it doesn't drip or slide off. It remains on his skin like a pair of black beads.

"This doesn't have a name either, I'm afraid. Not the best marketing, I'll grant you, but then again, my product sells itself. Put your tongue out."

This situation has long gone past the point where you can tell yourself that none of this is real, that it's all some elaborate practical joke. You may not understand exactly what's happening, but you damn well know that it's real, all of it. You can feel it in the core of your being. And whatever that black goo is, you know it will deliver the experience Liza promised. All you have to do is open your mouth and stick out your tongue.

So you do.

The man in the too-white shirt places the drop on your tongue, but before he can place the second on Liza's, she grabs hold of his wrist and shoves his index finger into her mouth. She sucks on it, sucks *hard*, as if she's trying to pull the meat off his finger, too. The man's lips purse in disgust, and he places his other hand on Liza's head and shoves her backward. His finger comes free from her mouth with a wet schlurp, and she stumbles backward, almost falling. She doesn't care, though. She's too busy laughing.

You watch this happen, but it barely registers on your consciousness, for the drug has already been absorbed into your tongue and is beginning to do its work. The first thing it does is shut down your senses. Sight goes first, followed swiftly by hearing. The drug left a sour tang in your mouth, but when your taste goes, the sourness goes with it. The apartment's dead earth odor cuts off as your smell dies, and then your nerve endings follow, and you can no longer physically feel anything. It's like you no longer exist, except you're still conscious, still *you*, but you're nowhere and nowhen. This non-sensation should be the opposite of a high. After all, it's nothing. But there's an almost euphoric feeling of deep peace, and rather than your sense of self being diminished, it instead feels enhanced, strengthened. You are, after all, the only thing that inhabits this noplace. That makes you God, doesn't it? You wonder what would happen if you said, *Let there be light*.

If this was as far as the experience went, if it was all the black drop had to offer, it would've still lived up to Liza's promises. But it's only the beginning, a mere appetizer for what's to come.

You feel yourself begin to expand rapidly, growing at a rate beyond comprehension. You become aware of the physical world again as you grow, becoming larger than the building, larger than the city, the state, the country, the continent, the hemisphere, the world…and still you continue growing, expanding outward in all directions, past the moon, the sun, the other planets in the system. And then, although you wouldn't have believed it possible, your growth accelerates exponentially, and soon you encompass hundreds of star systems, millions, then this galaxy, then the neighboring ones, then *all* the galaxies until you are everything that was, is, or ever will be. You are All.

It should be too much for a single human mind to withstand, and your tiny, limited psyche should be obliterated by the experience. You're overwhelmed, to put it mildly, but that's okay. You can handle it, with the drug's help. And you think this—*this*—is the ultimate, that there can be nothing beyond this. How could there be?

And then you feel it, feel reality dying. It's been happening since that timeless instant everything came into being, an inexorable process, unimaginably slow but constant, like the dripping mineral-rich water that over centuries forms stalactites on a cave ceiling, or the trickling stream that over millennia carves out a vast canyon. You are All, and you can feel yourself dying, giving forth an endless moan of pain and despair that is the true song of existence, a discordant symphony of glorious hopelessness, of absolute and utter futility. The universe was born to die. It has no other purpose, and knowing this, *being* this, is truly the ultimate drug.

Then you're shrinking, even more rapidly than you grew, and with a dizzying rush and a hard jolt, as if your mind has been thrown back into a cage, the door slammed shut and locked tight, you are you again. Small, limited, and oh so empty.

You open your eyes, see the man in the too-white shirt

smiling at you, see Liza standing close by, looking even thinner now, little more than a skeleton, really, but with an expression of bliss on her skull-like face. Then her eyes, now sunk deep in their sockets, open and she lets out a despairing sob. You know just how she feels.

The man looks at her, eye holes growing wider, the darkness within them roiling. But when he speaks, his voice is not altogether without sympathy.

"Are you ready, Liza?"

You can sense she isn't. Who would be?

"Does it matter?" she says.

"Not in the slightest," the man replies. Then he opens his mouth and inhales deeply.

Liza remains standing for a moment, unaffected, but then bits of her begin to flake away like ash and drift toward the man, who's still somehow drawing air into his lungs, though they should've been filled by now. The man breathes the pieces of her into himself, only a few at first, but then more and more, faster and faster. Liza is being dismantled, pulled apart, as if she's a dying flower whose petals are falling away one by one. Her face is halfway gone when she looks at you, and the remnant of her mouth attempts to say three words. No sound emerges, but you think she says *It's worth it*, but you aren't certain, and then she bursts apart into thousands of tiny fragments which swirl and tumble as the man in the too-white shirt sucks them in. When the last piece of Liza passes between his lips, he closes his mouth and gives a contented sigh.

You don't know what he is, only that he's a terrible, awful *thing*, but still you step toward him, moving slowly on legs that are thinner than they were before, plastic crinkling beneath your feet. You reach out and grip his arms with hands that are weaker than they used to be, look into the dark holes where his pupils should be, and speak a single word in a tremulous voice.

"Again."

It's a demand as much as a plea. You'd do anything, sacrifice anything to experience the Dying All again. Absolutely anything.

"Easily done," the man says. "All you must do is leave here and come back with a friend, just as Liza did. Then you have to pay the same price. Sound fair?"

It sounds more than fair, sounds fucking *excellent*, in fact. You smile, showing your new teeth, now soft and gray, and your hands drop away from the man's arms. You turn and head for the door, already thinking about where you can go, who you can make your sales pitch to. You have no doubt you'll find someone who'll buy what you're selling. There are lots of fools like you out there. And after all, the first one's free.

VOICES LIKE BARBED WIRE

I've lived in Ash Creek most of my adult life, so when I pull into the parking lot of a fast-food restaurant that doesn't exist, I am—as you might imagine—more than a little surprised. I'm scared, too, but at the same time hopeful. Maybe I'll finally find what I've been searching for here— some small measure of peace.

I park my Prius between two vehicles that I can't identify. One is a monstrously large sedan that looks like it belongs in the 1950s, its body shimmering in the sunlight as if it's made from mother of pearl. The other vehicle has seven wheels and looks like it's been constructed from odds and ends of silvery wire soldered together. The other cars in the lot are equally strange, but I find them comforting rather than upsetting. They're an indication that I've come to the right place.

When I get out of my car and take a breath, I find the air has a chemical tang to it, as if an industrial factory is close by. There isn't one to my knowledge, but up until a few moments ago, I didn't believe there was a restaurant here, so what do I know? The asphalt of the parking lot is dry and cracked, and there are no lines painted on it to indicate parking spaces.

Vegetation grows upward from the cracks, some of it ordinary grass, but there are also weeds of a kind I can't identify. Sickly yellow-green things that are covered with thistles and which terminate in round crimson bulbs that glisten wetly. These bulbs sway slowly back and forth despite the absence of a breeze. I ran over several of these plants while driving into the lot, and I flattened them, the bulbs bursting open like tumors, squirting reddish-brown goo. The substance reminds me of how my daughters used to mix paints when they were little, adding more and more colors until they created a muddy brown soup.

It hits me then as it often does, so strong and unexpected that I'm unable to prepare myself.

An image of two girls sitting on a couch, one twelve, one seven. My daughters, Nancy and Lauren. Nancy's eyes are wet, but she's smiling, desperately trying to hold back her tears. Lauren is crying openly, tears streaming down her cheeks like tiny waterfalls. The girls are holding hands, fingers interlaced, gripping tightly. It's this detail that hurts my heart the most, I think.

I wish this wasn't happening! Lauren wails. *I wish this was a dream!*

Nancy's response to what her father and I have just told them is more restrained, and all the more awful for it.

That's okay, she says, lips trembling with the effort of maintaining her smile. *It's okay.*

The memory of their voices—of their shock and pain—nearly drives me to my knees. I can't breathe, and I wonder if the grief and guilt will finally kill me, and I'll fall dead in the parking lot of a place that shouldn't be real. But the memory retreats and I begin breathing once more. My heart is racing, but I don't think it's going to give out on me this time. I feel as much disappointment as relief from this knowledge.

Pandora's is the name of the restaurant, and it's spelled out in large red plastic letters on the front of the building, which —despite the oddities of the parking lot and the vehicles within it—looks pretty much like any fast-food joint. Beneath the name is a cartoonish depiction of a wooden box, the lid partway open, inside black shadows which almost seem to be swirling, like eddies of dark water.

How appetizing, I think, and although I'm still unsteady on my feet, I feel a little better. False bravado is better than none, right?

I go inside.

The weird chemical tang is stronger in here, as if the restaurant itself is producing it. My throat starts to hurt immediately and my eyes sting. I try not to think about what that odor is or what it might be doing to my body. At first glance, the interior looks the same as any other fast-food place: tiled floor, counter staffed by dull-eyed uniformed workers, menu above them displaying options and prices, along with photos of what's meant to be tempting food selections. Sandwiches, fries, and shakes, but not the normal offerings. The sandwich meat is greenish and covered with what looks like scales, and the seeds on the bun aren't seeds at all, but rather tiny eyes. The fries look more like small sections of bone sprinkled with salt, and the shake cups are filled with a purple-gray substance that looks like something that's been squeezed out of an infected wound. My stomach lurches, and I almost turn around and get the hell out of there, but the girls' voices come to me again.

I wish this wasn't happening! I wish this was a dream!

That's okay. It's okay.

I take a deep breath through my mouth so I don't have to smell the chemical stink, and then I approach the counter. The woman at the register is in her twenties, bald with a tattoo of a large purple eye on her forehead. Her left eye remains closed while her right blinks rapidly and continuously. Her short-sleeved uniform is blue, and she wears a square brown hat shaped like a wooden box. Her nametag reads OND. When she speaks, her voice is bright and chipper, but she doesn't smile.

"Welcome to Pandora's, where you won't believe what's in the box. Will this be cash, credit, or etheric transfer?"

I try to speak, but my throat's so raw—thanks to the chemicals in the air—that it takes me a couple tries to produce sound.

"I'm, uh, actually here to meet someone. Mr. Lim?"

Ond's right eye stops fluttering, just for a couple seconds, before starting back up again. She doesn't answer with words but instead raises her arm and points toward the dining area. Her hands are twisted and lumpy, as if she suffers from severe arthritis, but her face doesn't change expression as she points.

I turn my head to look where she's pointing, and I see a dozen people scattered around the dining area, some sitting alone, some with companions. They all look like the sort of people that would drive the strange vehicles outside, but only one captures my full attention. An older man sitting alone and eating a sandwich, a pile of fast-food sandwich wrappers on the table before him.

Mr. Lim, I presume.

I thank Ond, who gives no indication that she hears me—or maybe she simply doesn't care—and I walk over to Mr. Lim's table. The man's body odor hits me when I'm within five feet of him, a feral smell, like the scent of big cats in a zoo enclosure. His stink leavens the chemical odor and actually comes as something of a relief. He's a thin man in his fifties—about a decade older than me—and he's wearing an army jacket, jeans, and sneakers. His clothes are worn, colors faded, but overall clean enough. He's several days overdue for a shave, and his bristles are as white as the tangled thatch of hair on his head. There's a TV screen hanging from a ceiling mount. The sound is muted, but instead of news, it's playing a series of black-and-white images that look like clips from snuff films. Mr. Lim keeps his gaze focused on the screen as he eats. Although *eating* is too nice a word for what he's doing. He's *devouring* his sandwiches, tearing into them with the speed and ferocity of a starving dog. He has three other sandwiches waiting for him on the table, all wrapped in yellow paper. I do a quick count of the crumpled wrappers piled in front of him, and I get ten. Assuming he hasn't been sitting here all day and pacing himself, he's evidently ordered fourteen of Pandora's sandwiches for his meal, and while he's eaten the majority of them, it appears his appetite is nowhere near satisfied. I wonder if he's eating the sandwiches with the green-scaled patties, but I decide I don't want to know.

He doesn't look away from the TV to acknowledge my presence, so I stand there, unsure what to do. On the screen, a naked middle-aged man holding an electric drill approaches an equally naked teenage girl duct-taped to a wooden chair. The terror in her eyes is so strong it's almost a living thing in and of itself, and I cast my gaze downward, unable to bear witness to what happens next. I try to tell myself that it's not real, just some slasher flick, but I know better.

I almost leave then, but I hear my daughters' voices once more—maybe because the woman in the video is so young— and my gut cramps with pain. As bizarre and frightening as this place is, it's nothing compared to what that memory does to me and I stay right where I am.

"Sit down," Mr. Lim says through a mouthful of food. He still doesn't look at me.

I hesitate for a moment, then I sit down opposite him, my back to the TV. He continues eating, one sandwich after the other, until he's finished. It doesn't take long. When he's done, he wipes a bit of ketchup from the corner of his mouth and licks it off his fingers. At least, I hope it's ketchup. He lowers his gaze to mine then, and I see he has the most beautiful pair of sky-blue eyes that I've ever seen. The eyes of an angel.

I'm about to introduce myself when he asks, "Who referred you?"

His voice sounds normal, but my ears hurt when he speaks, as if his vocal cords transmit an ultrasonic signal that I can't consciously detect. I find my voice faster than I did with Ond.

"Marsha McLean. A friend from high school. She said you helped her and could help me."

"Said?"

"Uh, yeah. I posted about my problem on social media—just venting, you know?—and she sent me a private message about what you did for her and how I could find you."

Marsha gave me Pandora's address, but no result came up when I entered it into my GPS app on my phone. I figured it was just a glitch of some kind, and I set out searching for the restaurant. I drove up and down the street five times before I finally found it. A gas station was on this corner the first four times I drove by, but on the fifth, Pandora's sat where the station had been.

Mr. Lim raises and lowers his chin, as if to indicate my answer is satisfactory.

"I remember her."

He turns halfway in his chair and waves to get Ond's attention. She looks at him blankly, then she nods and shuffles toward the kitchen. He then turns back to me.

"What's your problem?"

I tell him about the memory that plagues me, the night Jacob and I told our girls that we were divorcing.

"I'm their mother. I'm supposed to protect them from hurt, not be the cause of it."

When I finish, I feel exposed, as if I've revealed too much.

But I have to tell him my story, don't I? How can he help me otherwise?

Marsha's problem was similar to mine. She lost her husband to cancer, and she was holding his hand in the hospital room when he died. She didn't regret being there for him, but every night she dreamed of that last moment with him. When it became too much for her to bear any longer, she told a friend, and this friend told her about a man she'd heard of who could solve any problem. A man named Mr. Lim. It took Marsha some time to track him down, but she did, and when she finally met him in person, he was indeed able to help her. Somehow, he removed the memory of her husband's death from her mind, and she's slept fine ever since. I pray he can do the same for me.

"What do you want me to do?" Mr. Lim asks.

"You took away a painful memory from my friend. I'd like you to do the same for me."

He looks at me for a moment with those unearthly blue eyes, and then says, "I can do that."

The relief that fills me is so overwhelming that it's all I can do not to burst into tears.

"But I'll need you to get something for me first."

Before I can ask what it is, Ond approaches the table carrying a tray of fresh sandwiches wrapped in yellow paper. Fourteen of them. Despite her arthritic-looking hands, she carries the tray without difficulty and sets it in front of Mr. Lim. Without looking at either of us or speaking a word, before she turns and shuffles back toward the counter. Given the way he was eating before, I expect Mr. Lim to tear the paper off one of the sandwiches and cram it into his mouth. But instead he calmly tells me what he wants me to do.

When he's finished, he asks if I understand. I don't really, but I'll do whatever it takes to be free of the voices.

Satisfied, he picks up one of the sandwiches, unwraps it

slowly, almost lovingly, and then falls upon it with an animalistic snarl.

***

As I wrote earlier, I've lived in Ash Creek for a long time, but I grew up on a farm outside a small town called Waldron. It wasn't a very successful farm. My dad inherited it from his father, but his heart wasn't in it. He didn't like the work and had no head for business. He grew soybeans mostly, and he didn't do a good job of it. By the time I was married and Nancy was born, he'd sold the farm, moved with my mother to a smaller house in town, and started doing odd jobs as a handyman.

One summer when I was six, I was playing in a field that Dad never planted nor maintained. I was running through the field, laughing as I chased butterflies, when my foot snagged on something. Fiery pain shot through my ankle, and I cried out as whatever had hold of me drew taught, sending me falling to the ground face first. I put out my hands to break my fall, and the impact hurt my wrists, but that pain was nothing compared to the agony in my ankle. Crying, teeth, gritted, I rolled onto my back and sat up. I bent over to examine my foot and saw my sock and shoe were both covered in blood. There was so much of it, and it was so *red*, that the sight of it almost made me pass out. I sat there whimpering for several moments until I worked up enough courage to examine my wound more closely.

Rusty barbed wire was wrapped tight around my ankle, the points caught so deep in my flesh that I imagine they touched the bone. I had no idea where the wire had come from, but later Dad told me there used to be a fence around that field when he was a kid, and the length of wire that caught me must've been left over from that time, lying in the field all those years like the world's most patient serpent, waiting for someone to come along so it could strike.

I needed stitches and a tetanus shot, of course, and I walked with a crutch for a couple weeks while the wound healed. Luckily, no tendons were damaged, as least not badly, and I was back to running again before summer's end. But not in that field. Never again.

The pain of that rusty wire biting through my skin and muscle down to the bone was the worst I'd ever experienced in my life—including labor with both of my girls. Until the night Jacob and I gave them the news we'd both hoped never to have to tell them. Until I saw their faces. Until I heard their voices.

It's worse in my dreams. There the memory plays and replays with vivid colors and crisp sound, like an expensive Hollywood production. I don't sleep much. Hell, who am I trying to fool? I hardly sleep at all. You'd think that the memory, painful as it is, would've faded over the years, especially since the girls are grown and in college, Lauren at Northern Kentucky University for her undergrad, Nancy at Wichita State for her graduate degree. But the memory has only become sharper with the passage of time. My brother once told me that's because I have a sick need to punish myself. Maybe so but knowing that doesn't make the memory go away.

I'm careful about what I watch on TV. Commercials are the worst. You never know when kids will be in one. And I'm cautious about the movies I see in theaters. I only go to shows that start after 9 pm in the hope I won't run into any parents taking their little ones to see the latest animated extravaganza. But for all my precautions, I still hear my girls' voices throughout the day, so many times that I no longer bother counting.

I'm back at Pandora's less than an hour later. I'm carrying a white cardboard box with the logo for Pets and More printed on the side. Mr. Lim is finishing the last of what I assume to be another set of fourteen sandwiches. The mound of crumpled wrappers on the table is so large now that there isn't room for them all, and several have fallen to the floor. I wait for him to finish his sandwich—I know it won't take long—but I don't look up at the TV. I don't what to see what it's showing. As before, Mr. Lim pays no attention to me until he's finished. He then glances over at me, then his gaze flicks to the box and he grins. His teeth are overlarge and so white they gleam. He sweeps the wrappers off the table to make room, and I gently set the box down before him. My heart pounds, and my stomach roils with nausea.

Mr. Lim leans over the box, closes his eyes, and inhales deeply, as if he's drawing in the scent of a fine wine. He reaches out with trembling hands and opens the box. His lips are moist and I realize he's drooling. He peers inside, then he turns and give me an angry glare.

"I don't eat anything that's still alive," he says, voice dripping with disgust. "I'm not a *savage*." He picks up the box and shoves it toward me. I don't want to take it, but Mr. Lim releases the box, and if I don't grab hold of it, the box and its contents will fall to the floor. So I catch it, and there's a panicked scuttling from inside.

I look down at the rabbit, a black-and-white fluffball that looks back up at me with frightened eyes.

"I... You can't..."

"What I *can* do is give you the relief you desire," he says. "But I don't work for free."

I don't look at Mr. Lim. Instead, I continue looking at the bunny. After the divorce, Nancy and Lauren begged me to get them a pet, but back then I lived in a small two-bedroom apartment, and I didn't want to deal with looking after an animal on the days the girls were with their father. And by the time I found myself a new house, the girls were older and had stopped talking about pets. So they never had any growing up. One more regret to add to my list.

I wish this wasn't happening! I wish this was a dream!

That's okay. It's okay.

I take hold of the rabbit by the scruff of its neck and pull it out of the box. I let the box fall to the floor, put one hand around the rabbit's neck, the other hand on its head, and I quickly turn them in opposite directions. There's a snapping sound, and the rabbit spasms once and then falls still. I toss the dead creature onto the table, and Mr. Lim gazes at it for a moment, gorgeous blue eyes shining. Then he snatches it up and brings it to his mouth. It takes him longer to finish it off than it does a Pandora's sandwich, but that's because he has the fur, bones, and internal organs to deal with, too—all of which he eats. When he's done, his army jacket is splattered with crimson, and the lower half of his face is a red smear. As he starts to lick blood from his fingers, I say, "Now will you do it?"

Between finger-licks, he glances at me and says, "It's already done."

I don't feel any different, and doubt must show on my face, for Mr. Lim sighs and says, "Why did you come to me?"

"So you could remove one of my bad memories. The worst one."

"And which one is that?"

I open my mouth to reply, but then I realize I have no idea.

I remember everything about my interactions with Mr. Lim from the moment I first stepped into Pandora's, but I can't recall which memory I wanted him to take from me.

I smile in wonderment.

"I can't believe it! It's *gone!* Thank you, thank you *so—*"

He waves away my thanks. Ond approaches with a tray of fresh sandwiches, and Mr. Lim turns his attention to whatever new atrocities are playing out on the TV screen. I take this as my cue to go, only too happy to take my leave of Mr. Lim and this strange place.

As I push open the entrance door, a mother and her two young daughters enter. The faces of all three are mottled, the flesh swollen and gently pulsating. I try not to stare as they pass me, then I continue outside and walk toward my Prius. I don't hear any voices in my head, and I don't know if I should be relieved by that.

<hr>

I'M A PHLEBOTOMIST, and I took the day off work so I could meet with Mr. Lim. It's still early enough that I could go to the hospital and put in a few hours, but I feel so good, so much *lighter*, that I decide to take the rest of the day to celebrate. I don't know exactly what burden Mr. Lim relieved me of, but given that I'm so happy I'm almost giddy, I know it has to be a huge one, and no longer being tormented by memory like that is definitely worth celebrating. I feel so great that I don't question how Mr. Lim performed this miracle or even what he is precisely, or where exactly Pandora's is in relation to what I've always thought of as the real world. In truth, I don't really care about those details, and I suspect that if I had answers to my questions, I wouldn't like them.

I'm debating whether to get a relaxing massage at my gym or a strong margarita at my favorite Mexican restaurant when my phone starts buzzing. I left my purse on the floor of my passenger seat both times I went into Pandora's, but I moved it back onto the passenger seat before I left the parking lot. I reach inside, remove the phone and accept the call without looking to see who it is. Like most people, I usually screen my calls to avoid salespeople or political polltakers, but right now I'm too happy to care who it is.

"Hello?"

"Hi, Mom!"

I frown. "Who is this?"

Silence on the other end for several seconds.

"Mom, it's *me. Nancy.*"

I'm not sure why this woman is calling me *Mom*, but I search my memory, trying to recall if I know a Nancy. There's a nurse named Nancy that I've worked with a few times when I've been on nights, but this isn't her. She's in her late sixties, and this woman is young, in her twenties, maybe. Besides, why would that Nancy call me *Mom*?"

"Sorry, you must have the wrong number." I pull the phone away from my ear, intending to disconnect, but before I can the woman—Nancy—speaks hurriedly.

"Is this some kind of joke, Mom? Please tell me it is, because if it's not, you're scaring me."

I should disconnect anyway. If there's anyone joking here, it's her. But I don't. Instead I put the phone back to my ear.

"I'm sorry but not only don't I know a Nancy, I don't recognize your voice."

The pause is longer this time, and I think *she's* ended the call, but then she says, "Do you remember the hospital where you work?"

I'm not sure what disturbs me more: that she knows where I work or the forced calm in her voice, which does a poor job of masking the fear underneath.

"Yes."

"Go there. Right now. Tell them you're having trouble remembering things. I'll book a flight and be in Ohio as soon as I can. I'll call Laura and—" She breaks off. "Do you remember Laura?"

My silence is answer enough.

"I'll call her, and I'm sure she'll come, too. She's close enough to drive, and she'll get there first. Don't worry, Mom. You're going to be okay. Everything's going to be okay. I love you."

She sounds on the verge of tears as she disconnects. I hold the phone to my ear a moment longer before returning it to my purse. This incident is as strange as anything I experienced in Pandora's, and while I have no idea who Nancy or Lauren are, there was something about Nancy's parting words, something about the way she repeated *okay* that chilled me. Whoever these girls are, they must be part of the memory Mr. Lim removed from my mind. I wanted that memory gone, *needed* it desperately. My continuing sanity depended on it. So maybe I shouldn't think about this too closely, shouldn't try to recover that which I worked so hard to be free of.

To hell with the massage and the margarita, and to hell with the hospital. I needed to go home. *Now.*

I pressed down on the gas and prayed I wouldn't catch the attention of any cops on the way.

A COUPLE HOURS LATER, I'm sitting in Pandora's parking lot again. It isn't as full as it was earlier, but the vehicles here now are just as weird as the ones before. I was afraid that I wouldn't be able to find the restaurant again, that once my wish was granted, the place would go back to wherever it came from, never to return. But I found it again, and on the first try. I've been sitting here for five minutes, gripping the steering wheel and looking straight ahead. Once I got home, I checked my phone and found contacts for both a Nancy and a Lauren. No last names, though. I checked my text messages and found conversations with both women. The latest exchanges were about their upcoming Spring breaks. Their schools didn't do their Spring breaks during the same week. Lauren's was first, and Nancy's was the week after. The three of us wanted to take a cruise, but we were having trouble figuring out the logistics of the trip.

I have no memory of these texts.

There are saved voicemails from both girls, too. I didn't recognize either of their voices. There are pictures on my phone, most of which are of one or two young women who I assume are Nancy and Lauren. I'm in some of those pictures, but I have no memory of them being taken. I checked my social media accounts and found more pictures of them, along with their comments on my posts. I checked out their profiles, went through their pictures, saw bits and pieces of two lives I know nothing about. I saw both girls are connected to Jacob on social media, and they share his last name—Haynes. That was my last name, too. I didn't change it after the divorce. It seemed like too much of a hassle, and Jacob and I don't have hard feelings toward each other, Well, not *too* many. I haven't spoken with him in years, not since he remarried, but I'm tempted to call him now and ask him about Nancy and Lauren, if they really are who I fear they are. I have others I could call, too. My own mother. My brother. But there's no point. I understand what happened—if not exactly why—and I know what I need to do.

I get out of my car and head into the restaurant once more.

OND IS STILL STANDING behind the counter, and the place still smells like a chemical factory. The dining area isn't as full as it was earlier, but the people that are here are strange, just like—

Mr. Lim is sitting at the same table, a new mound of crumpled wrappers in front of him and scattered piles of them on the floor around his feet. He has only one sandwich left, but he seems to be in no hurry to eat it. Maybe he's finally full? He holds onto the sandwich with both hands, almost as if cradling it. His jacket is still stained with rabbit blood, thick and wet. He's watching a woman use a butcher knife cut off a man's balls on the TV. I'm so relieved he's here. I was afraid he might have left while I was gone. I then wonder if he ever leaves, or if he's always sitting here, devouring one sandwich after another, watching an endless parade of televised murder and mutilation, doing favors for people willing to pay his price.

I head over to the table on the edge of panic. I don't have any memories of Nancy and Lauren, but now I believe I *should* have, and I'm horrified at what I must have lost, what I must have willingly given up. I don't know what I was thinking, and I don't care. I just want my memories back. But before I can speak, Mr. Lim turns to me with a smile that's almost but not quite mocking.

"No one realizes that when you remove *one* memory, all the others associated with it have to go, too. It's like a house of cards. Take one from the bottom and the entire structure collapses. You'd be surprised how many of my clients come back after they understand this, but I must say, you may have set the record for the fastest return visit."

"So you can give them back—the memories?"

"Of course, I can!" He sounds offended at first, but then he smiles again, slowly this time. Slyly. "But like I told you earlier, I don't work for free."

He unwraps the sandwich, crumples the paper, and tosses

it to the floor. He lifts the sandwich up for my inspection and removes the top bun to reveal a bloody hunk of raw meat sitting there. A very particular cut of meat.

"It's hard to find a steady supply," he says. "Especially when you have an appetite like mine."

I remember how during my first visit, when I told him Marsha had *said* something to me about him, he questioned my use of the word. Now I know why. Marsha can type just fine, but she can't *say* anything. She went through this same ritual, as I imagine most of Mr. Lim's customers do—if they want back what they so foolishly gave away.

He replaces the top bun and gobbles the sandwich down. Afterward, he wipes away a splotch of crimson from his lips which I now know for certain isn't ketchup, and then points to the counter. Ond holds a butcher knife that looks very much like the one wielded by the ball-cutter on the TV. I think of how scared Nancy sounded on the phone even though she fought so hard to sound calm. I think of Lauren, who even now is driving back to Ohio from Kentucky, worried sick that her mother had a stroke or is suffering from early-onset dementia. I'll see her soon, Nancy too, and when I do, I may not be able to say I love you, but I will hug them, hug them *hard*. I think they'll get the message. Most importantly, I'll remember them. Remember everything, good times and bad.

I walk to the counter and stick out my tongue. Ond takes hold of the tip between a thumb and forefinger and pulls it taut. Then, without any change in her expression, she raises the knife and cuts. It hurts worse than the barbed wire around my ankle, but still not as bad as—

I hear my girls' voices again, and as Ond heads back to the kitchen with her grisly prize, I smile with my empty mouth, blood pouring over my chin and splattering onto the counter with a sound sweet as music.

IN THE END THERE IS A DRAIN

"Daddy, why did he go?"

Dwayne glanced up at his daughter's reflection in the rearview mirror. Hannah was strapped into a forward-facing car seat, swinging her legs, the backs of her heels thud-thud-thudding onto the seat. It was dark out—the sun set early this time of year—but enough light filtered into the Prius from the streetlights outside to enable him to make out Hannah's face. She was tilting her head back and forth, as if she was matching the rhythm of her feet, which sounded loud as a jack hammer to him. He already had the beginnings of a headache after watching an animated movie about talking flamingos with Hannah and several hundred other children of various ages, all of whom couldn't keep quiet throughout the film. It had been the longest ninety minutes of his life. It hadn't helped that the damn thing had been in 3-D. He always got headaches from 3-D.

He wasn't sure what she was asking.

"Do you mean why did Fernando fly away at the end of the movie?"

"Yeah."

"He finished helping that family of flamingos, and he left to find someone else who needed his help."

At least that's what he *thought* had happened at the end. But at that point, his head had been pounding so hard that he could barely think. His headache had lessened somewhat since they'd left the theater, but it still bothered him. He wanted to tell Hannah to quit kicking the back seat, but he didn't want her to feel as if she was doing something bad. *Go, Go Flamingo!* had been the first movie she'd seen in a theater—her first *big girl* movie—and he didn't want to say anything that might tarnish the experience for her.

"He should have stayed," she said. "It was sad."

Dwayne wasn't sure what, if anything, to say to that. The ending *had* been sad, at least to a four-year-old, and it was okay for Hannah to recognize that. Healthy, even. Part of him wanted to protect his child from experiencing anything negative, including uncomfortable emotions. But parents had a duty to prepare their child to live in the world the way it was, not at they wished it would be. Maybe he should provide some context for—

"Daddy!"

Hannah's cry of alarm shocked Dwayne out of his thoughts. He looked in the rearview and saw that she was pointing forward, eyes wide, mouth open in horror. He looked out the windshield in time to see the cat. It sat in the road, legs tucked underneath its body. It was a calico, small and delicate, probably no more than a year old. It turned its head to look at the Prius as it came, headlights starkly illuminating the animal. The cat didn't move, didn't so much as twitch as whisker. It seemed completely relaxed and calm, and it watched placidly as four-wheeled death bore down upon it.

Dwayne had two simultaneous reactions. The first was confusion. What the hell was a cat doing sitting in the road like this, and why wasn't it hauling ass to get out of the way? There had to be something wrong with the animal. His second reaction was to a feel a profoundly disturbing sense of recognition, as if he had seen this cat before. Not merely another calico but this exact same one, although he had no idea where he knew it from. He only knew that the feeling of recognition made his stomach churn with nausea, and his head began pounding harder, to the point where he started seeing flashes of color in his vision.

He checked the left lane for oncoming traffic and saw a pickup coming toward them. If he swerved to try and miss the cat, there was an excellent chance they'd get into an accident, and he couldn't risk that. He remembered something his father had told him when he'd been learning to drive. *If it comes down to your life or an animal's when you're on the road, you choose yours. Every time.*

Dwayne took his foot off the gas, ready to press the brake. He couldn't jam the pedal all the way down. If he did, their car could swerve, and they might hit the pickup. But if he could manage to slow down a little, give the cat a few extra seconds to get out of the way… But Dwayne had run out of time, and more to the point, so had the cat. Dwayne felt the impact through the steering wheel as well as the floor. He was surprised that hitting such a small, frail-looking animal felt like slamming into a bowling ball. Adrenaline jolted through his system. His headache diminished and his nausea vanished —at least for now—and he looked at Hannah in the rearview. Tears streamed down her cheeks, and her hands were balled into small fists, as if she wanted to strike out at something but there was nothing close enough to hit.

Dwayne's foot remained off the accelerator, and the Prius began to slow. *Too late now,* he thought. He wasn't sure what to do next. He thought he should find a safe place to pull over and go back to see if the cat was still alive—although its survival seemed doubtful given how hard they'd hit the poor thing. But what if it *was* still alive, hurt and suffering? Although if it was, he wasn't sure what he could do about it. He supposed he could get the tire iron out of his trunk and use it to put the cat out of its misery, but he didn't know if he could go through with it. Hannah wouldn't see him do it. She wouldn't be able to turn around in her car seat and look out the back window, but she was smart and would probably guess what he did. He didn't want to traumatize her further. His primary responsibility—his *only* responsibility—was to his daughter. What had happened to the cat was a shame, but it couldn't have been avoided. Something had to have been wrong with the animal to make it act so strangely. Maybe it had been sick or had already been injured. Whatever the case, there was no way in hell the cat would live much longer, assuming it wasn't already dead.

Get Hannah home, he thought. *It's all that matters now.*

Yes. Get her home, try to calm her down, and help her process the horrible thing that had happened.

That decided, he pressed down on the accelerator again, and the car began to pick up speed. Hannah whimpered softly in the back seat.

"It's okay, sweetie," Dwayne said as he continued to drive. "It's okay."

DWAYNE WAS TWELVE. His family lived only a few blocks from the middle school he attended, so instead of riding the bus, he walked. It sucked when the weather was bad—when it was pissing down rain or it was freezing out—but overall, he liked it. He enjoyed having some quiet time to himself in the morning and afternoon.

There was only one problem with walking: passing the Cat

Lady's house. Cat Lady wasn't her real name, of course, but that's what all the kids in the neighborhood called her. Most of the adults, too. According to his mom, the woman's real name was Mrs. Figueroa. Dwayne didn't have anything against her personally, but her property was a *mess*. The yard was overgrown with long grass and thick weeds, and her small one-story house was falling apart. Shutters hung at awkward angles, flanking grime-streaked windows of cracked glass. The siding was a pale yellow, and the color reminded Dwayne of diseased mucus. The roof sagged in several spots, and there were a number of shingles missing. As her neighborhood nickname implied, she had cats. *Lots* of cats, and she kept her windows open just far enough so the animals could come and go as they pleased. You could always see a half dozen cats, maybe more, prowling through the miniature suburban jungle that was Mrs. Figueroa's yard, and even if you couldn't see them, you knew they were there. You could hear grass rustling, the sound punctuated by the occasional meow. Every time Dwayne passed by—even when he made sure to walk on the other side of the street—he had the feeling that dozens of small inhuman eyes were watching him. But that wasn't the worst part. No, the worst part was the *smell*. The air was heavy with the harsh tang of ammonia—which he supposed came from cat pee—but beneath that was another scent, a thick greasy odor like rotting meat, along with a curdled sourness that reminded him of spoiled milk. The stink was so strong that even across the street, Dwayne would hold his breath as he hurried past, wondering—as he did every day—if it was possible for a person to be stanked to death. If Mrs. Figueroa's house hadn't been located on the most direct route to Dwayne's school, he might've chosen a different path. But he was twelve-going-on-thirteen, and he was too old to walk farther than he had to because some crazy old woman lived like a pig.

But one morning in early March—chilly but not too cold —a two-man construction crew was tearing up the sidewalk opposite Mrs. Figueroa's house. The sidewalks were old around here, the concrete chipped and broken, and evidently the city had finally decided it was time to replace them. Unfortunately, this meant Dwayne had to use the sidewalk in front of Mrs. Figueroa's house.

The odor of decay was so strong around her property that Dwayne felt like he was walking through a semisolid wall of stink. His exposed skin started itching, as if the foul air were eating away at the surface of his flesh. He told himself he was imagining the sensation and began walking faster.

He heard a rustling in the grass close by, and he jumped backward when something small and furry dashed across the sidewalk in front of him. As the cat—a calico—reached the middle of the street, a car—driven no doubt by a parent in a hurry to get his or her kid to school then head off the work— struck the animal. There was a *thump*, a high-pitched yowl, and the car passed over the cat and kept going.

The cat lay on its side, a thin coil of intestine protruding from its burst belly. Its head was twisted at a sickening angle, and Dwayne knew its neck had been broken. He hoped the animal had died instantly, but that hope was shattered when he heard the animal meowing pitifully.

The traffic didn't let up. Cars continued zipping by, all of them swerving to avoid inflicting any further injury on the cat, but none stopped or even slowed. The two men working on the other side of the street had witnessed the accident, but it hadn't seemed to faze them, and they continued to work. The next driver that attempted to swerve didn't do so in time, and the two wheels on the passenger side rolled over the cat, first the front tire, then the rear. The cat didn't yowl this time, but more guts were squeezed out of the animal's stomach, along with a significant amount of thick gray fluid. Dwayne had no idea what the stuff was, but it was *gross*.

At first, Dwayne had been numb with horror at what he'd seen, but now he felt a strange calm settle on him. Without making a conscious decision to do so, he dashed out into the street.

He ran to the calico cat, bent down, and picked it up. He carried the animal back to the sidewalk, the exposed organs dangling from its body cavity and dripping that weird gray muck onto the ground. The cat's injuries were fresh, but they were far from the only things wrong with it. There were bald patches on its body, and the exposed skin was riven with fissures through which more of that thick gray substance oozed. The smell was awful, a stomach-churning stench of rot that seemed to coat his nasal passages with a greasy film. Worse than that, though, the cat didn't *feel* right. It felt squishy in his hands, like it was only a flesh bag filled with that sickening gray muck.

Revulsion gripped him, and he wanted to hurl the cat into Mrs. Figueroa's yard, but he resisted the impulse. The cat had already suffered enough indignities, and no matter how disgusting the animal's corpse was, he didn't want to subject it to one more. So when he reached the sidewalk, he knelt and gently placed the cat in the yard.

Some of the gray gunk had gotten on his hands, and the areas where it coated his flesh felt hot and tingly. He would've wiped his hands on the grass, but he couldn't bring himself to touch the vegetation growing in Mrs. Figueroa's yard. Instead, he wiped his hands on the sidewalk to get off the majority of the stuff, and then he stood and wiped the remaining residue on his pants.

"I saw what you did."

He wanted to run, but a hand fell on his shoulder and bony

fingers tightened, holding him in place. He held his breath, too afraid to speak.

"Her name was Nala. She was one of my favorites."

The woman's voice came from close to his right ear. Her breath was cold on his skin and smelled of the gray gunk that had oozed from Nala.

"You feel guilty for what happened, don't you?" A deep inhalation, a slow release. "I can smell it on you. But you should rejoice. Your actions have hastened Nala's union with the Magna Mater."

She turned him around to face her.

He had never seen Mrs. Figueroa before, didn't know anyone who ever had. Her face was lined with deep wrinkles which reminded Dwayne of the fissures in Nala's skin. Her nose was crooked, as if it had been broken sometime in the past, and her lips were so thin they were almost nonexistent. Her teeth were crooked, but they were a startling white—*like bone,* he thought. Her gray hair was a wild, unkempt mop, and her eyes were large and filled with a shining intensity.

"Have you heard of the Magna Mater?" she asked.

Dwayne managed to shake his head.

"It's Latin. It means Great Mother."

He heard rustling in the grass, coming from numerous directions. Small forms slunk between the weeds as a dozen cats—maybe more—approached.

"She's inside us," Mrs. Figueroa said. "She's part of us from the moment we're conceived, and she remains with us until we're nothing but old bones and dust. She speaks to us constantly, but most don't hear her. Some of us do, though, and we *listen.*"

Cats emerged from the grass, padded onto the sidewalk and gathered around them. There were more than a dozen— *way* more—and they filled the sidewalk for ten feet in both directions, and their numbers spilled onto the street. All the cats had bald patches like Nala's, and gray gunk oozed from fissures in their skin. They were eerily silent as they watched Dwayne with their inhuman eyes.

"Cats know," Mrs. Figueroa said. "They *listen*. You ever want to see the truth—the *real* truth—look into a cat's eyes."

"I have to get to school," Dwayne said, and then added a plaintive *"Please."*

Mrs. Figueroa gave no indication that she was aware he'd spoken.

"Most people do everything they can to postpone the Mother's embrace, but by doing so, they only prolong their own suffering. But to those who understand, she grants the mercy of the Benefaction."

She removed her right hand from his shoulder, reached toward her face, and touched her bent, swollen-knuckled index finger to her left cheek. She pushed, and the finger slid through one of the lines in her flesh, disappearing all the way to the knuckle. She rooted around for a moment, and when she withdrew her finger, Dwayne saw it was coated with gray slime. She extended the finger toward his face, as if she wanted him to examine it. The stink was so fierce that he thought he might vomit.

"The Benefaction helps us grow closer to the Mother. We honor her by becoming one with her blessed decay." The woman's eyes gleamed with madness, and gray muck oozed from the spot on her cheek where she'd inserted her finger.

Dwayne was on the verge of panic now. He looked toward the men working on the other side of the street. Maybe if he could get their attention, they would realize something bad was happening to him, and they'd come over to help him. But the men were no longer there. It was too early for lunch. Had they gone on a coffee break? Had they seen Mrs. Figueroa leave her house and been so creeped out by her that they'd decided to leave? Or had they been helping her? Had they set up a fake work site to purposely divert him to this side of the street so she could finally get her hands on him? Had they heard the Mother, too?

The cats began making *mmmrrrr* sounds deep in their throats.

"It's a lot to take in all at once, I know," Mrs. Figueroa said. "But when you taste the Benefaction, you'll understand."

She smiled and moved her finger toward his mouth.

The thought of the old woman sliding her muck-covered finger past his lips and depositing the gray sludge onto his tongue was more than he could bear. Sheer animal panic took hold of him, and he yanked free from her grip with such force that he stumbled backward and fell on his ass. Cats scattered when he fell, darting off in all directions. Pain erupted in his tailbone and shot up his spine, but he barely noticed it. He crab-walked backward several feet to gain distance from the woman, then he sprang to his feet, turned, and ran like hell, Mrs. Figueroa's laughter following behind him.

HE TOOK a different route home that afternoon. It took ten minutes longer, but it was worth it. His mom was there, and he told her about his bizarre encounter with Mrs. Figueroa. She didn't quite understand all the details, but she understood that the woman was crazy. That night, she told her husband what had happened to Dwayne, and he called the police to report the incident. Social services quickly became involved, and Mrs. Figueroa was declared incapable of caring for herself. A judge ordered her to be taken to a hospital for a mental evaluation, but before she could be removed from her home, she sealed her head in several layers of plastic wrap and suffocated herself.

One night, he overheard his parents taking about her death.

They say she had a smile on her face, his mom said.

Dwayne had no trouble believing it.

AFTER DWAYNE'S encounter with Mrs. Figueroa, his mother started driving him to school so he wouldn't have to walk past the woman's property, but one morning she had an early dentist appointment and couldn't take him.

"I don't want you going past That Place," his mother said. That's what she called Mrs. Figueroa's now. *That Place.* "Take a different route, okay?"

He promised he would, but it was a lie. After what had happened to him there, how could he resist revisiting it?

When he arrived, Dwayne couldn't believe how drastically the place had changed. The lot was empty, like Mrs. Figueroa had never existed at all. But despite the town's best efforts to clean up the property, the air still smelled like ammonia and rotting meat.

The town had brought in a bulldozer to level her house, and no sign of it remained—even the foundation was covered. The earth had been turned over, like a farmer's field prepared for planting. Dwayne doubted anything would ever grow again in this diseased soil, not even weeds. The bulldozer had left behind rocks and chunks of broken roots, along with scattered bits of broken bones, remnants of the cats Mrs. Figueroa had buried over the years, he assumed. He wondered what had happened to her living cats. Some—maybe most—had run away, but the ones who hadn't? He supposed animal control officers took them somewhere, probably to be euthanized.

Gazing upon the empty lot, Dwayne felt guilty. Mrs. Figueroa might have been looney—and sick with some kind of weird disease that made gray muck ooze out of you—but she hadn't deserved what happened to her. And it wouldn't have happened if he'd kept his mouth shut. His mother told him that it had only been a matter of time before something like this occurred. *Better now, before she hurt anyone,* she'd said. *She hurt herself,* Dwayne had replied. His mother hadn't been able to respond to that.

He stayed on the sidewalk, reluctant to set foot onto the contaminated ground. Sure, he was wearing sneakers with rubber soles, but he didn't want to take any chances. He was several yards from where Nala's corpse had disappeared, and while he didn't want to examine the location any closer, he started walking toward it anyway. Why, he wasn't sure. Morbid curiosity? Or was something else drawing him forward, something even darker? When he reached the section of sidewalk in front of where he'd put Nala, he stopped. The ground here looked the same as in the rest of the lot, and he figured Nala's body had either been removed by workers or had been buried even deeper by the bulldozer. Whichever the case, he was relieved not to see it, and he was about to continue on his way when he noticed what looked like a tuft of black fur poking out from the dirt. There was a broken branch lying in the gutter nearby—another leftover from the lot cleanup, he guessed—and he picked it up. It was only a foot long and thin, but he thought it would do the job. He returned to where Nala was buried and began using the stick to excavate the cat's corpse. The soil was loose, which made the task easier, and after only a few minutes, he'd managed to expose most of Nala's head.

The animal's mouth was partway open, and a small greenish-gray tongue lolled from the side. Needle-sharp teeth were visible, and like Mrs. Figueroa's, they were a startling bone-white. The worst part was that Nala's eyes were open wide, and lines of crusty muck trailed from them, as if the animal had been trying to expel the Benefaction from its body as it died. Flecks of dirt stuck to the eyeballs' surface, but despite how disgusting the eyes were—or maybe because of it—he couldn't look away. He remembered what Mrs. Figueroa had said.

You ever want to see the truth—the real *truth—look into a cat's eyes.*

Mrs. Figueroa had said that the Magna Mater lived in everyone, that she was some kind of dark force that slowly ate away at everything that lived until there was nothing left. If it was true, then he—along with everyone else—carried the seeds of their own destruction from the moment they exited the womb. He'd become so obsessed by this idea that he barely ate or slept anymore, and his grades were starting to suffer. His mother and father were beginning to talk about sending him to see a child psychologist, but he knew no doctor could help him. There was only one thing that could: *knowing.*

Despite his misgivings about the soil, he stepped onto the property and faced Nala's corpse. He got down on his hands and knees and lowered his head toward Nala's, holding his breath so he wouldn't have to smell the stench of the animal's rot. He focused his gaze on both of the cat's eyes and leaned in close so he could *see.*

He remained in that position—not moving, barely breathing—for nearly three hours before a neighbor finally noticed him and called the police.

AFTER THE POLICE brought him home, he told his mom that he had no idea why he'd been staring into the eyes of a dead cat in the empty lot where Mrs. Figueroa's house had once stood. He slept the rest of that day, through the night, and well into the next afternoon. When he finally woke, he walked out of bed, staggered to the bathroom, peed, flushed, and then washed his hands. As he did, he watched the water circling around the drain before it went down, and he remembered.

In Nala's eyes, he'd seen an unfathomably vast gulf of darkness, not merely the absence of light, but a darkness that was its own thing, real and tangible, and it filled Forever. At the center of this darkness was something he wouldn't have thought possible: an object that was even darker. It was the absolute embodiment of nothingness, of emptiness. A name for it flashed through his mind then. The Big Dark. But around that emptiness light swirled, and he understood that this light was everything that ever was or would be. All existence—all space, all time, and everything and everyone within—had only one purpose: to satisfy the eternal hunger of the Big Dark. Together, the hole and the light rotating around it were called the Gyre, and the Magna Mater was one of its servants. She helped to break down reality, like a mother chewing food for her infant so that the child could digest it more easily.

That's all we are, he thought. *All we were ever meant to be. Food.*

He turned off the water and screamed until his throat bled.

IT TOOK a while to get Hannah settled, but after she was finally in bed and sleeping, Dwayne's wife wanted to have "words" with him in the kitchen. She accused him of driving recklessly, of not paying enough attention, of traumatizing their little girl due to his carelessness.

"It's your duty as a parent to protect her from things like this," Kate said.

He wanted to smile at her and say *Honey, you don't know what trauma is,* but he knew it would only make things worse, so he remained silent. Eventually, Kate's anger dissipated, although it didn't go away completely, and she went to bed, leaving Dwayne sitting in silence at the kitchen table, alone with his thoughts. Kate was right, of course. He *had* failed to protect Hannah. But that was because he hadn't prepared her to understand the true nature of reality. And if she didn't understand it, how could she face it?

He understood then what he had to do. He rose from the table, removed his car keys from the wall hook by the door to the garage, and departed.

"HANNAH? SWEETIE?"

Dwayne sat on the edge of his daughter's bed and shook her shoulder gently. She didn't wake right away. She'd had a difficult night, and her mind and body needed rest. But he persisted, shaking her a bit harder, until finally her eyes opened and she gazed at him blearily.

"Daddy?"

"I'm sorry for what happened tonight. I know it came as a shock to you. I want to make sure you never feel like that again. I want to show you something. Because once you know the truth—the worst thing that ever could be—something like hitting a cat will be no more remarkable to you than taking a breath."

He bent over to pick up the dead calico from the floor. He'd gone back to the scene of the accident to retrieve the cat.

Was the animal Nala reborn or a different animal entirely? He supposed it didn't matter. He held the cat before Hannah so she could look into its unseeing eyes, and as she did, her own eyes widened and she began to tremble.

Dwayne smiled as thick gray tears began to slide slowly down his cheeks.

CAST-OFFS

Valerie estimated it was sometime after midnight. She was sitting at the curb of her house—Number 164—wearing a thick winter coat and gloves, even though it was early May. It might technically be spring, but the nights were still pretty cold for her. But then, she was always cold, even at the height of summer.

You've got ice water in your veins instead of blood, Ian had teased her on more than one occasion. He'd meant it as a joke, of course, but she wondered if part of him wasn't serious.

The area where she sat was cluttered with junk that she and her husband had hauled from the house earlier that day. An old easy chair with a spring protruding from the back. A game table that you could play ping pong, air hockey, or pool on, which they never used. An artificial Christmas tree that had lost half its fake needles. A cheaply made hutch cupboard she'd inherited from an aunt which was on the verge of falling apart. And assorted other items, the cast-offs from nearly thirty years of marriage.

Exactly where I belong, she thought.

Her head pounded, her joints throbbed, and tendrils of

pain coiled through every part of her body. Her throat was tight, her lungs heavy. She considered using her inhaler but decided against it. It didn't matter that her breathing was weak. Not now.

Similar piles of discarded items sat at the curb in front of the other houses on the street. Some larger, some smaller, but they all had one thing in common: they were made of things no longer needed or wanted, broken or useless. Like her.

Tomorrow was Free Bulk Item Pickup Day, when the city collected unlimited refuse for no extra charge. It was like an official spring cleaning holiday, with waste collection vehicles moving up and down the streets like large hungry beasts gorging themselves on the detritus of people's lives. The city's waste collection vehicles wouldn't hit the streets until morning, but throughout the evening and into the night, people roamed the neighborhoods in vans and pickups, stopping to examine the refuse piles in hope of finding something worth salvaging. They picked through mounds of junk, sifting and searching, and when they came across something they thought worth taking—such as an old sofa, table, or chair—they loaded it onto their vehicle and drove to the next house. Ian looked down at these people, considered them freeloaders, but Valerie—while feeling a little uncomfortable at the thought of strangers going through their things—didn't share her husband's disdain. People had to do what was necessary to survive, and as far as she was concerned, it was better for items to be rehomed than wasted.

She heard her next-door neighbor's front door bang open, and she turned to see Jeanette Gibson step outside. The woman was in her sixties—not much older than Valerie—and she wore a blue robe and house slippers. She gripped the handle of a dog carrier in her right hand, and she walked across her lawn to the curb, where she'd deposited her own mound of junk to be picked up in the morning. Valerie thought the carrier was empty until Jeanette dropped it to the ground, eliciting a frightened *yip* from the animal inside.

Jeanette put her hands on her hips and glared down at the carrier.

"That's the last time you shit on my carpet, you little bastard!"

Then she turned and started back to her house. When she was halfway across her lawn, she glanced in Valerie's direction, as if only just realizing the other woman was there. Jeanette said nothing—she and Valerie barely knew each other and hardly spoke—but her mouth twisted into a cruel smile, as if she wasn't surprised to see Valerie sitting at the curb with the rest of the trash. Then she went back inside her house and shut the door with an authoritative slam. There was silence for a moment, and then Omar began to whine.

Omar was a black pug that had belonged to Jeanette's late husband, Wayne. Omar was an older dog, ten years, maybe more. He was missing his left front leg, but whether he'd been born like that or had lost it along the way, Valerie didn't know. Omar did just fine on three legs, though, even if he had to hobble-hop instead of running. *They should've named him Tripod,* Ian had once said and then laughed. Valerie hadn't thought it was funny. She'd always liked Omar, even though she and Ian had never owned any pets because of her many allergies.

She was horrified by what Jeanette had done. Omar was a sweet little thing, and for Jeanette to treat him as if he were just another piece of trash to toss out...

But then, she thought, *aren't you treating yourself the same way? Isn't that why you came out here? Because you see yourself as Unwanted?*

She rose to her feet, gritting her teeth against the fiery protests of pain in her joints. She intended to walk into Jeanette's yard, pick up Omar's carrier, and—assuming she was strong enough to carry it—take it back onto Jeanette's porch and pound on the door until the cold-hearted bitch answered, and then Valerie would go off on her for treating Omar so badly. But before she could start walking, she saw a pair of headlights as a vehicle turned onto her street. *Green* headlights, belonging to a vehicle that—as near as she could tell—made no sound.

Valerie stood and waited for whatever was coming.

EARLIER THAT NIGHT, after struggling to help Ian lug all their unwanted junk out of the house, her body was wracked with pain. She'd never been one to let her physical problems stop her from trying to live her life, such as it was, and she'd insisted on helping, even though Ian had encouraged her not to. She was, to put it mildly, a mess in the health department. She suffered from food allergies, seasonal allergies, asthma, migraines, fibromyalgia, and rheumatoid arthritis. To top it all off, her immune system sucked, and she regularly caught colds which progressed into sinus infections, bronchitis, and —if she was really unlucky—pneumonia. She and Ian never had children. The doctor said that her body wasn't strong enough for pregnancy, and besides, she didn't want to pass on her lousy genes to future generations. Better they die with her.

She'd managed to help Ian with the work, but by the time they were finished, a migraine seared her brain, her nerves were on fire, and she was so weak she could barely stand.

She went to the bedroom to take medicine and lie down in the dark, but Ian soon followed. He stepped into the room, but thankfully he didn't turn on the light.

"I'm sorry you're not feeling well, sweetheart. I shouldn't have let you help carry all that junk. I shouldn't—" He paused for a moment and then said, "I hope you feel better soon."

And then he'd left, closing the door softly behind him.

What had he been about to say? *I shouldn't have married you?* He did his best to be understanding of her physical condition, and while she was sure he got frustrated at times, he rarely showed it. She wished she was stronger and healthier, if for no other reason than so she could be more of a partner to Ian. She felt like she let him down so often, that even at her best she could only be a part-time wife.

Valerie, in pain and overwhelmed with sadness and guilt, wept.

SHE LAY awake for several hours, staring up at the darkness gathered on the ceiling. She was still awake when Ian came to bed, although she pretended to be asleep to avoid talking to him. She remained still and quiet as he slipped under the covers next to her, and within moments he was snoring softly. She envied his ability to fall asleep so easily. She was in pain most nights, and she had difficulty sleeping even when she took the powerful pain and sleep meds her doctor prescribed.

She listened to Ian snore for several moments—the familiar sound actually comforting to her—when she heard something else. A soft, breathy sound. At first, she thought it came from Ian, and she listened more closely. But it didn't sound like breathing so much as it did a gentle wind. The more she listened, the more she thought she detected a pattern to the sound, almost as if it was a voice speaking softly in a strange language. And even though she couldn't make out individual words, she still somehow understood the meaning they carried.

Bring out the Unwanted.

Just that, repeated over and over.

She listened to the voice—because that's what it was, a cold dark voice—for a time. And then she got out of bed, dressed quietly in the dark, and left the bedroom, closing the door softly behind her. She walked down to the closet in the front hallway, put on shoes, coat, hat, and gloves, and stepped outside.

AT FIRST, Valerie thought the vehicle was a car. But the pale-green headlights were too far apart and too high off the ground. Could it be one of the city's waste-collection trucks getting a *very* early start? She'd never heard of them collecting at this hour before, but with the amount of bulk trash people had put out, maybe starting six hours earlier than usual was a necessity.

There were no streetlights in this neighborhood, but most of the houses had porch lights on, and she could make out the vehicle's general shape—a roundish mound that resembled a giant snail shell—and its color, a glossy obsidian. The waste-removal vehicles she was used to were square-ish and painted green and yellow—and they made a ton of noise. This vehicle was completely silent. No rumbling engine, no hiss of pneumatic brakes, no machinery working to compact the waste its crew tossed in the back. She might've thought the vehicle was parked with the engine off, if it hadn't been for the fact that she could see it was moving down the street toward her. Slowly, to be sure, but moving.

The vehicle made its first stop four houses down, at the Claytons'. Valerie didn't know them well, just enough to wave to if they were outside when she drove by. They were an older couple, and she'd heard the husband—Arthur, she thought his name was—had Alzheimer's. The vehicle's green headlights provided enough light for her to see the silhouette of a person standing at the end of the Claytons' driveway. She couldn't tell if the figure was male or female, but she had no doubt she was looking at Arthur Clayton. After all, between him and his wife, which of them was more likely to be Unwanted?

A thought struck her then. How many more people had heard the voice and brought out whatever Unwanteds lived in their homes? Or, like her, had brought themselves out? And had the voice spoken only to people on her street, or to the entire town? Hundreds—men, woman, children, even pets like Omar—could be sitting outside in the cold and dark, waiting for whatever was coming to get them.

Doors opened on either side of the obsidian vehicle's cab, and two people got out. They were little more than shadows as they approached Arthur. One was short and stout, the other tall and thin, but those were the only details Valerie could make out. The two figures moved toward Arthur, making no more sound than their silent vehicle. In a moment, the three merged into a single large shadow, and then Valerie heard a sharp gasp, followed by a tearing sound and a thick splattering, as if someone were pouring milk onto concrete. Then came an eager slurping, and when that ended, a soft snuffling that might have been laughter.

When the snuffling ended, the short and tall shadows walked around to the rear of their vehicle. One carried something round (a head?) and the other carried something long (a body?). A moment later they returned to the vehicle's cab empty-handed, climbed back in, and closed the doors. The vehicle began sliding forward once more, but not as silently as before, Valerie heard a crunching sound, and a horrible thought came to her: those two—whoever they were —had killed Arthur and tossed his body into the back of the vehicle, where its machinery was working to compact him.

Terror welled up inside her, and she wanted to flee back

into her house. But before she could move, she heard the voice again.

Sit down. Wait.

There was extra force behind the last word, and with it a heaviness settled on her as if someone had draped several thick blankets around her shoulders. Accompanying the sensation was an emotional numbness, and Valerie found herself sitting on the curb once more. But she kept her gaze fixed on the vehicle as it approached.

The vehicle glided past the next two houses—evidently everyone was wanted in those families—and came to a stop next door, in front of the Tannreuthers' home. The Tannreuthers had a lamppost at the end of their driveway, and the light it cast gave Valerie a much clearer look at the obsidian vehicle—although *vehicle* wasn't the right word for it. In the dark and from a distance it had roughly resembled some kind of truck, at least in terms of basic shape and size. But the bulk of the object was a corrugated black shell from the bottom of which emerged six segmented legs. A bulge protruding from the front resembling a truck cab with doors, windows, and windshield, although the doors were made of the same shell-like substance as the rest of the object, and the windows—curved outward—looked more like tumorous growths than glass. She'd thought the thing was silent as it moved, but now that it was closer, she could hear a soft *tik-tik-tik* as its legs tapped against the hard surface of the street. The headlights—or what functioned as headlights—were receded into the shell, and now their greenish glow made Valerie think of the way fireflies' abdomens lit up on summer nights. The thing gave off an odor too, an oily metallic smell with an acidic tang. Once when she was a very young child, she'd been playing outside and a ladybug had landed on her tongue. The smell reminded her of the way the insect had tasted.

When the vehicle—creature—whatever-it-was came to a complete stop, the doors opened and the occupants emerged. Both the short one and the tall one wore gray coveralls, the cloth darkened by wet red stains. While the two stood upright, neither was human, or at least, not completely so. Their heads were avian—black feathers, beady eyes, sharp beaks—and their hands and feet were scaly claws. The bird-things stepped to the end of the Tannreuthers' driveway and waited, gazes fixed on the house. A moment later, the front door opened and a teenage boy stepped outside and started walking toward the creatures.

Jamey Tannreuther was gangly, with an unruly tangle of brown hair. He wore glasses which were perpetually in the process of sliding down his nose, and despite the cool night air, he wore only a T-shirt, jeans, and sandals.

He heard the voice too, Valerie thought. *Or maybe one of his parents did.*

Jamey was like her in that he had health problems. The difference was his issues were all mental. She wasn't clear on exactly what conditions he struggled with, but he wouldn't meet anyone's eyes when they spoke to him, and Valerie had never heard him speak. She did hear him shout sometimes— loud, inarticulate cries of frustration and anger that would cause his mother and father to shout back at him. These yelling matches could take place anytime of the day or night and could sometimes last for hours. They could get so loud the whole neighborhood could hear them. Ian had threated to call the police on more than one occasion when they got into it, but Valerie had been able to talk him out of doing so each time. She felt sorry for Jamey. More, she felt a kinship with him, just as she did with Omar.

We feebs have to stick together, she thought.

Had his parents finally run out of patience with him, and when they'd heard the voice had decided to send him out? Or did Jamey feel like a burden on his mother and father and had chosen to come outside on his own? She suspected the latter, given the way the boy walked calmly down the driveway without any sign of reluctance.

The emotional numbness that the voice had visited upon her kept her from feeling anything as she watched Jamey walk toward the bird-things. He displayed no reaction to the creatures, and he kept his head lowered to avoid meeting their eyes. That much was a blessing at least.

When Jamey reached the bird-things, the tall one grabbed Jamey under the arms with its clawed hands and lifted him to his feet with surprising ease, as if the boy weighed no more than a scarecrow. Both creatures looked at him for a moment, heads cocked to the side, while Jamey—silent—continued averting his gaze.

Valerie wanted to jump to her feet and run over to help Jamey, but her body felt too heavy to move. And although the numbness that had settled upon her remained, the bird-things terrified her, and even if she had been able to move, she doubted she could've made herself approach them.

The tall creature lowered Jamey just enough for the short one to take hold of his head with its claws, give it a savage twist, and then pull. Valerie heard Jamey's neck snap and saw the flesh tear as his head was separated from his body. The short bird-thing lifted Jamey's head over his open beak to catch the falling blood. The tall one leaned forward and dipped his beak into the body's ragged neck stump. The creatures drank for several moments—Jamey's body twitching as if it hadn't yet realized it was dead. As they finished, the bird-things let out snuffling laughs—just as they had when they'd killed Arthur Clayton—and then carried Jamey's remains to the back of their insectine vehicle. The vehicle shifted position slightly, and Valerie realized that what she'd thought was the rear was in fact the front, and now that it had turned, she could see its head. It was the size of a small car, and it had a pair of compound eyes the size of basketballs and huge jutting mandibles. The bird-things fed Jamey's remains into the mouth, and the mandibles pulled the meat and bone in and the monstrous creature made quick work of them.

The short creature got back into the vehicle's cab, but the tall one simply walked as the insect "truck" *tik-tik-tiked* backwards to Valerie's house and stopped right in front of her.

She still felt numb, still sat at the curb, but the terror that witnessing Jamey's death had roused deep within her began to rise to the surface. She started to tremble, and when Omar began barking in alarm, she jumped.

The tall bird-thing stepped up to her, and a moment later the short one joined her. Now that the creatures were close, a ridiculous, almost hysterical thought popped into her head. When she was a kid, she'd loved watching cartoons about a pair of mischievous magpies named Heckle and Jeckle. That's what these two things reminded her of now: distorted, nightmarish versions of those characters. She felt a laugh bubbling up, but she fought it down. She feared that if she started laughing now, she wouldn't be able to stop.

Heckle and Jeckle's coveralls were soaked with Arthur's and Jamey's blood, and the feathers around their beaks were matted with it. Their eyes should've gleamed with reflected illumination from her porchlight, but they were a dull flat black that reflected nothing. She had the impression that they didn't actually have eyes, that the sockets were empty, and what she thought were eyes were instead pockets of darkness. A glimpse, perhaps, into what the bird-things truly were behind their bizarre facades.

As the two creatures regarded Valerie, she fought to throw off the physical and emotional lethargy they had inflicted on her—for surely they had somehow sent the messages she'd heard.

Bring out the Unwanted.

Sit down. Wait.

She wanted to spring to her feet, whirl around, and make a mad dash for her house. She wanted to fling open the front door, rush inside, slam the door, lock it, and wait for the two bird-things and their monstrous vehicle to move on. She'd wait until dawn if she had to. Creatures like these were nightmares made flesh, and like all dreams—good and bad— they'd vanish with the sun's first rays. They had to, didn't they? For if things like this could exist in the light of day, that would mean the world truly was completely, hopelessly mad, and—worst of all—always had been.

But the most she was able to do was twitch her hands, and even then, only a little. And so she sat where she was as Heckle—the tall, thin one—stretched out his clawed hands, preparing to take hold of her and lift her up in the air, just as he'd done with Arthur and Jamey. And there was nothing she could do to stop him. She closed her eyes—she was able to do that much at least—and hoped the end would be swift and relatively painless, although she knew it would be neither.

But after several moments passed without her feeling Heckle's claws touch her body, she opened her eyes. It would've been nice if the creatures were gone—their vehicle, too—as if they'd never existed, but Heckle and Jeckle still stood there, gazing at her silently, heads cocked to opposite sides. She sensed that something was wrong, but she didn't know what. The bird-things continued looking at her a moment longer, and then they leaned forward and thrust their beaks toward her. She thought they intended to pierce her eyes, and she tried to scream but all that came out was a soft *eep*. Heckle and Jeckle didn't attack, though. Instead they sniffed the air around her head, at times touching their beaks to her hair. The contact, however brief, made Valerie's skin crawl, and she tried to scream again, but this time nothing came out.

What *were* these things? Did they always roam the streets at night, preying on the Unwanted? Or did they wait for this night in particular, the one when people sorted through their lives—literally and figuratively—because that's when people were most susceptible to their message? Whatever the bird-things were, and whatever reason they'd chosen this night to make their rounds, they were here, and now they were going to take her.

But both Heckle and Jeckle drew back then, and Heckle turned away and started walking toward Jeanette's house, while Jeckle got back in the vehicle, and its insectine legs began moving once more. Valerie realized then that the bird-things had passed her over.

She was going to live.

But before she could feel any relief, she understood why Heckle and Jeckle had moved on. She was too sickly even for scavengers like these to take. She hadn't been spared. She'd been *unwanted*.

With that thought, her paralysis lifted. Now able to move, she did what she could only imagine a few moments ago. She got to her feet and started running across the lawn toward her front door, limbs moving awkwardly at first, as if they'd fallen asleep while she'd been immobilized, but they limbered up fast, and soon she could move normally again. She was halfway to the door when she heard Omar's barking increase in intensity and pitch.

Don't look, she told herself. *Just get inside. You'll be safe there, and this will all be over.*

She looked anyway.

Heckle had picked up the dog carrier and was looking through the wire mesh opening, head cocked to the side the same way he'd looked at Valerie, as if he wasn't sure what to make of Omar. Or maybe he knew exactly what he was looking at and was disappointed that Jeanette had left a snack for them instead of a full meal.

The vehicle stopped and Jeckle jumped down from the cab and joined Heckle in examining Omar. The three-legged pug continued barking, and Jeckle thrust his head toward the dog and let out an angry hiss that sounded more like it came from a reptile than a bird. Valerie heard Omar's nails scrape against plastic as he scuttled backward from Jeckle, and the pug began to whine in fear.

She made no conscious decision to start walking toward the creatures, and she was almost there by the time she realized what she was doing. This realization didn't stop her, though. Omar was a good dog, and he didn't deserve to be tossed out like some old piece of trash, any more than Arthur or Jamey had. Or her, for that matter.

Jeckle was reaching for the carrier's lock when she said, "Hey!"

Heckle and Jeckle swiveled their heads and trained their darkness-filled eye sockets on her. She felt a cold flutter in her stomach, but she forced herself to continue forward.

"You can't have him. Put him down."

She didn't yell these words, but the tone of command in her voice was unmistakable.

Heckle and Jeckle didn't react. They just kept looking at her as she approached. When she reached them, she stopped, took a deep breath, and met their shadowy gazes as she repeated her command.

"Put him *down.*"

This time the creatures' response was swift. Heckle opened the cage, grabbed hold of Omar, and pulled him out, while Jeckle put a clawed hand on her chest and shoved her backward with startling strength. She stumbled backward, tripped over a battered suitcase Jeanette had put out for removal, and fell on her ass. The impact knocked the wind out of her, and all she could do was watch in horror as Heckle dropped the carrier to the ground and took a two-handed grip on Omar's middle. Jeckle then reached out and took hold of the dog's head. They were going to tear his head off and drink his blood, just as they'd done to their other victims.

Valerie felt an asthma attack coming on, and she struggled to draw in enough breath to speak.

"I…want…him."

Her words came out as little more than whispers, but that was enough to make Heckle and Jeckle pause.

Valerie rose to her feet and spoke again, her voice stronger this time.

"You can only take the unwanted, right? Well, I want Omar."

Heckle and Jeckle stood motionless, both of them still holding onto Omar. Valerie walked forward, reached out, and gently pulled Omar from their claws. She drew the little pug to her chest, and he began licking her face.

Valerie laughed.

Heckle and Jeckle sprang into motion then. They both made the same sinister hissing sound Heckle had used to intimidate Omar, and they turned toward Valerie, claws raised, ready to strike.

"And it looks like he wants me," Valerie said.

Heckle and Jeckle froze, and after a moment they slowly lowered their arms. They regarded Valerie one last time, and then turned away and started back toward their bizarre vehicle.

Valerie opened her jacket and tucked Omar inside to keep him warm. But instead of turning and heading back to her house, she said, "Now Omar's *owner*… I doubt anybody in the world wants her. I'm sure Omar doesn't, not after the way she treated him." She opened her jacket a bit so she could see Omar's face. "Isn't that right, boy?"

Omar let out a snort, which might have been an answer or might not. Whichever it was, it was enough to make Heckle and Jeckle turn away from the insectine transport and start walking toward Jeanette's house. Valerie headed for her own home then, and as she heard the sound of knocking on Jeanette's door, she realized for the first time in a long while that she didn't feel any pain. In fact, she felt pretty goddamned terrific.

TIL DEATH

Audrey pushed the shopping car filled with metal odds and ends along the cracked sidewalk, her husband Edmund trailing behind her, struggling to keep up. Sweat beaded on her upper lip, despite the slight chill in the air. The temperature never varied in the World After, never grew colder, never grew warmer. But Audrey was seventy-three, and even though she worked every day and was in good shape for her age, pushing a full cart took it out of her. She had no idea how long she'd been working. Time didn't operate the same way it had before the Masters' arrival. There was no day or night now. The sky was a perpetually hazy sour yellow like diseased phlegm with no sun or moon ever visible. Audrey didn't know if there even *was* a sun or moon anymore. For all she knew, the rest of the universe might've ceased to exist once the Masters came to Earth. Without day or night, Audrey had no sense of time. She could've gathered metal for five hours or fifty. There was no way to know. She only knew that she was tired all the way down to the bone.

The thrall mark on her forehead hurt like a fresh sunburn,

and her head pounded with a rhythm that almost felt like language.

BRING, BRING…

Maybe it was her Master's voice, maybe it was her imagination. It didn't matter. Either way, she had to make her delivery—so much depended on it. She stopped pushing the cart, released her grip on the handle, and turned around.

Edmund, her senior by eight years, was twenty paces behind her on the sidewalk. He was naked, his parchment-thin skin drawn close to his old bones. His limbs had been rearranged, so he could only move by crab-walking backward, and his head was turned 180 degrees so he could see where he was going. Not that his cataract-covered eyes could see much. His sparse body hair was wiry and snow-white, but his head was bald. Instead of a beard, thick worm-like growths grew out of his chin and cheeks. The fleshy tendrils were tipped with oozing pustules, and Audrey thought of them as pimple-snakes. They writhed with independent life, and Audrey couldn't look at them without nausea twisting her stomach. His mouth hung open, jaw slack as if the muscles no longer functioned, and perpetual lines of drool ran from his mouth to moisten his pimple-snakes.

He didn't talk—or maybe he *couldn't*. Either way, Audrey was grateful. She had no idea how his mind functioned these days, but whatever distorted thoughts might spark and sputter inside what remained of his mind, she was glad he couldn't share them. He did make sounds from time to time: strange mournful hissings and tremulous bleats. His penis was always erect, so filled with blood it was purple-black, and a clear fluid that smelled like ammonia leaked from his ass. A line of the foul stuff trailed behind him on the sidewalk. In some ways, his body odor was the worst part. He stank like unwashed cock and balls that had been slathered in shit, and his breath was a sour-sweet reek that reminded her of rotting fruit.

Edmund hadn't always been like this, of course. Like so many things about the world, he'd changed since the advent of the Masters. So had she, just not outwardly.

It took him a while to close half the distance between them, but when he had, he stopped, gazed at her with eyes dull and lifeless as glass marbles, and lowered himself to the sidewalk. Audrey gritted her teeth in frustration. She *hated* it when he did this. She wanted to yell at him, shout that he should get his lazy ass moving, but she knew it wouldn't do any good. He understood so little these days. Not that he'd understood much in the last few years before he'd changed. She knew of only one way to get him going again, and while she was reluctant to do it, it was vital they made their delivery today...before she lost her nerve.

She hesitated a moment, uncomfortable about leaving her shopping cart unattended. She'd worked hard to gather this much metal, and she didn't want to risk another thrall stealing it while she was trying to coax Edmund to get moving. Then again, the longer she remained in one place, the more she risked being noticed by another thrall. Or by one of the deadly creatures that roamed the World After.

Damned if you do, damned if you don't.

She once thought she'd understood that phrase, but she hadn't known shit.

She started walking toward Edmund.

IN THE FIRST days after the Masters' advent, and the remaking of the world, Audrey had often thought it a blessing that Edmund's mind had been mostly devoured by dementia. He remembered her—more or less—but otherwise he wasn't aware of much. In a way, she envied him. She wished she was insulated from the World After with a comforting blanket of mental oblivion.

After the Arrival, she estimated they had remained in their home, doors locked and curtains drawn, for nine days before their supplies became dangerously low. Water was the biggest issue. Something still came out of the taps, but it was thick as tar, smelled like a mixture of cinnamon and turpentine, and had a corrosive effect on both metal and porcelain. She didn't want to know what it could do to flesh. Their only food was one nearly empty container of oatmeal and a few boxes of pasta. But she had no water or electricity to prepare any of it.

One evening—or perhaps morning, it was all the same now—she lay in bed, curtains closed so she wouldn't have to look at the phlegm-colored sky outside...or at whatever hideous abomination might go lurching past. Edmund lay on the bed next to her, so motionless he might have been dead.

She couldn't remember the last time she had slept, was certain that she wouldn't drift off no matter how long she lay there, but sooner than she expected, her eyes closed and sleep took her. She hadn't dreamed since the Masters' arrival, but she did so now.

In the dream, she stood on a patch of bare earth enclosed by a high wooden fence with barbed wire all around the top. The white paint on the fence was old and peeling, the wood beneath gray and weathered. Mounds of scrap metal were piled at the corners of the fence, each taller than she was. In the middle of the enclosure was an open pit, ten feet in diameter, she estimated, maybe fifteen. The edges were smooth, almost as if the pit was a natural structure, though the perfect roundness of it argued against that. She stood several feet away from the pit, but she still had a good view of the inside. All she could see was darkness, so black, so deep, so *absolute*, that it seemed to actually be absorbing light, pulling it into itself and swallowing it.

Gazing into the pit caused unreasoning atavistic fear to well within her. She couldn't move, couldn't think, could only stand and watch, heart pounding rapidly in her chest like a small bird caught by a predator's mesmeric gaze.

She heard the Master's wordless voice for the first time then. It asked her a question, offered her payment for her service—unquestioning, unwavering. She spoke a single word in reply.

"Yes."

Fiery pain seared her forehead then, as if an invisible branding iron had been pressed to her flesh, and she screamed herself awake. Edmund woke too, confused and frightened. He began to shout and then to cry, and Audrey held him for a time, comforting him while her forehead pulsed with pain. When Edmund fell back to sleep, she took a flashlight from her nightstand, went into the master bathroom, looked into the mirror over the sink, shone the beam on her forehead, and saw her thrall mark for the first time. Along with the mark came knowledge: the location of the Master's lair and what was expected of her. The Master wanted her to get to work immediately, for it hungered. There was just one problem, one that she hadn't considered in her dream.

She fixed her gaze on the thrall mark's reflection, as if by addressing it she could communicate with her new Master. "I can't leave Edmund alone for long. He's not strong enough to work, and his mind..." She trailed off, uncertain how best to explain it. But before she could speak again, she heard Edmund scream, a high-pitched shriek so intense it sounded as if he were tearing his throat to shreds.

She dropped the flashlight and ran back into the bedroom. Edmund writhed on the bed as his body reformed itself, bones breaking and resetting into new configurations. The transformation wasn't swift and it only become more painful as it continued, but when it was finished, Edmund had become a monstrously twisted thing, a creature strong enough to accompany Audrey while she worked. Her Master had done this somehow, she realized, in order to help her. It was, to the Master's alien mind, an act of kindness and generosity.

Audrey swallowed her rising gorge and forced herself to whisper, "Thank you," all the while unable to take her gaze off the horrible thing her husband had become.

THE MASTERS HAD COME from elsewhere. Space, another dimension, a different time...no one knew for certain. Some believed the Masters had ruled Earth in the far distant past, perhaps even created it to be their plaything—or feeding ground—and long ago they'd left Earth for unknown reasons, but now had returned to reclaim what was theirs. They had no individual names—at least, none that humans were aware of—and no one had ever seen a Master. No one who'd ever lived to tell about it, anyway. Most believed they possessed no physical form, not as humans understood the concept. They lived in separate lairs and worked through thralls and monstrous servants of their own creation. Thralls were rewarded for their service with food, clean water, and electricity in their homes, and while wearing a thrall mark didn't protect you from every danger in the World After, it usually gave predators—both those human and those not—pause.

A thrall's main purpose was to feed his or her Master. Sometimes this meant capturing other humans and bringing them—kicking and screaming, if need be—to the Master's lair. But Masters didn't always feed on human flesh. From other thralls, Audrey had learned of Masters that fed on blood, human waste, and specific organs such as pancreas. Some fed on inorganic objects such as used clothing, books, electronic devices, CD's, and DVD's. Some dined on more abstract fare: people's memories, emotions, or fantasies. All Audrey's Master required was metal. Any kind would do, although it was particularly fond of copper. Audrey had no idea exactly what happened to the metal after she threw it into the pit that served as her Master's lair, but she'd never heard it hit bottom.

Even though their Master gave them food and water—somehow made it materialize right in their home—Audrey was thin to the point of emaciation, as was Edmund. Masters might reward thralls for their service, but they were far from generous. They gave just enough for their servants to remain alive, and not a scrap more. And for this, thralls risked their lives day after day. But what else could they do? It was the only game in town.

IN THE WORLD BEFORE, Audrey's therapist had warned her about something called compassion fatigue.

It happens to long-term caregivers, she'd said. *Especially those whose loved ones suffer from conditions like dementia, which only worsen over time. You become emotionally exhausted, and—if you're not careful—that exhaustion can turn into feelings of resentment. Even hatred.*

That hadn't happened to Audrey. Not *before*, anyway. But now? Now it was hard to think of the loathsome thing that followed her around like some freakish dog as the man who had been her husband. She wanted to be free of Edmund as much, if not more, as she wanted him to be free of the nightmarish existence she'd inadvertently cursed him with.

The first time she'd tried to kill Edmund, she'd done it during a scavenging run, when she'd been picking through the ruins of a downtown office building. She didn't know what had caused the building's collapse. There was no sign of fire, no sign that something had struck the building. No wood rot, no crumbling concrete, no fatigued metal. It looked as if the pieces of the building had simply detached from one another and fallen into a jumbled heap. Edmund stayed away from the debris, guarding the shopping cart and watching as she walked through the odds and ends, searching for choice bits of metal. If anyone—or any*thing*—came near, he'd let out a loud hissing sound. She had no idea if this was a conscious warning on his part or merely an instinctive reaction. Either way, his warnings came in handy.

As she searched among the debris, she came across large shards of glass, pieces of a window that had been broken in the building's collapse. A couple of shards were the right size to hold in one hand, and one of those was the basic size and shape of a butcher knife blade. She gazed at the glass knife for a long time before finally crouching down to pick it up. She gripped it like a knife, carefully not to squeeze too hard so she wouldn't cut her hand. She was surprised by how heavy it felt, almost as if it were a real blade instead of merely a piece of broken glass. She gingerly touched the finger of her free hand to the pointed tip, then ran it along one of the shard's edges, again careful not to press too hard.

After a time, she stood, turned, and began making her way toward Edmund.

He watched her approach, no awareness showing in his milky eyes. His erection bounced several times, like he was a dog wagging its tail upon his master's return. He didn't react when she knelt next to his head. Didn't flinch when she touched the glass shard to his throat. Didn't do more than let out a soft hiss of air—was there a hint of surprise in that breath?—as she drew the shard across his neck, the sharp edge parting flesh and severing veins and arteries, bringing forth a gushing flood of crimson.

He turned to look at her then, blood dribbling past his lips onto his pimple-snakes. No expression, no recognition. And then he slumped to the ground and continued to bleed out.

She stood and stepped back to avoid the worst of the blood, but it was too late. It had spattered her clothes, slicked her hands…so what did it matter if the widening pool on the ground touched her shoes?

She watched her husband die, surprised by how long it took for his erection to subside. But subside it did, and Edmund let out a last choked gurgle and stopped breathing.

Heart pounding, she stepped forward and pressed two trembling fingers to the side of his neck. No pulse.

She stood. She felt mostly relief, although there was some sorrow and guilt as well. She contemplated what to do with his body. He was little more than skin and bones, but he was still too heavy for her to lift. She couldn't get him in the cart, and even if she could, what would she do with him? There were no funeral homes anymore. She supposed she could bury him in their backyard, but something had happened to the grass. The edges of the blades were sharp as razors, and if you got too close they emitted high-pitched cries that sounded like tiny voices screaming. She wasn't sure it would be safe to try to dig there. Maybe if she just took his head…

She heard the first predator then, approaching in the distance. A simian *hoot-hoot-hoot* accompanied by a leathery sliding, as of something large dragging itself across asphalt. The scent of Edmund's blood had drawn it, whatever it was, and she knew it wouldn't be the last. At least she wouldn't have to worry about what to do with Edmund's remains now.

She dropped the glass knife, took hold of the shopping

cart's handle, and began pushing it away from her husband's corpse as fast as she could.

SHE DIDN'T HAVE any metal to deliver to her Master that day, and her reward for her failure was an excruciating headache brought on by her throbbing thrall mark. Even so, when she got home she slept well for the first time since the Masters' arrival.

She woke to the sound of pounding at the front door. As she stumbled down the hallway, she already knew what she'd find waiting for her. She unlocked the door, opened it, and stood back as Edmund—who didn't have a mark anywhere on his body, including his throat—crab-walked inside. A thought drifted through her mind. *The cat came back...*

SHE TRIED THREE MORE TIMES. She used an iron poker to cave in Edmund's skull. She jammed a pair of socks down his throat to block his airway. Finally, in desperation, she took a screwdriver, rammed it through his left eye into his brain, stirred it around real good, and then did the same to the other eye.

He healed each time.

She had no idea if Edmund healed because of some quality his transformed body possessed or if her Master specifically healed him each time as a way to torment her. Whatever the reason, she knew she couldn't kill him by ordinary means. To end his travesty of a life, she would need *power*. The same kind that had transformed him in the first place.

She began to plan.

THE SKIN on Audrey's right hand was raw and blistered. Pushing the cart hurt, but she couldn't manage it with only one hand, so she endured the pain. Edmund followed behind her on the sidewalk, moving a bit faster now, with a decided bounce in his step. She'd jacked him off, and it hadn't taken him long to come. It never did. But while what shot out of his quivering cock looked more or less like semen, it was an unhealthy gray, stank like sulfur, and was boiling hot. Getting Edmund off was a sure way to motivate him. He'd be in a good mood for hours—but she only did it when nothing else worked, for no matter how hard she tried, she always got some of his cock lava on her. Usually on her hand, but if his orgasm was particularly strong, he'd blast like a firehose, and there was no telling where she might get hit. Today, she'd been lucky. Only her right hand and a small spot on her left wrist had been burned. Painful, but nothing that would slow her down, and now Edmund was trotting behind her like an eager puppy, cock already swollen purple once more.

Audrey didn't look down as she walked. She knew better than to gaze at the cracks in the sidewalk. Something—or many somethings—lived inside and whispered the most awful things. If they caught you looking down, they'd whisper louder. They'd urge you to do things to yourself and to others, and the longer they whispered, the harder it was to resist them. Better to not set them off in the first place.

The town's population was sparser now. Many people died during the early days after the Masters' arrival, and many more had died since. Some had been sacrificed to Masters, some had been killed by the new monstrous predators that roamed the world, and some died at the hands of their fellow survivors, people who'd been driven mad or had turned savage during their struggle to stay alive.

Because of this, Audrey saw few people along the route to her Master's lair, and those she did see were sitting in alleys or on front stoops, heads down, sleeping or—just as likely—gone deep into their minds to try to escape the horrors of the World After. Every now and again one of them would look up as she passed, and she always made sure to turn her head toward them so they could see her thrall mark. That was usually enough to make them look away and lower their heads once more.

She was aware of other creatures, moving swift and silent between buildings, or crouching on rooftops and watching, motionless and hopeful. At times she even had the sense that something was looking down at her from above, but when she looked up, she saw nothing in the sour-yellow sky. The land was filled with predators now—some large, some small, all deadly in their own ways. Her thrall mark would keep them at a distance, especially close to her Master's lair. She hoped.

Audrey had never had cause to visit the Third Street Iron and Metal Company before the Masters' arrival. She didn't live particularly close to the place, either. She had no idea why the Master who laired there had offered to take her on as one of its thralls. Maybe it had broadcast a general call and she'd answered. Maybe she'd been chosen for a specific reason, one she'd likely never know. Whatever the truth was, she'd come to wish she'd never accepted the Master's offer. If she hadn't, she and Edmund would've been dead by now, probably from lack of fresh water, but that end would've been preferable to what their lives had become. Serving as a thrall was a mistake, one she intended to rectify now.

The word *company* seemed too grand for this place. A high white wooden fence surrounded the property, with the business' name painted in red letters on one of the outside walls. A section of a wall served as a sliding door which could be closed and locked, although it was always open when

Audrey came here. Since the only thing that could threaten a Master was another of its kind, there was no need for simple physical boundaries like doors and locks.

Audrey's thrall mark burned hot as fire. Her Master knew she was close, knew the *metal* was close, and it was losing what little patience it had. Audrey had heard about what happened to thralls that displeased their Masters. It made what had been done to Edmund look like little more than a mild swat on the hand.

She began pushing the cart once more, Edmund crab-walking obediently behind her.

The instant she set foot on the barren earth inside the fence, she felt the Master's power wash over her. She was officially in its lair now, the place where it was strongest. The air here seemed to ripple, like the distortion created by waves of heat rising off hot asphalt. Edmund made a small bleating sound when he entered. He was never comfortable in the Master's presence, but he always accompanied her inside anyway. She was counting on this—habit? loyalty?—now.

The ground was smooth, the path to the pit well worn, and the squeaking wheels of the shopping cart rolled easily over it. Normally, Audrey would push the cart up to the pit's edge— not *too* close—and then start lifting out pieces of metal one by one and tossing them in. If the Master was especially impatient and the cart's contents not too heavy, she might try to dump the entire load in at once. She would do neither of these things today, though.

Her Master's impatience, its lust to feed, filled her, made her thrall mark feel as if white-hot coals had been slipped beneath her skin. She gritted her teeth against the pain, gripped the cart handle tighter, and started to run. She was seventy-three, malnourished and dehydrated, but fear, anger, and determination fueled her, and she ran with the strength and speed of a much younger woman. The cart's wheels squeaked so loudly they almost seemed to be screaming. The sound of the wheels combined with the sound of her heart pounding in her ears, and she couldn't hear if Edmund continued to follow her, if he too had picked up speed, his bare hands and feet *slap-slap-slapping* the earth as he fought to keep up with her. She hoped he was.

At first, she felt only her Master's all-consuming hunger, but then she detected a hint of puzzlement. Why was this thrall approaching the pit so fast? But before the Master could command her to stop, Audrey felt the front wheels of the heavily laden cart roll over the edge of the pit. She held tight to the handle as the cart tipped forward and fell into the darkness, pulling her with it. She looked back in time to see Edmund fling himself after her, and she smiled. The Master might prefer to eat metal, but she hoped it wouldn't mind an offering of flesh. *Two* offerings.

Audrey and Edmund tumbled down through black nothingness.

Audrey had no idea how long they fell. She'd lost her grip on the cart somewhere along the line, and she had no idea where it was. Edmund was close by, though. She might not have been able to see him, but she could still *smell* him. More, she sensed his presence the same way she'd sometimes wake in the night and know he was lying in bed next to her without having to reach over to confirm his presence.

The vertiginous feeling of falling had subsided around the time she'd lost contact with the cart, and she couldn't tell if she still continued descending. Without so much as a speck of light, she had no way of telling which way was up and which way was down, if such directions even meant anything in this dark limbo. For all she knew, she was hanging motionless in this void, and she might remain so until she died. Or worse, she'd stay like this forever, never dying, always awake and conscious. How long could a person exist like that before going completely insane?

She tried to speak but was unable to tell if her mouth produced any sound.

I'm so sorry, Edmund. I didn't know something like this would happen. I thought we'd die.

No reply from her husband. For once, she was glad his mind was gone. If they were trapped in this place, he wouldn't go mad. After all, he was already there.

After a time—how long was impossible to say—she sensed another presence, enormous and terrifying. It was as if she were floating in a sea and a silent ocean liner had drifted close without her being aware of it until the massive craft was almost on top of her. She knew she was now truly in her Master's presence.

She felt a wave of curiosity roll forth from the Master. It wasn't a word, wasn't even a human concept, but Audrey interpreted it as a single-word question.

WHY?

She didn't have to ask why *what*.

I couldn't let him go on living like he is. And I couldn't leave him.

She sensed only continuing curiosity, now tinged with confusion, coming from the Master.

He's my husband. We belong together.

The Master's confusion and curiosity vanished, followed by a sense of satisfaction, which Audrey interpreted as a single word.

UNDERSTOOD.

Pain exploded throughout her body as her bones, muscles, and organs began to shift and rearrange. She let forth a soundless scream, but she felt a hand clasp her shoulder—

Edmund's hand—and she knew that, whatever horrible thing was happening to her, at least she wasn't alone. And then she felt Edmund's fingers join with her flesh, their skin flowing together like liquid putty, and if she could've produced sound in this non-place, she would've screamed louder.

AUDREY AND EDMUND shuffled slowly into an abandoned building. The sign out front said the place once had been a night club called Spinners, but since neither of them could read anymore, the letters were only meaningless nonsense. They moved on four hands and four feet, two pairs of eyes scanning the debris inside the club for any metal. Poking out from beneath a splintered table, they saw a thin half circle of what looked like... Could it be? *Copper!* Once, Audrey would've recognized this object as a bracelet, but now she only saw it as her Master's favorite delicacy. Audrey and Edmund were excited to retrieve the bracelet, but their combined anatomy made it difficult to move the pieces of broken wood. Yes, they had four hands, but their arms no longer bent the way they once did. Edmund carried a silver serving spoon they had found in a restaurant a couple blocks away, and he put it on the floor. The two of them then took hold of the table fragments with their teeth and slowly, painfully dragged them off the bracelet. When the object was fully revealed, Audrey leaned her head down to it. She used her thorn-covered tongue to lift it into her mouth, and then she gently gripped it between her serrated teeth. Audrey and Edmund couldn't operate a shopping cart, and so they were limited in what they could gather for their Master, but hopefully their meager offering would still be pleasing. Their Master would understand. After all, hadn't the Master made them this way?

Edmund retrieved his spoon, and they left the bar. Because of the tangled arrangement of their limbs, they scuttled and lurched instead of crab-walked, and they were more awkward than either of them had been on their own. But they'd learn to make do. Everything would be all right, just as long as they had each other. Once outside, they turned left and began heading in the direction of the Third Street Metal and Iron Company.

Together.

HOW TO BE A HORROR WRITER

If you want to be a horror writer, be washed from your mother's womb in a river of blood, kicking and screaming, writhing like an annoyed insect larva released from its egg. Feel rubber glove-covered hands clamp tight on a tiny arm and leg and pull you all the rest of the way free. Wail at the loss of the warm wet dark which is all you've ever known, scream in terror as harsh light stabs your eyes, shudder as cold air rakes your skin like a thousand claws of ice.

You look upon the face of the giant that holds you, its eyes all that's visible, other features concealed by cloth. There's another faceless giant present, and together they carry you to a small table and place you on a scratchy white cloth beneath a blazing miniature sun. You continue screaming as these horrible faceless creatures touch and probe you. You fight as best you can, but you're so small compared to them, so weak. They can do anything to you that they want, anything at all, and there's nothing you can do to stop them. They could tear the limbs from your body with ease, place a hand over your nose and mouth, sealing them shut. They could jam a thumb into your fontanel, sink the digit into your small brain and stir shit around in there. And when they finish, when they've had their fun, they could hurl you to the tiled floor to see how many times you bounce, maybe kick you back and forth like some sort of grisly toy. But the Faceless Ones do none of those things. They clean you off, take some measurements, wash you, and then one of the giants wrap you in a thin, soft blanket. You like the cloth. It's tight against your body, and you find this comforting. You grow quiet then, as much from weariness as from relief.

You're carried to a bed where a third giant lies. This one's face is bare, skin wan and coated with a sheen of sweat. You are held out to this new giant, and it reaches ungloved hands to you, lips pulling tight, ends curling upward. You find the expression as hideous as it is alien. The giant takes you and draws you close to its chest. The giant gazes at you with an expression you cannot read. Maybe it's happy to see you, maybe it wants to sink its teeth into your tender flesh. How can you know for certain what dark thoughts swim behind those large eyes?

The giant's lips part and sound emerges from its mouth.

"Hi, little one. I'm your mommy."

You have no idea what the sounds mean, but they feel familiar, or rather, the voice that speaks them does. You think you've heard it before, numerous times, but it was always softer before, muffled. Now it's loud and grating.

It comes to you then, less of a thought than an instinctive realization, something buried at deep in your genetic code. This pale, sweaty thing holding you is your home. Only now you're looking at it from the outside. Until this instant, you had no concept of *inside* or *outside*, of being *a part* and being *apart*. This creature from which you emerged is large, yes, but when you were inside, the warm dark was the entire universe, and you were at the center of it. But now you begin to understand that existence is somehow both larger and smaller than the Warm Dark, and that not only aren't you the center of everything, you're so much smaller and weaker than everything around you.

You take a deep breath then, hold it for a moment, and then you let forth an ear-splitting shriek that, if it was a word, would be *No* repeated over and over.

IF YOU WANT to be a horror writer, go to your Uncle Red's funeral when you're nine. He's not the first dead person you've seen. He's your great-uncle, and you have spent weekends at his house—along with your great-aunt Becky and great-grandmother Alfretta—as long as you can remember. Uncle Red, Aunt Becky, and Great-Grandma have always taken you with them when they do old people stuff, like shopping at flea markets, visiting sick people in the hospital, or attending viewings of recently deceased friends and acquaintances. You have no idea how many viewings you've been to, maybe as many as a dozen, but while you found it awkward to be the only child present, the dead never bothered you. You knew they were dead in an abstract sense, but they all looked more like mannequins than people: skin waxy, eyes sunken, cheeks hollow, too much makeup on their faces.

But as Aunt Becky leads you up to the coffin, clutching your hand, her flesh thin as paper, bones underneath as light and fragile as a bird's, you know that this time is going to be different than those others. You're not afraid, and you don't feel nervous. Your stomach doesn't sink, there's no roaring in your ears, and you're not hit with a sudden wave of dizziness. You feel numb and disconnected, as if only part of you is present and the rest is somewhere else. As the two of you stand next to the coffin, your first thought—which you're too young to realize is a cliché—is that your uncle looks so natural, almost as if he might sit up at any moment, open his eyes, give a huge grin and say, *Gotcha!* Everyone would gasp and then burst into laughter accompanied by tears of joy and relief. But he doesn't move, of course. In fact, his body possesses a profound stillness that disturbs you on a primal level. The living are never so still, not even when sleeping. There's always some movement or sound, however slight. But there's nothing inside your uncle, aside from chemicals designed to slow his body's decay, and it's this Great Nothingness which disturbs you on a level so deep you cannot consciously touch it, let alone name it.

In the monster movies you love to watch on *Shock Theater*, hosted by Dr. Creep, death is embodied by some horrible creature emerging from the darkness, eyes wide with hunger, teeth bared, claws outstretched. In the movies, death is both awful and awesome, in the original sense of those words. It is, in its dark way, majestic and special. A monstrous beast, a servant of ultimate darkness, comes for you—*especially* for you—because you are the *victim*, and without victims, there can be no monsters. But there's nothing special about what's happened to Uncle Red. What's happened to him is no more remarkable than someone flipping a light switch to the off position. An everyday event—common, mundane, and utterly banal.

In the weeks and months to come, you will become obsessed with the idea that Time robs us of our life one moment after another, that it steals whatever happiness we can find even as it gives it to us. This obsession grows worse after you almost drown in a lake while on vacation with your family that summer. You ask your mom and dad what they would've done if you'd died. *We probably wouldn't go on vacation ever again*, they answer. They don't take you to see a psychologist. Only crazy people need a psychologist. It takes a couple years, but eventually you make an uneasy peace with Time. Yes, it takes, but it also gives. It brings new experiences, growth and healing. None of those things would be possible without Time. This realization helps, and you're able to go on with your life, but you never smile as broadly as you did when you were a child, never laugh so easily.

IF YOU WANT to be a horror writer, learn to live with depression. It's your heritage, after all. Your mother is an agoraphobic who sometimes goes days without speaking, and your father—the very definition of an enabler—does little to help her. Only crazy people go to psychologists, remember? You don't know why she's like this. Your maternal grandmother, who you've always known as Nana, once told you that your mother was married before she met your father, and that her first husband abused her, although Nana didn't elaborate on the nature of this abuse, leaving your imagination to fill in the details for you. You wonder if whatever that man did to her made her like this. Years later, you'll decide her depression—like yours—is primarily biochemical, but for now you live with her stillness and silence, and while she'd not as still or silent as the dead, she might as well be.

IF YOU WANT to be a horror writer, internalize your parents' warnings—often unspoken or given obliquely—that the world is a dangerous place, that's it's safest to stay home, but if you do go out, always be careful, always keep watch. Your sister's high school boyfriend is killed when he flips his car over one night after they argue, and when your brother is twenty, he'll have a stroke that changes him forever. Your older relatives begin dying one by one, and you hear stories of kids you knew in school dying in accidents, or by their own hands or—once—because they are stationed in Beirut and happen to be sleeping in the barracks when a terrorist drives a truck filled with explosives into the building. You get married and develop testicular cancer when your first daughter is only a few months old, and you're terrified that you'll die before you have a chance to be a father to her. You survive, but you'll always know that your body can betray you at any moment, that it eventually will one way or another, thanks to your old friend Time.

Your mother dies at fifty-nine, when your daughter is two, and you won't cry at her funeral. People will think it's because you're being strong, but it's really because you're relieved that she's gone. It's like someone opened a window and let fresh air in. You think it's a profoundly sad thing when someone's death makes the world a better place, but there it is.

You have a second daughter. Nana ends her days in an "assisted living" facility, really an unassisted dying facility as far as you're concerned. It takes years for her to go, and by the end her mind is almost gone, and she'll think your teenage daughter is your wife.

So yeah, the world's a dangerous place. When has it ever been otherwise? But it's the only world you have.

———

IF YOU WANT to be a horror writer, divorce your wife. It's not a spectacular break-up. No hurled epithets or objects. Just a slow withering as your wife finds more excuses to avoid spending time with you. You come to understand that she finds your need to be connected to her emotionally burdensome, and that she's never truly enjoyed your company. A therapist will ask you to describe your marriage, and you'll say it's like you're a rock on the shore of a cold ocean. The sky is always gray, and wind and rain constantly buffet you. You end up in a shitty one-bedroom apartment that you share with too many roaches. You see your daughters half of the week, and the other half you feel like a ghost haunting your own life. You watch too many true-crime shows on TV because after paying spousal and child support—not to mention the debt payments on the bankruptcy your ex forced you into—you don't have any money to go anywhere or do anything. You only keep the damn cable so the kids have something to watch when they're over. Your ex takes the kids to her mother's for Christmas, and you spend the holiday watching police solve crimes with the latest forensic technology while you eat a festive meal of a single poached egg on a slice of toast.

You don't drink much, and you don't start now. You fear if you start, you won't stop. You find yourself contemplating suicide, not *too* seriously, but the idea seems increasingly appealing. Periodically, you find yourself staring at your reflection in the bathroom mirror—you're not sure why—and you speak these words: *There is no point to your continued existence.* Your reflection doesn't disagree with you. A friend of yours refers to depression as the Black Dog, and you think that's as good a name as any. You start taking meds to hold your own Black Dog at bay, and while they help, the damned thing remains close by, patiently waiting for a chance to bound forward and sink its teeth into your throat.

After a while, you start dating again, not that you have the money for it, but you're sick of being alone, and you're afraid of what you might do if you remain on your own. You try online dating, but the women you're matched with are incompatible at best and downright psychotic at worst. Still, you keep trying.

A blonde woman arranges to meet you on Valentine's Day at a bar in a town an hour-and-a-half from your shitty apartment. She has large breasts, and she refers to them constantly during your conversation, as if they're the most important thing about her. She downs one drink after another, and she eventually asks you back to her condo. You didn't date much before you married, and you're surprised by how many women ask you to go home with them, or go to your place, after only talking to you for a couple hours. Don't they know that the world is a dangerous place?

She continues drinking once you get to her home, slamming down so much alcohol that you don't see how she remains standing. It's winter and an ice storm is starting outside, and while you know you should start heading home before the roads get too bad, you can't bring yourself to leave. You're not especially attracted to this woman. She's physically beautiful, but her personality is repellent. But you can't stand the thought of going back to your empty excuse for a life, so you stay, and before long the two of you end up in her bedroom, naked. She displays the breasts she's so proud of, and then smacks her fists into their sides.

"I don't have any sensation in my tits," she says. "You can do anything to them, and I won't feel it. Weird, huh?"

You don't have a condom on you—you'd think by now you'd learn to bring some considering how many women are eager to hop into the sack on the first date—so you take care of her with your mouth and hands. She comes, and you're surprised she feels it, considering how much alcohol is in her system.

"Your turn," she says with a drowsy smile. And then she starts going down on you.

The woman doesn't just suck your dick. She suctions it as if she's an industrial vacuum. The pressure is constant and unrelenting, and you find nothing remotely sexual in the action. There's a kind of mechanical desperation in the woman's efforts, and while you've avoided drinking much tonight—you've got a long drive home, after all—you wish you were drunk now, because what she's doing doesn't feel good. It *hurts.* You wouldn't be surprised if she sucks your dick off and swallows it, like a constrictor devouring its prey. You are so repelled by what's happening, your dick goes soft, but the woman doesn't stop. If anything, she works more frantically to get you hard again. You're about to ask her to stop when you feel a strange sensation. It's kind of like you're about to orgasm, but how can you if your dick's soft? You do come then, quickly and perfunctorily. When you're finished, the woman raises her head from your crotch and gives you an accusing look.

"What the hell was *that?*" she demands.

"I don't know," you say truthfully.

She says it a couple more times, placing emphasis on a different word each time.

"What the hell *was* that? What the *hell* was that?"

You quickly get dressed and get the hell out of there. It's after two in the morning, and icy rain is coming down heavy, but you don't care. You get in your car—a beat-up Camry that you haven't been able to afford having serviced for over a year —and start driving. The roads are coated with ice so thick that it feels like your car skates across the surface. The highway's even worse, and you can barely see because the streaks of ice form a white wall in the glare of your headlights. You should drive more slowly, more cautiously, but you don't. You think that it wouldn't be so bad if you lost control of your car, spun out, and crashed. With any luck, you'd die, and your daughters would believe it was an accident, never guessing it was really suicide, or at least a surrender to the darkness inside you.

But you make it home in one piece a couple of hours later, and the disappointment you feel at still being alive is like a ten-ton weight crushing down on you.

There is no point to my continued existence, you think.

YOUR AGORAPHOBIC MOTHER becomes a ghost who not only haunts a house, she *is* the house. The lake you almost drowned in as a child becomes a setting for many of your stories. Your Uncle Red's corpse—or more to the point, the Great Nothing it represents—becomes the dark force of entropy which lies at the center of your fiction. And entropy, of course, is just another name for your old foe Time. The rest of it—your cancer, the divorce, the guilt over failing your daughters, the women you couldn't connect with—they're all there in your words, sometimes obvious, usually not. Your life is a funhouse mirror, and you look upon the distortions in the glass, and you write.

IF YOU WANT to be a horror writer, answer questions from people, like *Where do you get your ideas?* and *How can such a pleasant person write stuff so dark?* And the kicker: *When are you going to write something* real? *You know, something true and meaningful?*

You'll stand there, Black Dog growling at your side, the taste of lake water on your tongue, still and quiet as a corpse inside, and you'll smile.

ACKNOWLEDGMENTS

Thanks to Michael Dolan for his editorial guidance and enthusiasm. Every writer would count themselves lucky to work with an editor like him. Thanks to all the other editors who originally brought out these stories. Most of these tales wouldn't exist if you hadn't kindly asked me to submit something to you. And as always, special thanks to my agent Cherry Weiner. To paraphrase the movie *Mystery Men*, someone must've torn out the Q section in her dictionary because she doesn't know the meaning of the word *quit*.

PUBLICATION HISTORY

- "A Touch of Madness." *The Pulp Horror Book of Phobias.* Lycan Valley Press, 2019. Reprinted in *Year's Best Hardcore Horror 5,* Red Room Press, 2020.
- "The Crying Man." *Tales from Arkham Asylum.* Dark Regions Press, 2023.
- "No One Sings in the City of the Dead." *Literally Dead.* Alienhead Press, 2022.
- "The Girl Who Bled in the Tree." *Tales of the Lost 3.* Plaid Dragon Publishing, 2022.
- "In the Monster's Mouth." *Apex Magazine* 131, 2022.
- "The Garden of Love is Green." *Tales to Terrify, 500* Part 2, 2021. Reprinted in *That Which Cannot Be Undone,* Cracked Skull Press, 2022.
- "God Spelled Backward." *Shadow Atlas: Dark Landscapes of the Americas.* Hex Publishers, 2021.
- "Forever." *Tales of the Lost 2.* Plaid Dragon Publishing, 2020.
- "Old Monsters Never Die." *Classic Monsters Unleashed.* Black Spot Books, 2022.

- "Ashes of Our Fathers." *Borderlands 7*. BP Press, 2020.
- "The White Road." *The Horror Zine's Book of Ghost Stories*. Hellbound Books Publishing, 2020.
- "Going Home." *Tales of the Lost: We All Lose Something.* Plaid Dragon Publishing, 2019.
- "Negative Space." *Nightmare*, Issue 111, Dec. 2021.
- "The Gray Room." *Ashes and Entropy*. Nightshade Press, 2019.
- "Voices Like Barbed Wire." *Tales from the Lake V.* Crystal Lake Publishing, 2018. Reprinted in *Year's Best Hardcore Horror 4*, Red Room Press, 2019.
- "In the End There is a Drain." *Tails of Terror*, 2018.
- "Cast-Offs." *Chopping Block Party*. Necro Publications, 2017. Reprinted in *Night Land*, 2022.
- "Til Death." *Don't Fear—The Apocalypse. 13Thirty Books*, 2017. Reprinted in *Year's Best Hardcore Horror Vol. 3*. Comet Press, 2018.
- "How to be a Horror Writer." *Vastarien 2*, Grimscribe Press, 2018.

ABOUT THE AUTHOR

Tim Waggoner's first novel came out in 2001, and since then he's published over fifty novels and seven collections of short stories. He writes original dark fantasy and horror, as well as media tie-ins. He's the author of the acclaimed horror-writing guide *Writing in the Dark,* which won the Bram Stoker Award for Nonfiction in 2021. The follow-up, *Writing in the Dark: The Workbook,* also won a Stoker in the same category in 2023. He won another Stoker in 2021 in the category of Short Nonfiction for his article "Speaking of Horror," and in 2017 he received the Stoker for Long Fiction for his novella *The Winter Box.*

In addition, he's been a multiple finalist for the Shirley Jackson Award and the Scribe Award, and a one-time finalist for the Splatterpunk Award. His fiction has received numerous Honorable Mentions in volumes of *Best Horror of the Year*, and he's had several stories selected for inclusion in volumes of *Year's Best Hardcore Horror*. He's also a full-time tenured professor who teaches creative writing and composition at Sinclair College in Dayton, Ohio. His papers are collected by the University of Pittsburgh's Horror Studies Program.